No

Books for young people

SOMETHING TERRIBLE HAPPENED LAST NIGHT

Sam Blake is a multiple number one bestselling adult thriller writer, whose books have been shortlisted three times for Irish Crime Novel of the Year. Under her real name of Vanessa Fox O'Loughlin, she is the founder of Writing.ie, the Inkwell Group and Murder One, Ireland's acclaimed International Crime Writing Festival.

SOMETHING TERRIBLE HAPPENED LAST NIGHT

SAM BLAKE

GILL BOOKS

Gill Books
Hume Avenue
Park West
Dublin 12
www.gillbooks.ie

Gill Books is an imprint of M.H. Gill and Co.

978 07171 9714 9

Designed by Bartek Janczak
Illustration by Derry Dillon
Edited by Esther Ní Dhonnacha
Proofread by Ciara McNee
Printed by Clays Ltd, Suffolk
This book is typeset in 11 on 14pt, Minion Pro.

The paper used in this book comes from the wood pulp of sustainably managed forests.

A CIP catalogue record for this book is available from the British Library.

5 4 3 2 1

For Sarah Webb.
For *everything*.
And for the best advice I was ever given:
'Just keep writing'.

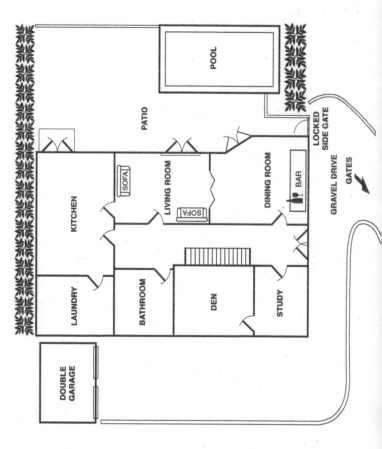

KATIE'S HOUSE

PROLOGUE

Sitting at the bottom of the stairs in Katie's black-and-white-tiled hallway, Frankie put her head in her hands and tried to shut out the chaos that was unfolding around her. She could feel the tears coming again, hot on her cheeks. Even with her eyes shut, the blue strobes of the ambulance and Garda cars outside were imprinting themselves on her brain. Bursts of garbled radio conversation came to her from the living room, together with the low voices of the paramedics.

She felt a hand on her shoulder and Jess bumped down to sit beside her. Unspeaking, she pulled Frankie into a hug. They'd only known each other a few weeks, but after tonight Frankie felt like they would be bonded forever. She still couldn't believe how an evening which had started so well had ended like this. She needed the hug. There were no words for right now.

'Miss, was it you who called the Guards?'

A male voice cut through her thoughts. Frankie opened her eyes and looked up at the man. He had a notebook in his hand and a radio clipped to his navy bomber jacket. He was about the same age as her dad, his hat blocking out the light from the chandelier above them. All the LEDs had been turned off earlier and now the house was flooded by the main lights.

Frankie wished Ollie would get here quickly. She still had his sweatshirt on. It came down almost to the hem of her dress and she hugged it to her now, even though it was warm in the house. She pulled her hands inside the sleeves and crossed her arms, glancing back up the stairs at her cousin Sorcha and then at Jess as she answered.

'Yes, that was me. Frankie O'Sullivan, Francesca. I live at the Berwick Castle Hotel. My mum and dad run it.'

'Ah, you're Ollie's sister?'

She sighed. One day she was going to be able to introduce herself in this town without someone saying, 'Oh, you're Ollie's sister.' Frankie didn't know if it was because he was the oldest of the five of them, or because his band was the only vaguely decent one in Kilmurray

Point, or because he was spending his 'gap year' – you had to do the rabbit ear thing because it was turning into almost two years at this stage – working behind the bar at the hotel. There didn't seem to be anyone in town who hadn't been in their bar.

'And this is?'

Frankie turned to look at Jess. The light was catching the diamond stud in her nose and making it gleam. Frankie wondered for a split second if she could capture its sparkle somehow, put it in a bottle to take home and uncork a bit of magic that would bring everything back to normal, to how it was before the party.

Right now, she didn't know if she'd ever be able to sparkle again.

'I'm Jessica McKenna – Jess.' Her English accent sounded strong after the Guard's soft country vowels.

'She wasn't here for the party.' Frankie rubbed her eyes. 'And that's my cousin Sorcha – she wasn't here either. They just came to help clear up.' Frankie turned to indicate the dark-haired girl curled up at the top of the stairs, where the staircase swung around in a big arc. Sorcha was tiny, and with her knees drawn up to her chin and her huge eyes dark in a very pale face, she looked even more pixie-like than normal. 'Ollie dropped us off, before …' She couldn't say it.

The Guard nodded like he was taking it all in, then made a note on his pad.

'So, what happened, love, can you tell me?'

Suddenly Frankie was back in the living room with the dogs yapping and running in circuits around the enormous beige leather sofa by the kitchen door. Katie had pushed it back to make space for dancing. It had been like the dogs couldn't cope with the change in the furniture and all the party smells.

At that point, Frankie had really had enough drama. First the fight, then trying to make sure everyone got home safely. Then coming back to Katie's house to help her clear up and finding bottles and cans and spilled drink everywhere, the living room stinking of weed and the patio furniture floating in the pool. They all needed some calm to just plough through the clear-up and get the place straight before Katie's parents got back. The dogs' yapping had started to set her teeth on edge.

Then Frankie had glanced up and realised Katie wasn't looking at the dogs. Instead, she was standing by the door that led into the kitchen and staring at the floor behind the sofa, her face totally drained of colour. Putting one hand on the door frame to steady herself, Katie had started trembling, the other hand moving towards her mouth in what felt to Frankie, like slow motion.

Sorcha had noticed Katie shaking at the exact same moment as Frankie, and as their eyes met, fear ricocheted between them like a basketball, hitting them both hard in the stomach as they turned to look across the devastated room at their friend. But Katie just continued to stare, like she was caught in some sort of alien ray beam and couldn't speak.

They'd both known something was wrong straightaway. Really super wrong. As if the whole party-chaos-house-smashed-Katie-grounded-forever thing wasn't bad enough.

The two dogs were going wild, barking and running around the sofa. The smaller one had something red all over her curly white fur. Frankie started to pick her way across the room, thoughts flying at the speed of the dogs – had the little one cut her paw on broken glass? Could this night get any worse?

Frankie was just envisioning calling Ollie back to help with a dash to the emergency vet when she spotted the heel of a white Nike Air Force 1 sticking out from behind the sofa.

And attached to the Nike was a body.

BEFORE

ONE
60 HOURS TO THE PARTY

'And who is *that*?'

Sitting on the sofa in the Fifth Year common room, Jess leaned towards Frankie, muttering under her breath. The blonde girl who had just flounced in was standing in the doorway as if there was a camera on her, pausing to see who had turned around to look at her arrival. Her red-and-brown-checked kilt was about four inches above her knees, and her false eyelashes – Frankie could hear her eldest brother's voice in her head – looked like two spiders had died on her face.

Frankie couldn't believe it was the first day of school already. The three-month summer holiday had gone past in a flash. It didn't help that she'd spent most of it working in the hotel rather than hanging out at the beach, but now they were back and beginning the Leaving Cert syllabus.

Leading up to the biggest exams of their lives.

Exams that would, apparently, decide how their lives would turn out forever.

Fun.

This morning Frankie had messaged Jess to say that she was meeting her cousin Sorcha at the DART station and they could walk up to school together early. Getting in early meant they managed to bag the lockers they wanted. Which was actually huge. Last year there'd been a plumbing crisis at the hotel and Frankie had been late in on the first day, ending up with the only free locker, one at the bottom in the middle that you could never get to because everyone else was always standing in the way getting their own books. It had been a nightmare the whole term.

Now, lockers sorted, the three of them were ensconced on the slightly moth-eaten sofa, waiting for everyone else to come in. Sorcha had thrown a blanket over it just to be sure nothing crawled out before she sat down – it'd had to be fumigated over the summer, which had been the first big news on the Rave-fess confession site – though the creation of Rave-fess itself was definitely the biggest news of the summer.

'*That* is Ruth Meaney. Head of the Mean Girls,' Frankie said out of the side of her mouth as, leaning on the open door, one hand on the frame, Ruth scanned the room to see who was in ahead of her. Frankie reckoned Ruth always wanted to arrive last so she could make a grand entrance. Ruth's eyes fell on them and she took a step inside.

'So, who do we have here, Frankie? Introduce us, please.'

Frankie smiled but could feel that it didn't reach her eyes. She'd tried really hard over the last few years, but Ruth was very hard to like. It didn't matter who you were – she always found something bitchy to say about you. When Frankie had discussed it with Ollie, he'd said it must be cold and lonely at the top of the mountain and if Ruth needed to look down on everyone to feel secure, then Frankie should feel sorry for her.

She was still working on that.

'This is my cousin Sorcha; she's moved from King's Academy to do the Leaving here. And this is Jess. She's just moved over from London.'

Ruth flicked her long blonde hair over her shoulder. 'Ah, Sorcha Bennett the famous swim champion? Frankie's told us about you.' Then she bent forwards slightly to look at Jess. 'We've met before somewhere, haven't we?'

Jess met her gaze, her face innocent. 'Have we?'

'Nose stud … but didn't you have purple hair? I don't think I'd forget.' Ruth pursed her lips, but it obviously wasn't coming. She smiled the fakest smile Frankie had ever seen. 'Welcome to Raven's Hill.'

She then spun around to look across the common room.

'Where are Amber and Ella? Oh, there's Georgia. I see them.' Ruth raised her voice: 'I hope you've got my locker organised, Georgia Swan? The top one on the end. I can't spend the whole year diving into the corner and fighting to get my stuff. Whoever decided to put the lockers on two walls like that needs to be sacked.' She flounced off to where her three followers, with their carbon-copy long glossy brown hair, were making toast in the kitchenette.

'So that's Ruth? I did wonder what she was like in person.' Sorcha's eyes were wide. Frankie glanced sideways at her, trying to remember when she'd mentioned Ruth before, then spotted Jess silently smirking beside her. 'What?'

'When Ruth turns up to that party you were talking about in vintage Chanel, you can remind her where she knows me from.' Frankie frowned, confused, as Jess continued: 'I've been volunteering at the Refugee Relief shop on the High Street over the summer. She came in with those two.' Jess indicated Ella and Amber with her head. 'Obviously I was only staff, so she barely spoke to me.'

'The High Street?' Frankie looked at her, confused for a moment. 'Do you mean the road down to the sea? The Main Street?'

Before Jess could answer, Sorcha leaned forwards, her mouth a big O, her Bambi eyes even wider. 'Ruth put that jacket on her Insta story, made it sound like she'd picked it up in Paris!'

Frankie did a double take. *Sorcha was following Ruth?* Frankie kept her school problems on a strictly need-to-know basis. When she'd been doing the big sales job on how great Raven's Hill School was to Sorcha and her parents, she'd deliberately left out Ruth's gang of Mean Girls. 'Do you follow her? How did you even find her?'

Sorcha raised her eyebrows. 'I wanted to be prepared, get to know everyone before I got here. Ella Diamond and Amber Weber have some interesting posts too. Knowledge is power.' She smirked. 'Although that Rave-fess site has everything on it. It's totally nuts.'

TWO

Frankie still couldn't believe that someone had been daring enough to put up a confession site for Raven's Hill. Now that term had started, it had taken off like it was jet-propelled.

Who'd have thought everyone was so prepared to put their secrets out there in public?

The students only knew that the common room had been fumigated because the Rentokil vans parked outside had been spotted and reported on Rave-fess, with photographic evidence. Ever since Frankie had started at Raven's Hill there had been gossip about the vermin in the common room, about fleas and mice in the sofa coming out to bite girls' fingers. All complaints had been put down to hysteria by the Head, but now, hey, maybe they'd been right all along.

Despite the critters, the common room was probably the best thing about being in Fifth Year – it was in the old part of the school, as far away from the staff room as you could get, and not on anyone's direct route anywhere. Which gave them all a bit of privacy – the chance to discuss any scandal, uninterrupted. And there was plenty to discuss on Rave-fess.

Over the summer, the walls of the common room had been freshly painted a sort of vomit yellow, and the yucky carpet tiles replaced with bright blue ones so – apart from the colour scheme – the place looked quite comfortable.

'Did you see that the bomb squad got called to the chemistry lab too? Was that for real?' Jess looked at them both like she really hadn't believed the post.

Before Frankie could comment on the bomb squad and the very fit soldiers who had arrived at school over the summer, the bell began to ring and the common room door flew open.

'Holy God, I can't believe I'm almost late on the first day. Are there any good lockers left?' Katie Cipriani looked like she'd run all the way from home. Her honey-coloured blouse was untucked and her red school sweater was tied around her waist. She threw her back-pack down beside the sofa and flopped onto the arm next to Sorcha to catch her breath. 'My parents woke me up going to the airport, and then I must have turned the alarm off. Sleeping me thought it was still the holidays.

'I can't believe they've gone to Italy without you over your birthday weekend.' Frankie couldn't keep the dis-belief out of her voice. Her parents had five kids and a hotel to run but they were always there on their birth-days, even if things got a bit chaotic sometimes and her parents had to fit the parenting bit in around the edges. All the O'Sullivans had been brought up to help out in the hotel since forever – Frankie and her brothers knew that five lots of school fees plus all their sports and music commitments were expensive and resulted in the long hours, but her parents never said no; they always found a way to make things happen.

Frankie often felt sad for Katie that her parents were hardly ever at home, leaving her with the housekeeper, or nannies when she'd been younger. But going away to their summer house, over her birthday, and right at the start of term, was bad even for them.

Katie nodded glumly, pushing a strand of natural blonde hair that had escaped from what looked like a hastily tied ponytail behind her ear. 'My dad's got work there and my second cousin's baby is getting chris-tened or something. I don't even know her. But …' She brightened up. 'He's left his credit card and they said it's fine if I have a few friends over while they're away.'

Frankie did a double take. 'So, you've actually got proper permission for the party?'

She grinned. 'As good as. We won't need to hold it on the sly now. Are you all coming?' Katie looked at Sorcha and Jess. 'I'm only going to be seventeen once, and I want everyone there. With a bit of luck, it'll still be warm enough to use the pool.'

'You've got a pool?' Sitting at the opposite end of the sofa, Jess sounded impressed.

Katie grinned, pulling at her hair elastic and shaking out her curls, trying to tidy them up. 'We do. Though it's only a small one and freezing cold most of the time. I'm Katie, by the way, usually the most on-time person in the whole class – and you're Jess? Frankie told me she met you at the induction day. I've been dying to meet you.'

Glancing at Frankie appreciatively, Jess smiled. 'The very same.'

Frankie still couldn't believe how well she'd clicked with Jess when they'd started talking that first day. They'd both been working non-stop over the summer; both had parents with crazy jobs that meant they ended up on their own a lot and had to be 'responsible'. Frankie sometimes felt like it was her middle name. That and 'boring'. Working in the hotel had fun moments, but it meant she'd missed half of the meet-ups and just about everything else interesting happening in Kilmurray Point over the summer.

Katie patted Sorcha on the shoulder. 'And fab to have you at Raven's Hill too, Sorch. Now we can hang out properly, instead of only seeing you at Frankie's birthdays.' Katie turned back to Jess. 'Frankie said you're from London? Did she tell you she wants to go to art college there? She takes the most amazing photographs.'

Katie paused. 'I'm not sure Induction Day gives you a *real* idea of what this school is like – food's always amazing, though. One of the best things about Raven's Hill being a boarding as well as a day school is that the catering is fantastic. The cooks make brownies to die for.' She glanced over at the lockers again. 'I can't believe I'm so late. I'm going to get stuck with that locker at the bottom, I know it. It's not even like I've got much stuff this year, it's all on my iPad.'

Frankie looked over her shoulder at the open locker doors. 'Share mine if you like. I don't have much either.'

'You're an angel, Frankie O'Sullivan – I might have to. Let me go see what's left. And Jess, you're welcome to use the pool any time. We'll swap numbers, and tell me what your Insta is, so I can follow. You and Sorcha have to come to the party. Promise. I don't want to be there on my own.'

THREE
36 HOURS TO THE PARTY

I t took ages for Jess to find the career counsellor's office. It was only day two of term, and even with the map she'd been given, she'd got thoroughly confused trying to find Ms Cooke's door. The school sprawled between the old main house, which was all narrow corridors and small rooms, and the new building, which seemed to be all glass and stairs. Most of it had been a blur yesterday as she'd met everyone and tried not to get lost.

She should have guessed that the careers office would have been in the old fancy bit at the front of the building, right beside the stairs to the boarding house and the school nurse. Obviously if you were a boarder having any sort of crisis you could come straight down those stairs and find an instant fix. Which would be useful to know for the weeks when her dad got caught up at work and she switched to boarding. But she didn't want to think about that yet.

The good news was that Raven's Hill wasn't bad for bullying, apparently – unlike, Jess had heard rumoured, its twin, Raven's Park College, the boys' school. But it was a bit heavy on pomp and circumstance in Jess's opinion. This hallway, with its chandeliers and oak panelling, was like a hotel. But then Raven's Hill was totally different from the schools Jess had been to before.

Jess knocked on the counsellor's door. She hoped this would be quick. The bell would be going for lunch in ten minutes and she wanted to catch up with Sorcha and Frankie. And she was starving.

'Come in!'

Jess pushed the door open to find Ms Cooke sitting on the other side of a huge carved desk that looked like it should be in a museum.

'Jessica McKenna, come in, come in, I've been expecting you. Sit down there. Can I get you a biscuit? I've got chocolate.'

Jess smiled. Frankie had told her about Ms Cooke's biscuit habit – it was one of the reasons for her nickname,

Cookie. Apparently at open evenings she always managed to get the chocolate ones with the jellies on the top almost before the lid was off the tin. Jess thought the teacher looked a bit like an alpaca, with her fuzzy hair and watchful eyes. She tried to push the image out of her mind in case she laughed. Which really wouldn't make the right impression. Apparently winning Ms Cooke over was the key to an easy ride in Raven's Hill, and Jess was going to do her best.

'Now, how are you getting on? Early days can be hard work, I know, trying to find your way around and meeting everyone. That's why we always start the new term on a Wednesday – it gives everyone a few days to find their feet before the real work begins. Have you been using the map we gave you at the induction day?'

Jess opened her mouth to say yes as Ms Cooke swept on. 'I know you're doing a few days of taster subjects, but I'm hoping you'll be able to give me an idea of your choices for the Leaving Cert by Monday. That'll give you the weekend to think about it. Will that be enough time?'

Jess cocked an eyebrow, waiting to see if she'd actually get a word in this time. She almost smiled as Ms Cooke continued, barely noticing she hadn't replied. 'Your father gave me an outline of the situation, so I wanted to make clear today that my door is always open.' She smiled broadly, finally giving Jess the chance to speak.

'Thanks, that's great.'

'If there's anything you want to talk about …' She left the sentence trailing and Jess did a mental eye roll. She didn't need to talk. Or want to. Everything that had happened in the last year was locked up inside a little box in her heart and she totally wasn't ready to share that with a complete stranger.

She didn't want to talk about her mum getting diagnosed with cancer, then dying only a few months later. Or about her dad having to move them to Ireland to be nearer to his mum, her gran, so he could keep working. Or about him being a war journalist – political editor, they called it, to make it sound less dangerous – and working in crazy places, at risk of being blown up at any moment. No, she wasn't going to be sharing any of that.

She bet Ms Cooke with her chocolate biscuits and posh accent didn't have any idea how any of those things could make you feel. Jess had had some counselling when the anxiety had got crippling, and had tablets that definitely helped, but as Frankie had said, Ms Cooke wasn't quite in the real world. And on top of that, she subscribed to the failing-the-Leaving-will-end-your-life nonsense. Jess's dad had warned her about that – he'd got to be a top reporter with a handful of C's and a couple of fails, working his way up through a newspaper from the post room. That was back in the dark ages when post was actually a thing, but he'd assured her there were lots of other routes to success that had absolutely nothing to do with passing or failing the Leaving Certificate.

But Jess *really* wasn't about to have that conversation now. She smiled. Humouring Ms Cooke was the fastest way to get out of here.

'I'm loving Raven's Hill; everyone's so friendly. I'm pretty sure I know which subjects now – I'm thinking Economics, History, Politics and Society, Music and Business.' She ticked them off on her fingers decisively as she said them. 'And I've an exemption from Irish, so French. I want to do Law in college.'

Ms Cooke paused significantly and raised her eyebrows. 'With English and Maths, that's eight subjects. That's a lot.'

'I know. It means if I need to drop one I can, but Business and Economics are very closely aligned, and so are Politics and History. I think I'll be fine. I did French and Italian in school at home. And English is my strongest subject. I was in an amateur acting company in London, so I've done *Macbeth*. I love Shakespeare.' Jess tipped her head to one side, employing her soothing, positive voice. 'My dad thinks it's all fine.'

'Excellent. Well, that all sounds excellent.' Ms Cooke was about to say something else when there was a knock on her door. 'Come in.'

Jess looked over her shoulder to see who was next in the queue and did a mental double take. It was Ruth

Meaney, her jaw taut. She looked, Jess thought for a split second, like she might have been crying.

'Oh Ruth, I won't be a minute.'

Jess sprang up. 'Thanks so much, Ms Cooke, you've been so helpful.'

'Super, Jess, I'll make a note of those subjects. If you change your mind, we'll do our best to accommodate.' Ms Cooke beamed at her from behind her desk.

Backing away from the chair, Jess was at the door in a second, opening it wide to let Ruth in. Ruth stalked past her, head held high like there was absolutely nothing wrong. Jess flicked her a smile and slipped out of the door.

Now, what could have reduced the great Ruth Meaney to tears?

FOUR

The canteen was heaving by the time Frankie got there, her stomach growling at the smell of hot food. It was her own fault she was so late. She'd overheard Amber and Ella in the loo talking about Ruth and what sounded like a complex relationship drama, and hadn't wanted to come out the cubicle in the middle of their chat and look like she'd been eavesdropping. They'd kept their voices down, and all Frankie had been able to catch was 'he' this and 'he' that, no names, and then they'd moved on to Ella's crush at her stables and how well her horse had done over the summer, until

Frankie had finally heard the door close as they left.

Thankfully Jess and Sorcha had arrived in the lunch-room ahead of her and saved her a place. She could just make them out on the Fifth Year table over the heads of legions of confused First Years. The new girls were super cute but there were always so many of them, especially at the start of term before they'd joined any of the lunchtime clubs. Raven's Hill had a buddy system where the Transition Year girls minded the First Years, so they always had older girls to hang onto, but it didn't help with crowd control.

As she dumped her iPad and school diary on the table, Frankie looked back at the queue, her mind moving rapidly from Ruth Meaney gossip to how she was going to get her lunch without having to join on the end. Fifth and Sixth Years got priority in the dining room because they had to study, but spotting an appropriate gap you could actually squeeze into to get served was a whole different story. Weaving between girls balancing trays, Frankie caught the eye of one of the blue-uniformed ladies behind the counter, and after a lot of pointing and gesticulating, two Transition Years passed Frankie back a plate of chicken korma and rice.

Back at the table, she sat down with a sigh of relief. 'I am *actually* starving. You were quick, Jess. Did Ms Cooke not give you the third degree?'

Jess grinned. 'She tried, but we'd just got past Leaving Cert subjects when we were interrupted by Ruth

Meaney, so I escaped.' Jess raised her eyebrows significantly and indicated the other end of the table. Frankie followed her eyes. Georgia must have saved Ruth's little posse places at the table. Amber and Ella were now sitting on the other side of a group of Spanish girls, who were all chattering away like birds. Frankie couldn't hear what Amber and Ella were saying but they were leaning together conspiratorially, probably filling Georgia in on their conversation from earlier. And it didn't look like it was about Ella's horse.

Frankie liked Georgia, although she really had no idea why she hung around with Ruth's gang, like some sort of junior sidekick. Georgia was so quiet and shy, *totally* unlike both Amber and Ella, and she was completely focused on doing theatre in college. Which made her even more of a strange fit with the other two, who didn't seem to have any imagination beyond selecting the latest lip gloss. Frankie had got to know Georgia quite well last year when the new drama teacher had seen some of Frankie's photos in the art room and asked her to take the cover shots for the school play programme. She'd got some brilliant pictures of Georgia, and Georgia had been so delighted that she'd asked Frankie if she could use them for her acting portfolio, which made it a double win.

Her mouth full, Frankie looked across the table at Jess. 'I just heard Amber and Ella talking about Ruth and her very tangled love life.'

'Interesting … Unless she's got really bad hay fever, she looked like she'd been crying when I saw her.' Jess's voice was so low Frankie almost couldn't catch what she'd said.

Sorcha finished her salad and narrowed her eyes. 'I heard in maths earlier that she's dating someone who's repeating Fifth Year. Like, maybe not dating but has been seen with. Perhaps she's got boyfriend trouble.' She paused. 'I wonder if that's got anything to do with this morning's Rave-fess post? Everyone was talking about it in the corridor on the way down.' Sorcha reached for her bag under the table and pulled out her phone, careful to look around before she used it. They weren't supposed to have their phones on in school, but as Frankie was always saying, hello, this was real life. It only took her a minute to open the site.

Have beef? Unfinished drama? Got tea?

Sorcha grinned mischievously as she scrolled down. 'Here we go: "Is it acceptable to date older guys? Discuss."' She frowned. 'No exclamation mark … that's interesting.'

Jess leaned over to try to see the screen. 'Why's that significant?'

'Because without the exclamation mark after *discuss* it's like a serious question.'

'I think you're overthinking that, Sorch.' Frankie put her fork down. 'What's the response?'

'Seem to be lots of vomit emojis on dating someone younger than you. Quite a lot of aubergines for older.'

Frankie rolled her eyes. 'That's the issue, really, isn't it?'

Just then, the screen refreshed and a new comment popped up.

Ella D might know all about that.

'Yikes,' Sorcha said. 'That's going to set fireworks off. Who is Ella dating?'

Frankie shook her head, wide-eyed. 'Apparently she had a fling with some lad at her stables but honestly, you couldn't keep up with Ella's love life if you tried. She should have her own gossip magazine.'

Sorcha glanced at her phone again, keeping it hidden under the table. 'And this just posted: "I hate messaging someone first. It always feels like I'm bugging them."'

'That's a bit sad.' Jess looked over at Sorcha. 'I know what they mean, though. And it's not just friends. Sometimes I don't want to message my dad in case he's in the middle of something.'

'In fairness, Jess, that's a legit problem – your dad could be anywhere. It's the complete opposite with me. I'm on speed dial with my family. Everything from babysitting to housekeeping, it's like "just call Frankie".'

Frankie sneaked a look at Sorcha's phone and read the next post loud enough for them to hear: "'Am I being too sensitive for getting upset that my boyfriend has started asking me to wear make-up when we meet? It makes me feel like I'm not enough.'"

Jess shook her head disapprovingly. 'That's just mean. She should dump him fast.'

'Who could that be? Not Katie? Didn't she say something to you about make-up earlier, Frankie?' Sorcha frowned. 'I hope not.'

Jess looked from Sorcha to Frankie enquiringly. 'Who's Katie dating?'

'Josh Fitzpatrick, Raven's Park College rugby captain. They've been together like forever. But that's definitely not her – Josh wouldn't be like that. You'll see when you meet him. He'll be at the party, with the *whole* rugby team …' Frankie paused as more Fifth Years arrived at the table.

'Are you guys talking about Rave-fess?'

Frankie grinned up at Maeve, who was followed by her girlfriend, Tara, their trays in their hands. 'Of course.'

Maeve rolled her eyes as she sat down beside them. 'That lunch queue is getting longer each year, I swear …'

Without a breath, Tara picked up the end of Maeve's sentence: '… there seem to be even more First Years this year. I hate skipping ahead of them.'

Maeve Andersson and Tara Li had been together since Transition Year and constantly held hands, as if one might drift away from the other if they let go. With Maeve's platinum-blonde bob and Tara's jet-black pig-tails, Frankie always thought they were just like the yin and yang symbols Maeve had on her pencil case. They seemed to fit together perfectly.

Frankie shunted up on the bench to make room for them. Then Caitriona Donoghue, her curly red hair tamed into a plait, and new girl Vivienne Smyth appeared, and squished in on the opposite side beside Jess and Sorcha.

Frankie gave Viv a smile. 'How are you settling in? Big change from Raven's Park?'

Viv glanced at her, her brown eyes anxious. 'Everyone's been really lovely. I'm so glad I got a place here.'

Part of Frankie wanted to hug Viv; she knew how nervous she was. Some of the boys had been supportive in Raven's Park College when she'd come out last year, but some really hadn't. Viv had started transitioning over the summer and her curly hair had grown into a cute bob. Caitriona had taken Viv under her wing from the moment she'd walked in. Moving schools was a big thing in a host of what Frankie knew were very big things.

Frankie did the introductions. 'This is Jess, new from London, and my cousin Sorcha.' Frankie introduced everyone. 'Are you all coming to Katie's party?'

Viv grimaced. 'Not totally sure yet.'

She trailed off as Tara leaned down the table for salt, her pigtails swishing around her face. 'We're going into town tomorrow to get new dresses, aren't we, Maeve? And I need new runners.'

Jess looked at Frankie. 'Would Katie be upset if I give it a miss? I hate big parties.'

Sorcha nodded. 'Me too. I don't really know enough people yet. But I'll be watching Rave-fess for all the gossip.'

'Is it just Raven's Hill?' Caitriona pushed her gold-rimmed glasses up her nose and hooked a stray tendril of red hair behind her ear.

'Raven's Park too. Sounds like Katie's invited the entire Fifth Year from both schools.'

Viv's beautifully formed eyebrows rose. 'Everyone? That may not end well.'

'She's got a huge house ...' Maeve chimed in.

'And a pool.' Tara grinned. 'It's going to be amazing.'

FIVE

'So, I hear you're the one to watch on the swim team?'
Sorcha jumped at the voice behind her, as
much at the nastiness of the tone as at the fact
that she wasn't alone after all. She'd been leaning on the
basin in the loo, scrolling through Rave-fess posts on her
phone, and hadn't heard the door. The others were still in
the lunchroom, but she'd wanted five minutes to catch up.

It had taken her three goes to find a toilet that wasn't
occupied. It was only day two of term and the first couple
had had girls sobbing in cubicles, their friends crowded
around the door, trying to persuade them to come out.

Sorcha put the phone screen to her chest so the new arrival couldn't see it, then turned slowly to look over her shoulder.

Ruth Meaney. She should have guessed. But Ruth on her own. At least she didn't have her followers in tow: they must still be at lunch. Perhaps Ruth had only just finished with the careers teacher and was on her way to the canteen. Jess was right about her eyes – whatever was going on, they looked distinctly red.

'Depends what you mean by "watch". I'm the fastest on the team if that's what you mean. And we're the best in the county.'

'Fastest at what? Leprechaun diving?'

Ruth towered over her, her long blonde hair slung over her shoulder. Sorcha scowled and looked at Ruth out of one eye, like she was talking an unintelligible language.

Sorcha had never had a problem with being small, and she knew she was fast with it, that she could duck out around Ruth before she'd even react. But Ruth Meaney interested her. As soon as Sorcha had found out she was moving to Raven's Hill she'd made it her business to check out everyone who would be in Fifth Year. And she knew Ruth liked to be the best at everything.

Well, maybe she'd try to take her down a peg or two.

'Is it tough being so tall? I mean, from what I can see, it's obviously hard to get nice clothes to fit.'

Ruth's mouth dropped open and Sorcha mentally chalked up Victory #1.

The thing that Ruth obviously hadn't realised about Sorcha was that she was fast in the water because she couldn't bear losing. Sorcha didn't come second; it just wasn't a thing.

The secret was preparation and having all the data.

Her parents were the same, both of them at the top of their fields – which was obviously great, but did mean they were away a lot, presenting research papers at conferences all over the world. When her sister, Beth, had been at home, it had been fun with just the two of them, but now that Beth was at university, Sorcha wasn't so keen on being on her own all the time. From next week she'd be boarding at Raven's Hill and she couldn't wait. She'd be able to fall out of bed and go straight to swim practice without fear of missing the bus. A whole extra hour under the covers would be heaven.

Even if she did have to put up with basic bitches like Ruth Meaney between times.

Sorcha looked at her, her eyebrows raised. 'You've had a busy summer. You're like a magnet to boys, aren't you?'

Ruth scowled at her, her eyes narrowing. 'What do you mean?' She leaned in closer to Sorcha and put one hand onto the basin beside her, creating a barrier between Sorcha and the door.

Sorcha looked at her innocently. 'You just seem to be

very popular. You're in lots of peoples' posts and stories.'

'I *am* popular, that's what happens. But you probably don't know anything about that.'

Sorcha looked pointedly at Ruth's hand on the basin. She was wearing a gold chain bracelet with an R on it. It was a heavy chain and the charm was very plain. Perhaps Sorcha was closer to the mark about Ruth's bad taste than she'd first thought. She was definitely wearing far too much make-up and her eyelashes looked like they had a life of their own.

'Winning isn't about being popular. Being the best means you leave people behind. It's like natural selection. I'm very focused.' Sorcha almost added, *and way ahead of you*, but she didn't need to explain herself to Ruth Meaney of all people, the very person who natural selection had obviously deselected in the brains department. Sorcha had a very low opinion of anyone who needed to be a bully to be on top; it said so much about them and their insecurities.

It took a second for Ruth to recover. 'But you hang out with losers. That doesn't make much sense to me.'

Sorcha looked at her hard. 'I think *loser* is a relative term. But you'd know more about that than me.' Without waiting for an answer Sorcha pushed roughly past Ruth and pulled open the door to the corridor, her heart thumping.

SIX
32 HOURS TO THE PARTY

'Here she is. *Finally.*' Frankie waved to Sorcha as she jogged down the drive towards the main gate where she and Jess were waiting. The last bell hadn't come soon enough, and they were heading to Starbucks for a much-needed afternoon caffeine and sugar hit.

'I thought you were supposed to be fast – we've been waiting ages.' Frankie gestured for her to hurry up. With four brothers at home, Frankie had always thought of Sorcha as the sister she didn't have. She'd been thrilled when Sorcha's move to Raven's Hill had been confirmed. And, even better, she'd be boarding. Which meant that she could get a pass to come home for dinner at Frankie's whenever she wanted. They definitely needed more women in the O'Sullivan household.

Sorcha scowled at her good-naturedly. 'At *swimming*, Frankie. I'm fast in the water, not at cross-country. I got stuck in the computer room and then realised I'd left my jumper in the common room. But I'm here now. Who else is coming to Starbucks?'

'Katie's heading up too,' said Frankie. 'Her boyfriend Josh should be there and – hopefully – the rest of the team.'

Jess grinned. 'Let's hope this Patrick dude is there, eh?'

'Has she been going on about him again? Did she mention he's super-hot, vice-captain of the rugby team and just a tiny bit dreamy?' Sorcha rolled her eyes theatrically.

'She might have done. In almost those words – maybe not "dreamy", but I sort of guessed that. Have you ever even talked to him, Frankie?'

Frankie shook her head, sighing. 'We've only spoken once. He's way out of my league.'

'Stop it, you're stunning!' Jess shook her head as Frankie blushed. 'How do you know him, then?'

'He's a good friend of one of Katie's best friends, Conor, but I only really know him from hanging out around the pier and stuff over the summer. And I haven't said anything properly to Katie.' She looked pointedly at Sorcha as she continued, 'So don't either of you dare. I'd die if he didn't like me like that.' Frankie let out a sharp breath. She'd almost told Katie a few times over the summer, but as soon as she'd brought up Patrick's name, Katie had changed the subject and the moment had passed. She glanced at Jess. 'He doesn't do much that's not rugby-related, that I can see on Insta, anyway. Not that I'm stalking him or anything, obviously.'

Jess grinned at Frankie. 'Obviously. Just due diligence. Research is important.'

Frankie laughed. 'Research is *very* important. According to his socials, rugby is his whole life. His dad's a lawyer, and they must be loaded because they go to amazing places on holiday.' She paused. 'And his clothes are gorgeous. I think he gets his shirts custom made – he tags this company in London on his posts and they've got this lovely blue floral fabric inside the collar. Each one is a bit different, but it's the same blue as his eyes.'

Beside her Sorcha was shaking her head, laughing. 'You've got it bad, Franks. I can't believe you're noticing the detail on his *shirts*. Stalker much? I keep telling you, you should just say it to Katie.'

'I can't, Sorch. I mean, what if it all goes wrong and he hates me and Conor's mortified and Katie's embarrassed and it's all a horrible mess?'

Sorcha shook her head. 'You're overthinking it, Franks. Your head's ruling your heart.'

Jess shrugged. 'I can understand that. I'm the queen of overthinking. But the more you know about him the better. My dad calls that the big data. He likes to get a full picture of new people, practically wants to know their bank account numbers.'

'I'm good with that. What do you always say, Sorch, "Knowledge is power"?' Frankie said it so seriously, Jess laughed.

'My dad says you need to be prepared, and always curious. Which *does* mean I'm the best person to have around in a crisis, FYI. I'm always ready for anything. Seriously, overthinking is my thing.'

Frankie gave Jess a good-natured shove. 'Good to know. Anyway, we all overthink. C'mon, let's get going.'

✖ ✖ ✖

Starbucks was in a small shopping centre only a five-min-ute walk from the school, beside a mini-supermarket, a Chinese takeaway and a bookshop. As they got there, Frankie could see the tables on the paved area in front of Starbucks were already occupied by an untidy muddle of girls in red, brown and gold uniforms, mixed with boys in Raven's Park College's navy sweaters, the V-necks delineated by red-and-brown stripes to indicate the association between the two schools.

Josh Fitzpatrick was in the middle of the group, sitting at a table with Katie, surrounded by a crowd of duplicate boys who could only be his teammates. As well as being one of the oldest girls in Raven's Hill's Fifth Year, Katie was the prettiest, richest and actually one of the nicest. People were drawn to her like moths to a flame. Beside her, broad-shouldered, his hair a sun-kissed sandy brown, Josh had an easy way about him that made everyone around them relax. They really were the golden couple.

Frankie put her bag down beside the low wall that surrounded the paved area and sat down on it. 'Let's sit here. Maeve and Tara will be down in a minute and Caitriona was trying to persuade Viv too.' The others sat down beside her as she continued, 'Did I tell you, Sorch, Josh's been offered a sports scholarship to Stanford for when he finishes at Raven's Park? Some of the American universities have an early access programme or something where they find the most talented students and approach them.'

Sorcha glanced over at him, her face puzzled. 'Do they play rugby in America?'

'Apparently, but they also play a lot of American football, similar game, more padding. He could end up being famous.' Frankie opened her eyes wide. Katie thought the whole American jock thing was hilarious.

Jess raised her eyebrows. 'Won't Katie be devastated if he goes away? I mean, it's not like she can visit at weekends.'

Frankie leaned down to unzip her backpack. 'She's going to apply to Stanford too. She's got it all worked out. She's got loads of family in the States and her parents can afford to send her. She bought him a really gorgeous gold Saint Christopher's medal necklace to celebrate – he hasn't taken it off since she gave it to him.'

'Aww, the patron saint of travellers to keep him safe. That's so cute.' Sorcha was looking across at the group again when Frankie nudged Jess beside her.

'Oh my God, he's here. There's Patrick, in the middle of the group.'

Jess looked discreetly over. 'Which one?'

'He's the gorgeous guy with dark hair over there, talking to Conor, the shorter blond one. Just on the other side of Katie's table. She's known Conor for years. He's on the team too.'

'Is Patrick the one talking to Katie now?' Jess asked.

Smoothing her hair, Frankie casually looked over her shoulder to where Patrick Kelly was standing. He was laughing at something Katie had said, leaning over Conor's shoulder. Frankie whipped her head back around. 'Yes. That's him.'

Jess took a proper look. 'Is he thinking of applying for college in the States too?'

'Feck, I hope not.' Frankie pulled her wallet and KeepCup out of her backpack. 'Mind the bags, Sorcha, and I'll get the drinks. What does everyone want?'

SEVEN

As Frankie manoeuvred her way back out through the glass door with their three drinks in her hands, she tried to get a sneaky glimpse of the group gathered around Katie and Josh, without looking like she was looking. The last thing she wanted was to appear too interested. That would just be embarrassing.

As she headed past them, the breeze picked up her hair and blew it across her face at the exact moment that Patrick looked up and caught her eye. He gave her a little smile. *Oh God, timing.* She tried to return it while also looking like a mouthful of hair wasn't a problem. She swished her head trying to get rid of it, but the breeze was getting stronger.

Walking faster, her cheeks burning, Frankie tried to juggle the cups so she could push the strand away. This was typical – she'd dashed into the loo after class with her brush and lip gloss before she met Jess, and now her hair was sticking to her gloss and the whole illusion of poise and polish was being blown away.

Sitting on the wall with their backs to the road, Jess and Sorcha were trying to see something on Sorcha's phone as Frankie got back to them.

'Quick, grab these so I can fix myself.' Frankie put the cups down on the wall and pulled her hair out of her mouth.

'Yikes, where's the fire?' asked Jess.

'Over there. And he smiled at me …'

Sorcha looked at her reproachfully. 'Frankie, get a grip, *please*! He's hot, but honestly.'

One eye on Patrick, Frankie sat down beside Jess on the wall, reaching for her cup.

'And breathe …' Theatrically she took a deep breath, gesturing with her hand as she let it out. She went to take the lid off her cup. 'Sorry, Sorch, I know how ridiculous this is, but I'm in love. It's a thing. I don't want to be single forever.' She paused, shaking her head, her eyes wide. 'It's mad, I've fancied him since the start of the summer but he's been posting way more on Insta this last month – he's there every time I look. It's like a sign.'

Laughing, Jess reached over to Sorcha for her own cup, taking off the lid as she spoke. 'How long have Katie and Josh been dating?'

Frankie took a sip of her mocha. 'They got together over Christmas in Third Year. Feels like forever.'

Sorcha tapped Frankie on the knee. 'There's no point in being in love from afar. You need to go and talk to Patrick. He's with Katie – go and ask if she's okay for everything for the party.'

'What? Now?' Frankie almost spluttered out her mocha. 'On my own?'

Jess laughed. 'What's the worst that can happen?'

'I make a complete fool of myself and Patrick thinks I'm a total eejit? How's that for starters?'

Sorcha stared at her impatiently. 'You won't – just be friendly. I know, pretend you need to get sugar from inside and wander over as you come out, see if you can catch Katie's eye, she'll say hello, and you can go over to them. It'll be completely natural.'

Frankie felt her heart rate increase. Sorcha was right, it *would* be completely natural, and if she changed her mind, she could come right on back here. She glanced at Jess and Sorcha.

Sorcha gave her a push. 'Go on, you've nothing to lose. Even if you only say hello, it means it'll be easier to speak to him at the party. Ice broken.'

Frankie bit her lip, her mouth dry. They were right. She closed her eyes and took another deep breath. 'Just pray I don't trip over and fall on my face on the way over.' She stood up. 'Are you sure?'

Both of them looked like they were about to burst out laughing. Frankie gave them a withering look and took another deep breath, trying to slow her heart. She could feel their eyes on her as she skirted the tables to the door. She tried to look sideways at Katie on her way in to see if she was looking in her direction. A moment later Frankie was inside and picking up sugar sachets and a wooden stirring stick.

Now she just needed to look super casual and wander over to Katie on the way out and ask how the plans were going.

'Sweet tooth?'

A deep voice right beside her made Frankie jump, almost dropping the sugars. She spun around and froze, her mouth open but no words coming out.

'They're not all for you, though, right?' Patrick leaned forwards and picked up a plastic lid from the stack behind her, brushing against her as he did so. He was a good foot taller than Frankie, his shoulders broad, dark hair cropped at the side and back, and slightly too long on top so that it sort of curled. He was wearing the Raven's Park College uniform sweater over its pale blue shirt, the exact colour of his eyes. *He had amazing eyes.*

Before Frankie could think of something to say, he continued, 'I wanted to talk to you, actually. I saw that photo you took of your brother's band in the newspaper. You're a really good photographer.'

'Thanks.' Frankie could feel herself starting to blush as she cleared her throat. 'I want to study photography in college. Really I want to work for *National Geographic*, but my brothers are as wild as it gets at the moment.'

His face cracked into a grin. 'That Battle of the Bands was mad all right. Amazing night.' Part of Frankie froze – Patrick had been at the Battle of the Bands? She'd been there in the club all night and hadn't spotted him. Part of her died inside – she'd been wearing grungy dungarees and an old long-sleeved T-shirt so she could get down on the extremely sticky floor to get the best angles. By the end of the night she'd been soaked in sweat and looked horrific; even Ollie had said so. Fortunately, Patrick didn't seem to be able to read her mind.

'I was wondering ... I need some new shots for the rugby club website.' He smiled. 'It's not as glamorous as a gig, I know, but I was wondering if you did any portrait-type pictures?'

For a split second Frankie thought she was actually going to pass out. *Patrick wanted her to take his picture?* Her heart was thumping so loudly that she almost didn't hear what he said next: 'Are you going to Katie's party?'

EIGHT
28 HOURS TO THE PARTY

**Are you home? Can you cover Sinéad's
break for 30mins? You can do your
homework, it's not busy.**

Frankie scanned the text that had arrived just as
she'd walked through the pedestrian entrance
beside the main hotel gates. She just wanted to go
to her room and process her day. How could her mum
need her now?

For a moment she wondered if she could pretend that she hadn't got the message. But someone would see her, she knew it. She changed direction to head in through the front door. Beyond the car park, on the other side of the road, she could hear the sea breaking on the shore.

Her head was still buzzing after her much-too-brief conversation with Patrick. She had no idea how she was going to focus on Shakespeare when her whole life might be about to change. He wanted her to take his photo – how mad was that?

'Oh, Frankie, thank goodness. I'm desperate for a cup of tea.' Sinéad, the Berwick Castle Hotel's head receptionist, stood up behind the mahogany reception desk as soon as she saw Frankie. 'I'll hang on while you get changed. It's fairly quiet – there are Americans in 202 who are struggling with the TV, but Danny's just arrived below in the kitchen, so call him if they can't get it working?'

'No problem. I'll be two seconds.' Coming around the back of the desk, Frankie dropped her backpack in under it and disappeared into the tiny room behind reception. Balling up her school sweater and shirt, she changed quickly into the hotel's generic plain blouse and skirt – a uniform that could be worn anywhere, whether she was waiting tables or hoovering the stairs. Back outside, she flopped into Sinéad's chair.

Sinéad put her hands on her hips and looked at her critically. 'You look how I feel.'

'The first few days back are *always* so tiring. It's so warm and they've the heating on for no reason. I was melting in history – the sun comes right in those windows.'

Sinéad smiled sympathetically. The Berwick Castle dark green pencil skirt looked great with her crisp white blouse, its puffed sleeves trimmed in green and gold, and a big bow under the chin. Frankie always thought Sinéad's red lipstick made her look like a Hollywood film star; it was like her trademark.

'You relax, it's lovely and cool in here. Will I send Danny up with a Coke and some ice? You can check on 202 when he gets here.'

'That would be fab. And take your time, I've got tons of homework. If it's quiet here, I can get a bit done before dinner.'

Sinéad leaned over and grabbed her green uniform jacket from behind Frankie where it was hanging on the back of her chair, and turned to head towards the kitchens, her high heels loud on the stone tiles.

Pushing off with her feet, Frankie rolled the reception chair along the desk, pulling her backpack with her. She bent down to unpack it just as the phone rang. So much for it being quiet.

By the time she'd dealt with the customer enquiry – no, they didn't have a pool; yes, they had a hot tub; yes, the middle of the hotel was Georgian but it had modern wings, air conditioning *and* central heating; and yes, they were a two-minute walk to Kilmurray Beach so they had rooms with sea views (*obviously*) – another text had come through from her mum.

> **Max is in the creche, can you collect**
> **him on your way up and give him a**
> **snack.**

Frankie flopped her head forwards dramatically and groaned. Her little brother Max was eight, the ultra-embarrassing bonus child and adorable when he wasn't being a total demon. Surely Cian and Kai, her twin brothers, would be home pretty soon and could pick him up from the hotel's childcare? As if her mum had heard her, another text came through.

> **K&C at lifesaving. Ollie's in the bar. I'll**
> **be back 6.30.**

Frankie was going to need lifesaving if she didn't get this homework done – *and* she hadn't worked out what she was wearing to Katie's party yet.

'You rang, m'lady?' Frankie jumped and turned around to see Danny, the part-time-kitchen-porter-who-actually-did-everything, with a bottle of Coke and a pint glass full of ice balanced on a tray. Keeping a straight face, he laid it down on the desk in front of her and bowed, doing a sort of twirling flourish with his hand.

She tried to throw him a withering look, but he was such a clown, it was hard not to smile around him.

'How was school?' He raised one eyebrow and she shook her head, laughing.

'You should be on the stage.'

'Not with this haircut.' His blond hair had been almost completely shorn around the sides. 'Reckon my mam thinks if it's short enough at the start it'll last all term. I had to fight her off to keep the top long.'

'Having a hairdresser for a mum would be so handy.'

'If I was a girl, maybe.'

Frankie picked up the Coke. 'How's it feel to be back?'

He sighed, leaning on the counter, his chin on his arms. He had the sleeves of his white shirt rolled back, the green epaulettes that matched his trousers making him look like he should be flying a plane. 'Grim, but only to be expected. They aren't too crazy about my TikTok. It's only the second day of term and I already got "the call". The headmaster doesn't want Earlsbrook Comprehensive to appear in any of my videos, apparently.'

'As if you'd be remotely interested in filming anything at school.'

'True, but you never know. Look at how big school stuff is on Netflix.' He pulled a face.

Frankie laughed. Danny was refreshingly normal after the super-posh boys from Raven's Park College who all thought they had a God-given right to be the centre of attention. He was seventeen already, had been working in the Berwick Castle Hotel since the day after his sixteenth birthday, and in the past year had become pretty much indispensable, according to her mum, covering everything from peeling potatoes to making beds and walking guests' spoilt dogs.

She took another sip of her Coke, pointing at it. 'You're a life-saver, Danny Holmes, don't let anyone ever tell you different.' She took a long slurp. 'But look, you have to see this.' Frankie pulled out her phone. 'Someone's started this Raven's Hill confessions page, it's *mad*.' She scrolled through until she found it. 'Take a look.'

Danny's eyebrows raised with interest as he took the phone, reading out the first post. '"U ever want to delete all your socials and just disappear?" That would be a yes.'

'Don't be silly, keep going.'

Danny glanced at her and continued reading: '"Dumped by text. Discuss."'

'Oof, what do the comments say?' Frankie had missed that one today.

'"Sometimes it has to be done." That's a bit brutal.' He scanned the page. '"Makes me so mad I want to kill." Yikes, nice young ladies you have in that school.' He rolled his eyes, moving to the next comment. '"Devastating, but if he can't say it to your face, he's not worth the oxygen." Well, that's for sure.' Danny's mouth twitched into a grin at the next post. 'This is hilarious: "Saw Mr Munro at the beach in Speedos. I am officially traumatised."' He burst out laughing. 'Speedos are really not a good look.'

Frankie snorted. They'd had a laugh about that one at breaktime, but the real discussion had been over the next post. She resisted the urge to grin. 'Keep going.'

'"What do you do when you realise you might have accidentally hooked up with the new hockey coach over the summer? Asking for a friend." Ooh, spicy. What do they mean "might"?'

'She means "did" and is dying of mortification. I'd guess alcohol "might" have been involved too. How awkward is that?'

Danny laughed, shaking his head. 'That's really bad.' He scrolled down, 'What's this one about?' He angled the screen towards her.

Not everyone on Raven's Park College Rugby Team is as straight as they pretend to be.

Frankie pulled a face. 'Nasty. That doesn't sound like someone from Raven's Hill – Raven's Park must have heard about the page.' She rolled her eyes. The confession site was brilliant while it was just the girls; she didn't know how it would go if the boys' school started commenting and posting too. But it wasn't a private site and now that term had started word seemed to have travelled. 'That's such a mean thing to put up. I mean, being gay is no big deal but if someone's not out, it's for a reason. Now everyone's going to be wondering.'

'It's pretty easy for these things to get toxic, but there must be admins – who set it up?' Danny scanned the next few posts as she answered.

'We've no idea. It started over the summer but it wasn't all that exciting to begin with.'

He crooked an eyebrow at her. 'I can't believe you didn't tell me about it.' He looked at her reproachfully.

'I kept forgetting, with work and Max-minding and stuff. And it's only started to get really interesting now.'

He frowned for a moment. 'I'd be careful about posting on it – what if the admins suddenly decide to make the identities of everyone public?'

Frankie looked at him, shocked. 'You mean like it's a giant prank to get everyone to share their secrets and then out them?' Frankie hadn't thought of that. 'God, I hope not …' She shook her head. 'What are you doing working on your first week back at school, anyway?'

'I'm down to two evenings during the week and a day at the weekends this term, but one of the junior chefs called in sick.'

'Make sure everyone knows it's your exam year. You know what my family are like for taking advantage.'

'Your mam's still trying to persuade me to do Hotel Management.'

Danny had his heart set on a course in Film and TV. He had his whole career path mapped out, starting as a cameraman in TV news and graduating to documentary directing as he got his qualifications.

'She won't give up, you know. She doesn't think TV is a real job.'

Danny looked at her despairingly. 'I got that impression.' He shook his head. 'Maybe I'll come back when I'm famous and make a documentary about this place. People wouldn't believe some of the stuff that happens here.'

Before Frankie could answer, the phone rang. She picked up. It was room 202.

'Of course. I'll send another one up right now and you can try that.' Rooting in one of the drawers under the desk, Frankie pulled out a spare TV remote control and passed it to Danny. 'Danny's on his way. He'll be right with you.'

She hung up. '202, and they need some Irish charm by the sounds of things.'

Grabbing the remote, Danny threw her a salute and headed for the lift.

NINE
28 HOURS TO THE PARTY

Sorcha leaned into the window of the train, smiling to herself, as the DART pulled out of Kilmurray Point heading back towards Dublin City. She loved the novelty of getting the train to and from school. As the dark evenings drew in and the temperature dropped, she knew she'd be very glad she was boarding, but for now commuting was great.

The DART pulled into the next station, and the noise level rose as the doors opened. The platform was packed with loud boys and a scattering of girls in grey-and-black unforms from Kilmurray Manor. The boys seemed to fall through the doors, pushing and shoving, completely oblivious to the other passengers. Sorcha could hear the elderly lady across from her tutting loudly. Not that any of the boys noticed. Behind them a small group of girls came into the carriage, their black skirts shortened to above the knee. Two of them had taken off their sweaters and tied them around their waists, but they had to be baking in their thick black tights.

Sorcha didn't know what year they were – the girls looked like they could be Fourth Years, but the boys seemed to be a mix of ages, shapes and sizes, sweaters and shirts untucked. She swam against Kilmurray Manor regularly; some of their teams were really good, but they had to train at the public pool, which meant their training time was limited. What they lacked in pool hours they made up for in pure determination though, and were rapidly climbing the league. Kilmurray was already consistently top in debating and had an incredible maths team, as well as their rugby team being the sworn rivals of Raven's Park.

Looking out at the platform, wondering why the train hadn't moved yet, Sorcha suddenly caught a glimpse of a Raven's Hill uniform and long blonde hair she thought she recognised. She leaned forwards to see better as an announcement came over the tannoy, the driver's voice betraying his annoyance at being held up. 'Will everyone please stand *clear* of the doors.'

Laughter broke out and a pile of the younger boys fell out of the doors, running back down the platform to the next carriage. The tutting got louder across from her. With the view now cleared Sorcha could see it was Ruth Meaney standing just under the platform canopy, beside a tall boy in a Kilmurray Manor uniform who had to be a Sixth Year. They looked a bit awkward. Ruth was staring at the platform, fiddling with her phone, while he seemed to be explaining something to her. She looked up with an exaggerated sigh and Sorcha could see her face was set in a scowl. Whatever was going on, Ruth wasn't very happy about it. Was this the boy Frankie had overheard Amber and Ella talking about? The Rave-fess post about dating across years shot into Sorcha's mind.

Sorcha lifted her phone and, pretending to use it as a mirror, took a quick photo of them through the train doors. They were a good distance away, but when Frankie zoomed in she might know who the boy was.

Her curiosity burning, Sorcha shifted in her seat to get a better look at him. He had his head down now, but he was definitely older than them, tall and good-looking, his hair cut in a mullet, a cigarette hanging out of his mouth. He looked away from Ruth, down the platform, and she suddenly moved off, heading towards Sorcha's carriage, leaving him standing alone as if she was making a point.

Sorcha bent down quickly as if she had to get something out of her bag. Thank goodness she'd taken off her bright red jumper on the walk down to the station. The last thing she wanted to do this afternoon was get into another confrontation with Ruth Meaney. Praying Ruth went to the other end of the carriage, Sorcha held her breath.

A moment later whoever had been messing with the doors obviously moved the obstruction and they closed.

Straightening up, hiding her face with her hand, Sorcha took a look down the carriage. She could see Ruth in her distinctive Raven's Hill uniform sitting down in the other half of the carriage, thankfully with her back to Sorcha. She had her head down, like she was looking at her phone.

When the train pulled into the next station, Sorcha's heart lurched as Ruth stood up, turning her way. She seemed to be making sure her bag was safe on the seat. Sorcha slipped down as low as she could beside the window, praying the couple in front of her would block Ruth's view. But Ruth wasn't looking Sorcha's way. Sorcha peeped up and watched as she walked over to the doors, leaning out of the train as if she was looking for some-one. A second later, a boy in a Raven's Park College navy sweater jumped on, laughing, as if he'd been running for the train, the doors closing immediately behind him. He moved so quickly Sorcha couldn't see him properly, and now he had his back to her. He had the handles of a Raven's Park sports bag looped over his shoulders like a backpack. Someone stood up and blocked her view so Sorcha couldn't see what happened next, but as they moved, Sorcha could see Ruth was laughing, playfully pushing him. He followed her back to her seat.

Now who was *this*?

Sorcha straightened up, trying to see. There were no free seats nearby, so the boy stood over Ruth as she sat down. They seemed to be chatting easily and Ruth was definitely flirting with him. Sorcha could see her touching her hair and laughing, although she couldn't see if he was flirting back. They seemed to know each other well, though.

Curiosity was eating Sorcha up when suddenly the woman who had been sitting in the window seat beside Ruth stood up to get ready to leave. Stepping aside to let her out, the boy glanced down the carriage straight towards Sorcha and her eyebrows shot up as she recognised him.

It was Josh Fitzpatrick. She was sure of it. The same Josh Fitzpatrick who had just been hanging out at Starbucks – the captain of the Raven's Park College rugby team. *Katie's boyfriend.* What did Ruth think she was doing, flirting with him?

TEN
24 HOURS TO THE PARTY

Frankie still couldn't believe Patrick Kelly had spoken to her. Finally alone in her bedroom, Max fed and entrusted to the care of Cian and Kai, she leaned her head against the cool glass of her window, her stomach flipping.

Outside she could see movement in the darkness as feral cats crossed in and out of the security lighting in the delivery area, Ollie's two huge Rottweilers barking frantically any time one of them jumped onto the wall that bordered their yard. Danny was sure the cats were teasing the dogs, sitting just out of their reach. He'd been trying to film them all summer for some documentary he was making for school.

Frankie's room was at the end of the family wing of the hotel and had an incredible view of the bins, the tarmacked back entrance and the edge of the dogs' yard. She was working on swapping with Ollie, who had a view of the sea that was utterly wasted on him because he never spent any time in his room. She loved her own room with its purple feature wall, silver-grey bedlinen and furry throw, but she knew she'd love Ollie's a whole lot more. And he probably wouldn't even notice the lilac paint in her room by the time he'd covered it in all his music posters.

Frankie glanced over at the photo she'd taken during the summer of her friends by the bandstand on the pier. She'd had it blown up to poster size to fill the huge wall beside her dressing table. Everyone was laughing or pulling faces, Katie and Josh in the middle, arms wrapped around each other. They looked like the cast of a Netflix show, as if they were about to burst into song. Frankie smiled to herself. She loved taking movement shots, capturing a moment. That day had been the first time she'd 'met' Patrick; he'd been walking past with Conor and they'd jumped into the frame, photobombing at the back. It was the perfect shot; the evening sun on everyone's faces, the holidays stretching out ahead of them.

Frankie sighed, remembering their laughter. She'd seen later on Instagram that Patrick had gone for hotdogs with Conor and got ketchup all over himself. He'd got really mad and the shots had been hilarious.

Frankie closed her eyes, frozen for a moment as she relived their conversation yesterday. Patrick had known her name. And he was going to Katie's party. And he wanted Frankie to take his picture.

It was mad. She'd literally been trying to bump into Patrick Kelly ever since she'd taken that photo on the pier – the whole summer.

When she'd got back with the sugar, Jess had tried hard not to laugh at Frankie's excitement. 'Maybe he's actually really shy and needed a reason to talk to you. Taking his portrait is perfect – you might even need to have a few sessions to get it right.'

The possibility that Patrick might be shy made him all the more adorable in Frankie's book.

Turning away from the photo, Frankie looked at her bed. Her whole wardrobe was laid out over it, skirts and tops and all her dresses.

Because the problem now was what to wear to the party.

Frankie could feel anxiety and excitement starting to grip her stomach. She'd seen Patrick down at the beach and hanging out at the pier with his friends a few times over the summer. She hadn't thought for one moment that he'd noticed her. And now this. She shut her eyes and remembered his smile.

Tomorrow night couldn't come soon enough.

ELEVEN
3 HOURS TO THE PARTY

Frankie looked anxiously at her alarm clock. It was already after six. Her hair was wet, tied up in a towel while she let the expensive conditioner she'd got for her birthday soak in, and all her final clothes options were spread out over her bed.

She was down to three possible outfits, but she really needed Jess and Sorcha's input on the final decision. They were on their way over, but honestly everything was going wrong this evening – you really couldn't make it up. As if getting stuck minding Max for an extra hour wasn't

66

bad enough when she had vital decisions to make, now Jess and Sorcha had both been held up too. She would have loved to have helped Katie set up for the party, but Friday was her Max evening and she'd only just managed to escape when her brothers got home.

The girls were on their way over now, but it really felt like the universe was conspiring against her and her plans to finally have a proper conversation with Patrick.

The only good thing was that it wasn't raining. Frankie glanced out of the window to check the weather. She was going to so much trouble to get her hair looking good she did *not* want it to frizz.

Behind her, Frankie's phone pinged with a message. She spun around to look at it, her stomach somersaulting. Jess was almost here. Thank goodness. Hurrying into her bathroom, Frankie unwrapped her dark wavy hair and switched the shower on to rinse off the conditioner. With a bit of work and a lot of product, she was aiming for sleek, glossy tresses tonight. Jess was going to blow-dry it for her and do her make-up, and then she and Sorcha would help Frankie decide what to wear.

As she was coming out of the bathroom, there was a knock on her bedroom door. Jess, looking like she'd run up the stairs.

'Sorcha's coming, she'll be as fast as she can. Sorry it took me so long. I got in and found Dad getting ready to head for the airport early, so I didn't want to abandon him.'

'You're so good for coming over when he's going away. How long's he gone for?'

'He said just the weekend, but then he thought he wouldn't be going until tomorrow, so I'm not sure. If it looks like longer I'll need to let school know and move into the boarding house.'

Frankie unwrapped her hair. 'Sorcha will love that. She's moving in next week too.'

Jess grinned. 'I know, double trouble. Right, bring me up to speed. Has Patrick messaged you?' Jess folded back one of the dresses on the bed, making a space to sit down.

Frankie shook her head glumly. After he'd asked for her phone number to talk about the photo shoot, she'd thought Patrick might her contact her, but so far nothing.

'Don't worry, he knows you're going to the party so he's probably planning to talk about the photos there. Did you see Katie's stories?'

'Of him and Conor helping cut up all the fruit for the punch? I did.' Frankie pulled a face. 'Am I being stupid even thinking he might like me? Maybe he does just want a decent photo. I mean, this is Patrick Kelly – he's gorgeous.'

'He's the one who went into Starbucks and talked to you, not the other way around. And you said his family are loaded – he could book a professional photographer if it was just about pictures.'

Frankie sighed. 'I supposed you're right, I'm just so nervous.' She put a hand to her wet hair. She was being ridiculous. She needed to calm down. She took a deep breath. 'But you're right. Okay. Let's do the hair. Then we need to think clothes. I need to look so amazing that he'll wonder why he didn't call.' Frankie picked her hairbrush up from the dressing table. 'Ollie's dropping me over at about nine-thirty so I'm not the first in the door. I so wish you guys were coming with me.'

'Sorch and I are going to get takeaway and watch a movie instead,' said Jess. 'Much more chill. We'll follow the action on social and you can tell us all about it after. Where's your dryer? Sit down and I'll get started on Frankie 2.0.'

Frankie's hair was almost dry when Sorcha appeared at the door, her own hair still wet from the pool.

'Sorry I'm so late – training went on for ages, I couldn't get away. Have you seen Katie's Instagram? I know she said she was getting her make-up done professionally, but her nails are fabulous too.' Sorcha drew in a breath. 'Wow, your hair looks *amazing*, Franks.'

Frankie looked at her in the mirror, swishing her hair. 'All Jess's doing. Look how shiny she's made it.'

Sorcha put her swim bag down. 'Are you going to do smoky eyes for her, Jess? With that black winged eyeliner you use on yours? You really need to show me how to do that. I'm strictly mascara and lip gloss.' Sorcha turned to the three outfits lying on the bed. 'Which one are you thinking?' She held up her hand as if she needed total silence to make the final decision. 'The bronze sequins, definitely. You want to sparkle. The red is trying too hard, and the black is really nice but better for your first date with Patrick.' Sorcha threw Frankie a cheeky grin.

From her seat at the dressing table, Frankie leaned over and gave her a shove. 'Shut up, Sorch.'

Jess laughed. 'That dress is gorgeous. It'll look fab with your hair and a slip dress is perfect for a party. It'll go great with your boots.'

'You sure?' Frankie swivelled around on the seat and looked anxiously from Jess to Sorcha.

'Absolutely,' they said in unison.

Sorcha grinned at her. 'You're sorted. Your hair's fabulous, Jess is going to do your make-up, you've got a cute dress and a photo shoot to discuss. What could possibly go wrong?'

THE
PARTY

TWELVE

'Phone charged up?' Frankie's brother Ollie asked as he pulled up outside Katie's gate in his battered white van.

'Of course.' Frankie rooted for her lip gloss in the tiny crossbody bag that also contained her phone, tampons and a mini-hairbrush. Jess had made her bring extra make-up, a tiny packet of tissues and some gum too. She was glad of the gum now: she was so nervous that the inside of her mouth felt sour and the last thing she wanted was to have bad breath.

Would she get to dance with Patrick tonight? And

maybe ...? The thoughts flew around her head like fire-works, leaving a trail of sparks behind them. She tried to put them out; she was getting ahead of herself here. They hadn't even had a proper conversation. But even as the thought vanished into the darkness of her mind, there was still a glow, an ember alight, just waiting for a breeze to ignite it.

Jaysus, the anticipation was killing her. Could she even walk in knowing he was already there? This would all be so much easier if she'd said something to Katie, but there really hadn't been the right moment. Frankie had missed so much having to work over the summer, and then Katie had been away ...

Frankie took a deep breath, trying to focus. Pulling down the mirror in the van's sun visor, she re-glossed her lips for the hundredth time, then rooted out the gum. Jess's meticulous planning was working out already.

'Okay.' She took a deep breath. 'I'm ready.'

Out of the corner of her eye, she saw a smile flit across Ollie's face. He knew this was a big one, but thank goodness he wasn't teasing her about who would be there – she didn't think she could cope with that.

'What time am I collecting you?'

Frankie wrinkled her nose. 'Not sure.'

Ollie instinctively checked his mirrors and catch-ing sight of something, grinned. He glanced at her and then swivelled it around to show her two girls walking along the lane towards them, coats draped over their arms.

'They think no one will know they've got bottles under there. Look at their faces, a picture of innocence.' He chuckled, then looked over at Frankie. 'I'm in the bar until eleven-thirty and then once I've cashed up I'm going down to the studio – the lads are practising tonight, so I'll probably be there late. If you don't call by two a.m., I'll swing by for you. That okay?'

'Cool, I'll call when I know. It might be terrible and I'll need rescuing.'

'Don't be silly. It'll be deadly.' He put his hand on her arm. 'Make sure you do call, now. No walking home, and the faintest sniff of trouble, call me immediately.'

'Will do. Thanks, Ol.' Frankie smiled at him gratefully. He wasn't bad for an older brother once you forgot about his terrible taste in music, awful driving and very strange friends. The guys in the band were all way older and still thought they were going to be discovered. Even Ollie thought they were delusional, but he loved playing and his guitar solos were pretty awesome.

Frankie unclipped her seat belt and slipped out of the door, her Docs silent on the grass verge. She slammed the van door, and waved as Ollie pulled off, grinding through the gears. It had taken him six goes to pass his driving test, and at times like this Frankie could see why.

Turning to look at Katie's huge gate posts, she suddenly felt really sick. From out here she could already hear the music. It was just as well Katie had no neighbours who would complain – the nearest house was at the bottom of the lane where it joined a narrow road, the woodland thick on both sides.

Katie had been Instagramming #Katiesparty pictures as she got ready, rolling back rugs with Conor, making the punch, sticking up LED lights, and greeting the first people as they arrived. From the posts, it looked like there was quite a crowd there already. Frankie didn't know if that was a good thing or not. More people to talk to, yes; but also they would all be talking to each other by now. *Oh God.*

Frankie felt her mouth get even drier and sucked harder on the gum. She just had to go in, pick up a drink and find someone to talk to.

Easy.

Katie's drive snaked through dense yew trees, revealing the house on the final turn. Frankie had been here lots of times before, but she never failed to be impressed. She started walking up the drive, her boots crunching on the gravel.

Katie had put tea lights in jam jars all the way up to the house. When Frankie got to the final turn the music was even louder, the front door standing open, guarded by two classical pillars. More tea lights were scattered over the broad, semicircular front doorstep and along the edge of the flower bed.

The double-fronted house looked beautiful lit up at night. The windows to the study on the left were dark, the dining room window surrounded by flashing LED lights on the right. The sound of voices spilled out over the music into the garden. As Frankie stepped up to the door her movement must have created a breeze as the tea lights suddenly flickered madly, creating sinister shadows.

The hall with its black-and-white tiles and huge staircase was in semi-darkness and full of people, pulsating strips of LEDs wrapped around the banisters all the way up. Lots of girls from her class, and others she didn't recognise, were mingling with boys from the Raven's Park College rugby team. But there seemed to be more than just the rugby team here. There were definitely some boys she didn't know.

Even in the hall with the front door wide open, the heat was overpowering. Katie had closed up the rooms on the left-hand side of the house, her dad's study and the den with its cinema-sized TV. On the right, over the racket of raised voices, chatter and laughter, music was thumping from the main reception rooms – the dining room at the front of the house, and the living room behind it, both reached through double doors off the hall. Frankie had seen online how Katie had pushed the furniture and interior connecting doors back, so the two rooms linked together to create a huge space for the dance floor and bar area. At the end of the hall, running the full width of the house, was Katie's gorgeous kitchen with its marble island and huge pine table.

Where would Katie be?

Frankie took a deep breath and started down the hall, trying to weave through the crowd without bumping into anyone. The noise was almost overwhelming. Ahead of her she thought she saw Rob Doyle from Kilmurray Manor disappearing into the living room. It was hard to see in the darkness, but he towered over the girls, so she was fairly sure it was him. What was he doing here? He was always in trouble with the Guards and she'd heard rumours that he was Kilmurray Manor's main dealer – not someone Katie hung out with at all.

'Frankie!' Over the beat of the music, Frankie caught her name as Katie emerged from the living room, the double doors pushed right back against the brilliant white walls. She had a red Solo cup in her hand and Frankie could see from the fruit bobbing in it that she was drinking the punch that she'd made with Patrick and Conor earlier. Where was Patrick now? Frankie felt her stomach flipping again. She was so nervous.

'You look *amazing*. Who did your make-up?' Katie didn't stop to let Frankie reply. 'I'm so glad you're here. I'm not sure I know everyone at all.' Katie was very merry. She'd obviously already had good bit of punch. Frankie didn't drink herself, but she didn't make a big deal of it. She smiled and gave Katie a hug, but a flare of worry was igniting in Frankie's stomach. Katie seemed very relaxed about not knowing who was here. She didn't notice Frankie's hesitation as she continued, 'Come into the living room, this is where the dancing is. I'm looking for Josh, he was here a minute ago ...' She looked confused for a moment. 'Maybe he's gone out to the pool.'

Despite the glass doors on the far side of the room standing open to a patio and the pool, it was still roasting inside, the air swamp-thick with a heavy blend of perfume and aftershave. Frankie was glad she hadn't worn a jacket. The living room was dark and the dance floor in the middle was packed, the only light coming from pulsating LED lights strung along the walls that changed colour and rhythm with the beat of the music. They switched from blue to purple as Katie propelled Frankie forwards, leaning in so Frankie could hear her. 'Come on. Look, there's Conor.' Katie paused. 'With Ruth.' Her voice went up at the end in surprise.

Frankie watched them. Ruth had her hand on Conor's shoulder, dancing with him to the track that had just come on. She was wearing hotpants and a short silver crop top. They seemed to both be concentrating on their footwork.

Did Ruth like Conor? That was news. And was Conor bi? There had been loads of rumours about him and

Katie before she'd started dating Josh, and even though Frankie was sure they were nonsense, there had been times when she'd wondered about Conor. He seemed to spend loads of time at Katie's. Frankie suddenly realised she was staring and turned back to Katie.

And felt her heart leap.

In her peripheral vision, Patrick was leaning on the fireplace with a bottle of beer in his hand. He was chatting to a boy she didn't know who was sitting on the arm of one of the two living-room sofas that Katie had pushed back almost to the wall. Lit by a strip of LEDs, Patrick looked casually amazing in one of his designer shirts with the distinctive floral fabric inside the collar, his free hand stuck in the pocket of his jeans. Frankie had screenshotted Katie's story of him and Conor in the kitchen earlier to add to her collection of Patrick pictures, and he looked just as good now as he had done earlier. Pretending not to notice him, Frankie met Katie's eye. Frankie indicated Ruth and Conor with an exaggerated movement of her head. 'Sorcha saw Ruth with Rob Doyle at the DART station yesterday. She took a photo to show me because she didn't know who he was – do you think she's after Conor as well?' Now really wasn't the time to tell Katie that Sorcha had also thought she'd seen Ruth flirting with Josh.

Katie raised her eyebrows. 'I'm not going to be the one to ask her. I'm going to find Josh. He must be out

by the pool. Punch is on the table in the dining room.'
She pointed to the other side of the packed dance floor,
where more lights gleamed like strings of jewels, the
colours rippling. Beyond the mass of bodies moving to
the music, the dining room was like a cave, the curtains
closed and a table pulled to the far end to act as the bar.
On Frankie's right, the other living-room sofa had been
pushed right up against the wall just inside the concer-
tina doors dividing the two rooms. Tara and Viv were
curled up on it, laughing at their phones.

Frankie could feel her heart thumping in her ears.
She didn't want to look in Patrick's direction yet. She
needed to get a drink and then wander over, so she could
appear surprised to see him. If she didn't pass out en
route. Had he seen her come in?

Viv and Tara looked like they were deep in conversation, taking photos, filming and giggling. Maeve and
Caitriona had to be close by. Glancing up and seeing
Frankie, Viv and Tara gestured for her to come over,
waving their phones at her. They were uploading the
action on the dance floor to their TikTok and Instagram.
Laughing, Frankie pointed towards the bar, indicating
she was going to get a drink. She pulled her phone out
of her bag. She'd promised Sorcha and Jess updates, and
somehow she felt safer with it in her hand, like it was
some sort of a lifeline.

THIRTEEN

By the time Frankie had found the soft drinks under the 'bar', grabbed a clean cup off the stack and turned around, Patrick had vanished from the other side of the living room.

The track changed and the dancers packed into the middle of the dance floor shifted, the bodies thinning out, giving her a clear view for a moment.

Leaning on the doors dividing the two rooms, Frankie tried to look relaxed and very definitely like she wasn't looking for someone. She cursed herself. Scanning the dance floor and trying to look over everyone's heads towards the fireplace, she couldn't see Patrick anywhere. She should have gone over to say hello when she'd first arrived.

'Frankie, come and sit down,' Viv shouted at her, waving from the sofa.

The music picked up again. Katie seemed to have speakers in every corner of the room. But Frankie could see that Viv was patting the seat beside her. Still holding her drink, Frankie slid in between her and Tara.

Viv leaned over to speak into her ear. 'We've got the most brilliant view of all the shenanigans.' Viv was wearing sparkly rainbow eyeshadow to match the laces in her hi-tops. She looked fabulous.

Frankie took a sip of her Coke and sank into the soft beige leather, her eyes on the dance floor. Perhaps she'd be able to see Patrick from here.

'Have you had any of the punch?' Tara opened her eyes wide. 'It's quite strong.'

Frankie laughed; Tara looked like she'd had quite a bit of it already. Even over the music, it sounded like she was slurring. 'Katie said she made it from just about everything in her parents' drinks cabinet.' Tara giggled. 'She took measures from each bottle so they won't notice the change in levels and added it all to the vodka. It's *very* nice.'

Viv nudged Frankie. 'Where are Sorcha and Jess?'

'Jess doesn't like crowds and Sorcha said she didn't know enough people yet. I think she wanted to keep Jess company.'

Tara cut in. 'Sorcha's going to be boarding soon, then she'll know everyone. Well, all the boarders anyway.'

'Why did she change school?' Viv took a sip of her punch. She seemed to be taking it a little more slowly than Tara.

Frankie leaned in close so they could hear her. 'She's skipping TY and wanted to come to Raven's Hill because of the pool – she's in the county swim team.'

Viv took another sip of her drink. 'Oh yeah, someone told me that. She's super clever, right?'

Frankie laughed and nodded ruefully. 'Her side of the family have all the brains.'

Viv grinned. 'Yours got the looks – your twin brothers are gorgeous. I heard Ella and Ruth talking about them the other day.'

Frankie rolled her eyes. Cian and Kai *were* both very good-looking, but they were also both eighteen and doing their Leaving this year at the Institute of Education in Dublin. She'd had friends make comments about the twins before, but the thought of Ruth and Ella properly setting their sights on them was more than a little unsettling.

Before Frankie could comment, Tara leaned across so she and Viv could both hear her. 'Did you see the latest on Rave-fess? "I love lying about things for no reason." Who on earth would post that?'

Frankie pulled a face. 'Makes you wonder what they've been lying about …'

'There's going to be a *huge* row when the teachers find out about Rave-fess.' Tara took another sip of her punch.

Viv pursed her lips, her eyes gleaming with mischief. 'They can't take it down, *especially* when no one knows who set it up. Did you see the post about hooking up with the hockey coach? Maybe someone was lying about that? I really hope it's true – can you imagine the coach's face when they see whoever it is come running onto the hockey pitch?' Viv laughed, shaking her head. 'Which coach could it be, do you think? There are three new ones if you include the girl that's looking after the juniors.'

Tara smothered a grin. 'The teachers'll be mortified when they see it.'

Viv rolled her eyes. 'Does Jess like it? Raven's Hill, I mean, not Rave-fess.'

Frankie grinned. Viv was getting tipsier with every sip. 'Some stuff's taking time to get used to, but I think so. She says Ireland is really different to what she expected but she loves working in the charity shop. The women there really look after her. You know her mum died? Her dad's away a lot too – that's why she's at Raven's Hill. He didn't want to leave her on her own in London, and her gran lives here so coming back made sense.'

Tara wound a stray strand of black hair around her finger as she chimed in. 'Ms Cooke loves her. Having a high-profile TV journalist as a parent is good for PR.'

Frankie pulled a face at the thought of Ms Cooke crowing. 'True. Jess thought it'd be awkward being the only British person in school, but there are so many different nationalities at Raven's Hill, she's loving it. And she doesn't have to do Irish, which would have been a whole other level of stress.'

Viv smiled ruefully. 'Lucky her. She's lovely, she'll settle in. I can understand why she didn't want to come tonight though, it's rammed. It's so hard to find anyone. Caitriona and Maeve went off to dance ages ago and totally vanished. You should see Caitriona. She's got all her hair down, it's totally wild, she looks incredible, like some sort of goddess. I wish I had red hair.'

Before Frankie could comment, Tara nudged her. 'Is that Rob Doyle? The tall guy? Did Katie invite him?'

Frankie craned her neck to see where Tara was pointing. 'I thought he was in the hall when I arrived. Katie said there were more people here than she expected, and that she didn't know everyone. It must have got around Kilmurray Manor that there was a party happening.'

Tara leaned in closer. 'I heard Rob got arrested. He attacked some guy, stabbed him, something to do with drugs. I'm not totally sure, but I heard he ended up in a detention centre. Apparently he missed a whole school year with the trial and everything.'

As Frankie looked across the room, the dancers moved and she caught a glimpse of Rob Doyle heading out onto the patio. Frankie had been surprised when Sorcha had sent her the photo she'd taken on the DART; Ruth was such a snob, Frankie couldn't understand why she'd hang out with someone rumoured to be a drug dealer. Frankie knew she wouldn't herself, and Ruth was all about having the right image.

Unless, of course, he had something she wanted.

FOURTEEN

'You really do have a fabulous view from here.' Sorcha leaned on the edge of Jess's fourth-floor balcony and looked out across the harbour. It was a calm night, with a slight nip in the air that made it feel like autumn was just around the corner, but for now summer was trying to hold on. In the distance a huge cargo ship waited to go into Dublin Port, its lights bright in the darkness.

'Beats our view in London by miles, not gonna lie.' Jess came out through the sliding doors from the living room to stand beside her, popping the last piece of pizza into her mouth.

There were times when she came out here and breathed in the sea air and felt like she was in some alternate universe. It was so different to London, it was incredible. Jess felt sadness welling up inside her, tears pricking at her eyes. It would be so much more incredible if Mum was here too. Jess still hadn't got out of the habit of wanting to share new experiences with her. They'd been so close. Sometimes she found herself turning to say something to her, before remembering she was no longer there. Then the enormity of her loss would hit her again, like a tsunami.

She'd been to see a grief counsellor when they'd first got the news that her mum's cancer had spread, but Jess wasn't sure it had helped. The counsellor had said that the pain would never go away, that you just learned to live with it, but she hadn't told Jess how to stop reliving the shock of her mum's absence, over and over again, whenever there was something that she wanted to share. Sometimes the moments of realisation were paralysing, the loss like a gaping black hole inside her chest.

Jess sighed. Sorcha was saying something about the view but she wasn't sure what. She looked up to the sky, stars now dotting the heavens. Sometimes she just wanted a sign, anything to show that her mum was near, was watching over her.

Sorcha waved her phone and Jess tuned back into what she was saying.

'There are a *lot* of people at this party. God, I'm so glad we didn't go. I really can't do crowds. Being stuck in a room with that many people all drinking and getting off with each other is my idea of hell.'

Jess smiled. 'Me too.' She didn't say more. She'd been at a class birthday party when her dad had called to say her mum was finally slipping away. It would be a long time before she'd be able to go to a house party again. 'What's happening?'

'Snapchat and Insta are going mad. Everyone's putting up stories. I think it's better than being there – we get to see everything but without the noise and vomit.'

Jess laughed. 'I wonder how much of it will end up on Rave-fess?'

Sorcha smirked. 'Plenty, I bet. Did you see the posts earlier?'

'The one about unrequited love or the one about eye-lashes?' Jess shook her head. 'I'm so glad my life isn't going to be ruined by getting eyelash glue in my eye.'

'And what's the point of posting on an anonymous confession site where everyone is going to read it, and every single person you meet is going to see your one red eye and know that it was you?'

Jess laughed. Sorcha's eyes were wide, marvelling again at some of the posts. Jess pulled out her phone from the pocket of her hoodie to see if anything new had appeared on Rave-fess.

How can I tell you how super-hot you look when you're dating my best friend?

Sorcha pulled a face. 'That's a bit of a dilemma. I *cannot* see that ending well.'

Jess glanced at her before she read the next one. 'Oh my God, listen to this: "Karma is a bitch. Hope when ** is the only person you have left, she cheats on you and then maybe you'll experience the pain you've put me through. Life choices have consequen ... sences."' Jess said the last word phonetically, the way it had been misspelled.

'Is that someone at the party?

'Looks like it. I think they've had too much to drink. Why the stars, do you think?'

Sorcha glanced over at her and raised her eyebrows. 'Maybe it was initials and it was too obvious who they were talking about?'

Jess nodded slowly as she read the next post out loud. '"What is it with hot guys being so perfect when you meet in person but so shitty over text?!"'

Sorcha shifted against the balcony rail. 'Sometimes I wonder why people don't look a little deeper when they say something like that, like maybe have a think about motives.' Before Jess could comment, Sorcha glanced back at her own phone. 'Wow, there's some serious action happening on that sofa by the fireplace.' She swung the phone around to show Jess two boys tangled in a clinch. 'They're going to be thrilled with @TiernanTheGreat for posting that.'

Jess laughed. She hadn't known Sorcha long, but she felt like they had connected, and this evening was proving it. They had the same curiosity and sense of humour.

'That speaker behind the sofa is pretty awesome, though. The sound must be incredible in that room.' Jess paused. 'Anything more from Frankie yet?'

Sorcha shook her head. 'She's arrived, she's spotted Patrick, but he's vanished. She's found Viv and Tara, but all quiet for now.'

'Oh no, she needs to find him.' Jess turned her back to the view and leaned on the balcony. 'That house looks so huge he could be anywhere.'

Sorcha turned around too. 'Let's see if we can find him. He must be in someone's video somewhere and they're putting them up in real time, so we may be able to guide her in.'

'I love how your mind works, Sorcha. Okay, Operation Find Patrick begins.'

FIFTEEN

The one thing Frankie had *not* expected to happen at Katie's party was that she would end up spending half the night in the bathroom with Amber.

'You'll be fine soon, honestly.'

Frankie caught a stray piece of Amber's hair and held it back behind her as the girl leaned in over the toilet and retched for what felt like the hundredth time. Frankie closed her eyes and held her breath. The stench was making her want to vomit too.

When Amber had stumbled out of the crowd on the dance floor, her face had been as close to green as

Frankie had ever seen. Frankie had literally grabbed her and steered her straight for the downstairs bathroom, which, miraculously, had been available. Well, not exactly available, but the girl who'd been about to go in had taken one look at Amber's hand clamped over her mouth and jumped out of the way. Frankie's '*Patient incoming. Stand clear!*' had hardly been necessary.

They'd got inside just in time, Frankie slamming the door closed as Amber fell on her knees in front of the toilet bowl.

Thank God.

The thought of someone vomiting in the middle of the dance floor, or on the dining room floor, was just, well, vomitsville.

'I think I'm going to die ...' Amber's voice wasn't much more than a croak.

Frankie rubbed her shoulder. The other girl was shivering uncontrollably. Frankie wasn't sure if it was shock or alcohol poisoning. Neither were good.

'You'll be grand once everything's out of your stomach.' She sounded like her mum. 'Did you have a lot of that punch?'

Amber reached for a piece of toilet roll to wipe her mouth. 'I had a lot of everything. Me and Ella started at Georgia's before we even got here. Ruth's not drinking because of some tablets she's on – I should have kept her company.'

Before they came. That could have been where things went wrong. Frankie mentally shook her head.

'Oh crap.' Amber retched again.

Frankie felt her own stomach contract as someone knocked hard on the door, making Amber suddenly sit back on Frankie's foot.

'Could you get me some water?' Her voice came out in a whisper.

'Do you think you're done?'

Amber grunted as the knocking came again.

Frankie shouted through the door: 'There's a bathroom upstairs. This one's engaged. You really don't want to come in here right now.'

There was some cursing and a thump on the door as whoever was outside gave up.

Frankie emptied her Coke into the sink and rinsed out her cup. The basin was Victorian style with super-fancy soap and moisturiser in pump dispensers on a table beside it. Huge, scented candles lined the windowsill, flames flickering. At least the vanilla scent was helping mask some of the bitter stink of vomit.

She handed Amber the red plastic cup.

'I'm not sure I can stand.'

'There's no need to. Stay there for a minute.'

Frankie was interrupted by more frantic knocking.

'Busy in here, try upstairs,' she yelled back through the door again.

Amber put her hand to her forehead. 'I need – need to go home. Can't let anyone see me like this.'

Frankie looked at her; she did look pretty horrific. Her mascara was all smudged where her eyes had watered and her eyes were bloodshot, her face covered in pinpricks of what looked like bruising where the blood vessels had burst from the vomiting. And she was as white as a sheet. There was no point in saying she didn't look too bad. Frankie reached forwards to flush the toilet.

'Can you call your parents or will they go nuts?'

Amber looked miserable. 'My mum's gonna kill me but I'll say it was food poisoning. I'm allergic to mussels.'

Frankie looked at her. She wasn't sure why Amber's mum would believe that Katie had been serving mussels but …

'I can say it was in a Chinese.' Amber reached for her phone on the floor and put it on speaker as she hit speed dial. 'I'll get her to pick me up.'

You had to give Amber marks for resourcefulness in the face of adversity. 'It's after half eleven, will she be okay with that?' Frankie sighed inwardly. They had to have been in here for over an hour.

Amber's mum answered her phone before Frankie finished speaking. She didn't sound completely convinced by the scenario, either. Amber knocked off the speaker and put the phone to her ear. 'Please come, Mum, I've been so ill. Frankie's with me but I can barely stand up. It's like when I was in France.' Amber glanced at Frankie. 'Thanks, Mum, love you.' She ended the call.

'She'll be about ten minutes.' She started to struggle up from the floor. Frankie put out her hand to help her. 'I was supposed to be going back to Georgia's with Ruth and Ella – can you find them and say I had to leave early?'

Frankie looked at her, confused for a moment. 'Why don't you text them?'

'I'll text Georgia but Ella looked pretty busy on the dance floor when I saw her last. Please make sure they see the message. Oh God, I feel so bad.' She groaned pitifully.

'I'll come down the drive with you and find them when I get back.'

'Thanks so much. Can you tell my mum you had the Chinese too?'

Frankie sighed. 'Let's get you out first.'

They didn't have to wait long for Amber's mum once they got to the end of the drive. She looked less than impressed when Amber climbed, shivering, into the front seat, but her daughter was so pale that she could hardly get cross.

As they drove off, Frankie checked her phone. Jess had texted.

> P on patio with other boys. Tell us when
> you find him xx

How does she know that? Frankie smiled. Sorcha and Jess were hilarious. She could see from her notifications that they had been following #Katiesparty closely and sharing posts.

It was almost twelve. If she didn't find Patrick soon, the way things were going, she might not see him at all. Frankie shivered in the cool night air as she turned to go back up the drive. She'd go out to the patio now and look for one of Ruth's gang on the way so that she could pass on Amber's message like she'd promised.

The whole evening had been a disaster so far. It could only get better.

SIXTEEN

Sitting on Jess's sofa, Sorcha scrolled through her phone, looking at the posts and stories of the party being uploaded minute by minute. They'd started watching *Pitch Perfect*, but neither of them was paying much attention: the party was way more interesting. She knew enough people from Frankie's friend circle to be able to recognise faces, but half the fun was working out who was who in the darkness of the party, particularly when they were wrapped around each other. Loads of people were dancing with the torches on their phones switched on, which made the stories more atmospheric but also harder to identify the dancers.

Sorcha looked across at Jess, curled up in an armchair, her iPad on her knee. 'Are you following Georgia Swan, Jess? Honestly, how does she have time to add video descriptions to all her posts? Listen to this: "a girl in a lime-green dress with long dark hair is dancing at a party with a blond boy in a white T-shirt. The room is dark and crowded, lit by multicoloured LED lights. She is dancing to a club track with her arms in the air. He puts his arms above his head too and they laugh."'

Jess reached for her mug of hot chocolate. 'Georgia's pretty quiet. Maybe she wants to be an influencer – I know she wants to act.' She took a sip. 'That's Ella dancing – she's really going for it. She looks like she's auditioning for a music video or something.'

When they'd come inside, Sorcha had suddenly had the brilliant idea (even if she said so herself) of screen recording all the #Katiesparty posts on Jess's iPad so they could make a birthday video for Katie. They both followed the same accounts, but as people tagged their friends, they had started following others. Tomorrow morning a whole bunch of people were going to wonder who @only_one_world999 and @bornwithflippers were, but right now they were getting a full 360-degree view of the party from the comfort of Jess's living room. And there was *a lot* happening.

As Sorcha scrolled, another story popped up on Georgia's account with a detailed description. 'I think you're right, she's doing it again now: "video description: three girls are chatting at the bottom of a curving stair-case. They are all wearing short tops and miniskirts with hi-tops. One of them has her blonde hair in space buns. One has dark skin and is checking her purple lipstick in a mirror. Her top and skirt are black denim. They all have red Solo cups in their hands. They are laughing at a shared joke. A girl with long blonde hair wearing a silver top goes up the stairs behind them.'''

Jess grimaced. 'I bet Georgia hasn't got anyone to talk to. That would be me if I was there. Out in the hall making videos. Oh, here's Katie again. That turquoise dress is so pretty on her, isn't it? It's her colour.' Jess put her mug down on the glass coffee table and leaned over to show Sorcha the iPad screen. As the camera of whoever was live-posting panned across the room, they could see the packed dance floor and, beyond it, Katie sitting on a huge sofa with Viv and Tara. The shot was a bit shaky, like whoever was holding the phone was dancing.

Sorcha reached for her own steaming mug. She was so glad she'd decided not to go to the party. Her first week had been exhausting, getting to know everyone and fitting in her swim training. And they hadn't even got properly into studying yet. Spending the evening relaxing with Jess, finding out more about her life in London, was exactly what she'd needed. She yawned. 'This is great, isn't it, being able to see what's going on without having to cope with the heat and the crowd?'

'Or the noise.'

'True.' She took another sip of the frothy hot chocolate Jess had made. 'Do you mind being on your own when your dad's away?'

Jess shrugged. 'It's okay. It's usually only for a couple of nights and Dad calls constantly – and Grandma too. I could go to her house, but he's away at least once a week so I'd end up practically living there.'

'Is that bad?'

'No, I mean, she's lovely. She's just quite inquisitive. I think that's where my dad gets it from. And she's just too far from school to walk, so it would mean getting the bus in, or using my bike, which means getting up about an hour earlier.'

'All time in bed needs to be treasured,' Sorcha agreed. 'Getting up for swimming is way harder than actually training. So, if your dad gets held up somewhere, will you move into the boarding house?'

'Let's hope he's not literally held up, but yes, that's the plan. Raven's Hill have been really great about being flexible. All the other schools wanted full boarding or nothing and I'm not ready for that yet.'

'Sounds like the perfect arrangement. Oh look, there's Frankie at last.' Sorcha held up her phone screen so Jess could see.

'I can't believe she got shut in the loo with Amber puking. I don't think I'd be able to do that.'

Sorcha put her head on one side. 'Me neither. It's not even as if Amber is very nice. I still don't get why Georgia hangs around with them. Frankie reckons Ruth's only half decent to *her* because she fancies Cian and Kai. As if they'd be interested in Ruth Meaney for one second.' She shifted on the sofa, getting more comfortable. Ruth obviously hadn't made the connection that Cian and Kai were Sorcha's cousins as well – it would be very satisfying when that penny dropped.

As the thought went through her head, her phone pinged with a new message.

> **Going to patio, wish me luck. Can you see Ruth etc need to tell them Amber's left.**

Jess leaned forwards. 'Is that Frankie?'

Glancing up, Sorcha nodded. 'She's going to find Patrick.' Sorcha felt excitement building inside her. She just hoped, when Frankie found him, that things went as well as she wanted them to. 'She wants to find Ruth.' Sorcha scrunched up her face. 'Georgia's story caught her going upstairs but I don't know when that actually happened. It was only posted a few minutes ago but those descriptions take ages to do.'

SEVENTEEN

lancing into the dining room, looking for Ruth. Frankie could see three girls she didn't know had started filming some sort of TikTok dance routine. She'd seen Ella on the dance floor, totally rocking it out in a tight knot of sweaty bodies, but Frankie wasn't about to plunge in and interrupt to give her a message that she probably wouldn't even hear. How had she got caught up in this Amber drama? God, she hoped she didn't smell of vomit. Assuming she ever found Patrick, that would be a serious passion killer.

Suddenly nervous at the thought of finally speaking to him, Frankie felt her mouth dry. She needed another Coke.

The white cloth on the table was even more stained with punch than it had been when she'd got her first drink. In the centre of the 'bar', the huge glass punch bowl was almost empty, chunks of orange and lemon left at the bottom like shells after the tide had gone out. Spread across the rest of the table were a jumble of beer bottles and lager cans. At one end were the remains of a stack of red Solo cups.

Frankie reached for one, careful to avoid knocking the phones the girls had propped up to film their set. She glanced over at them. An upbeat track had come on and they were dancing and lip-syncing, badly out of time with each other, but from the way they were pouting at the camera, they obviously thought they were amazing.

Frankie moved down the table, trying to see if she could find a bottle of something soft. What was left of the punch looked positively toxic: it wasn't surprising Amber had been ill. It took her a few minutes to sort through the bottles but she managed to find half a bottle of Coke. The ice bucket was almost empty too. Chasing the last few cubes around, she flipped them into her cup.

She just wanted to get a quick video of the dancing trio for Sorcha and Jess, then she'd go outside. Hopefully she'd find Ruth on the way.

Taking a sip of her Coke, she slipped around a couple she didn't know who were wrapped up in each other, and two girls who were trying not to snigger at the TikTok dancers. There was a corner between the two rooms where she could film. The girls would have been quite good if it wasn't for the fact they were woefully out of time with each other, and the tracks. Frankie watched, mesmerised, as they did a few routines.

The French doors, with the strip of lights running around them, created a frame, making the girls look even more serious about their routine. It was pitch dark outside now and the flashing LEDs made the house feel like a subterranean club.

Finally a track came on that the girls seemed to know better. Frankie got a few seconds of the trio and turned to film the dance floor. It was still packed. Was Patrick still outside? She hoped so. Perhaps he'd been looking for her when she was locked in the bathroom. She'd been in there long enough. *Wishful thinking, maybe.* Frankie searched for him with her camera as she swung the phone around. This party wasn't going anything like she'd imagined it would. She hadn't even *seen* Patrick since she'd arrived.

The music was booming as Frankie held her phone up high over the crowd. Everyone had their phones out, taking selfies. There was still no sign of Ruth. Conor was dancing with someone else now. He was a good dancer and looked like he was really enjoying himself. He had a spliff in his hand and was taking drags on it as he moved. Patrick *had* to be nearby – perhaps he was just on the other side of the room and she couldn't see him, or was still out by the pool. But Katie had a huge garden; he could be anywhere by now. Why hadn't he come to look for her? Maybe he *did* only want her to take his photo. Frankie felt her heart fall and her confidence wobble.

She was going to need a few minutes to get herself back on track.

Turning off her camera, Frankie went and perched on the sofa arm, next to Viv and Tara, who didn't seem to have moved since she'd last seen them. Frankie guessed Viv wanted to stay put. Tara was lovely to keep her company. 'Have you two got loads of photos?'

She leaned forwards as Tara showed her a picture of Ruth and Conor dancing. She'd added a bright pink arrow pointing to his hand on her bum.

'Oh my God, she's going to kill you when she sees that!'

Laughter made her feel better.

Frankie leaned in so Tara could hear her. 'I'm just going to go out to the pool to see who's there. I'll be right back.'

Focused on changing her phone settings so she could get some cool images for Katie, Frankie paused beside the dance floor, realising, as she did so, that something was happening there. Ella had stopped dancing. She was standing in the middle of the mass of bodies, looking over her shoulder and glaring at a boy. Ella's face was furious and the boy had his hand over his cheek like she'd slapped him, but he was laughing at her.

As Frankie watched, more people were beginning to notice something was up.

The boy Ella had slapped tried to put his arm around her and give her a kiss. She pushed him away and the boy's head suddenly flipped backwards like he'd been punched. He staggered, falling onto the people behind him. As Frankie watched, paralysed, another boy came from nowhere and threw a punch. She felt like she was watching everything in slow motion. More punches, more people piling in. Someone turned the music off and screams and shouts filled the space as the dancers reacted.

Suddenly more boys appeared from the hall and from outside, and now everyone was hitting everyone else. Frankie found herself pushed towards the fireplace, swept forwards in the movement of people rushing into the room to see what was happening. She couldn't even see Ella anymore. A spindly-legged dining chair came flying across the dance floor and more girls Frankie didn't recognise crowded in, grabbing at their friends' hoodies and trying to pull the knot of brawling boys apart. Frankie could see Raven's Hill girls trying to get out of the way. At least they had some sense. They didn't seem to have the same loyalty to the boys that the Kilmurray Manor girls did.

Some of the boys detached from the melee on the dance floor, pushing past people to get out into the hallway. Then someone threw what must have been a bucket of pool water over everyone, the smell of chlorine strong, battling the heavy scent of perfume, aftershave and body odour that already filled the living room.

The noise of screaming was so overwhelming that Frankie had no time to think. She felt like she was suffocating as she was pushed and shoved out of the way. She wriggled through the bodies, trying to get closer to the wall. Her phone was knocked out of her hand, and as she bent to grab it before it got smashed, she heard breaking glass and more screaming.

Someone stepped on her fingers as she reached for her phone, pain shooting up her arm, but she shoved her shoulder into the back of the leg of whoever it was and a moment later she had her phone firmly in her hand. She crawled backwards until she was curled up by the TV. Everyone was fighting now, and she couldn't see who was who, but it was getting nasty. Fear made her stomach churn and her head swirl as she realised she was trapped. Someone fell towards her and she curled up even tighter, protecting her head. Time seemed to stand still as the fight continued around her.

Then she felt it move away, the mass of bodies moving closer to the doors out to the pool, and Frankie grabbed her chance. Finding Ollie's number, she quickly dialled. She couldn't afford for him to miss a text. It was 12.11; he'd have put the cash in the safe by now and be getting ready to leave for the studio. After a couple of rings, he answered.

'Ollie, I need you to come. There's a fight. Really bad, come now.' Her voice was breathless with fear.

'I can't hear you properly, Franks – a fight, did you say? How many?'

'*Everyone*. Come now, Ollie, and bring help.'

'Get out of the house, go out onto the drive and wait for me. I was just about to go the studio, I'll bring the twins. Be there soon as.'

Frankie ended the call and, keeping low, doubled back along the edge of the living room, across the fireplace. Behind her the huge widescreen TV came crashing off its pedestal, the glass breaking.

All she could hear was screaming and boys roaring and swearing at each other, the smell of sweat and fear strong. She got to the sofa that was pushed back near the kitchen door and, edging along the front of it, made a dash for the double doors leading to the hall.

How could this be happening? Katie's beautiful house was getting wrecked. She was going to be in so much trouble.

In the hall, boys and girls were huddled together in tight knots, their phones in their hands.

Frankie spotted Issie, one of the Fifth Year boarders. 'Have you seen Katie, or Viv and Tara?'

Issie's normally glowing dark skin was dull with worry. She frowned as she spoke. 'Viv's gone, she went before any of us even really realised it had started. She was on the phone to a taxi when she passed me. Loads of people have headed home. They just left without their jackets or anything. I can't get through to any of the taxi companies – how are we going to get back to school?'

Fear shot through Frankie. It was pitch dark outside and a long walk to the main road. A load of drunk Fifth Years trying to get home unaided was another disaster waiting to happen.

EIGHTEEN

Frankie drew in a shaky breath, adrenaline kicking in as she thought fast.

'Go outside into the front garden where it's safe. My brothers are coming – Ollie will take you back to school. Tell the others. Don't go far. Stick together.' She pushed Issie towards the open front door. 'Go outside. Quickly.'

Behind her Frankie could hear things breaking, then more shouting and screaming. Where was Katie? It was hours since Frankie had seen her. She needed to make sure that she was safe. Frankie pulled out her phone and called Katie. It went straight to voicemail. *Where was she?*

Frankie turned to go back into the living room, but suddenly remembered there was a side gate. If it wasn't locked, she could get to the patio around the back and see if Katie was there.

She really didn't want to go back through the fight.

Running back down the hall and out of the front door, Frankie could see girls and a few boys gathered outside. Issie had found some of the other boarders and they were huddled together on the grass. Frankie ran to a group closer to the house, panic rising inside her.

'Has anyone seen Katie?'

Everyone shook their heads. Frankie ran across the front lawn and around the side, looking for the gate in the fence. It was hard to see in the darkness. Then she spotted it. She tried the latch. Locked.

Frankie tried Katie again. Voicemail, again.

Phone in her hand, Frankie took a step back to see if she could climb over the fence, but there was nothing to give her a leg up and it was super high.

She'd have to go back inside. She glanced towards the drive. No sign of Ollie yet. She knew she was mad going back inside to the fight, but she had to make sure Katie was okay.

In the hall were more girls she knew. 'Come outside! If you can't get a taxi, my brothers are coming with their van. They'll take everyone home.'

The girls started to move and Frankie ran on down

the hallway. The kitchen door was closed, and she was just about to open it when Katie appeared behind her at the living room door, her face streaked with tears. Seeing Frankie, she grabbed her, holding her so tight her fingers dug into Frankie's arms.

'Oh my God, Frankie, I thought you'd all left. What am I going to do? I keep shouting at them to stop, but they can't even hear me. Someone shoved me out of the way ...' She stifled a sob. 'The house is getting completely trashed. My parents are going to kill me, and I can't find Josh or Conor anywhere –' Katie was shaking. She looked like she was about to have a panic attack. 'I can't call the police. My parents will find out and I'll be grounded forever.'

Frankie hugged her. 'Ollie's coming – he'll fix everything. Go upstairs and shut yourself in your room where it's safe, and make sure the dogs stay inside with you. Ollie will be here in a minute. It's going to be okay, don't worry.'

Katie's mouth opened as if she was trying to say something but couldn't catch her breath.

'Go on, go quickly.' As she spoke, Frankie heard the screech of tyres pulling up on the gravel outside. 'That's Ollie, it'll be fine. We'll get everyone out of the house and get anyone who needs a lift home. I'll show him where to go to make it quicker, then I'll come back and help you clean up.' She tried to catch her breath as she thought fast. 'Sorcha and Jess will come and help too, they're both still up, they've been watching online. It's all going to be okay. Now go.'

As Katie reached the bottom of the stairs, Ollie appeared at the front door, Cian and Kai behind him. The twins were both Taekwondo blackbelts, and a year older than most of the partygoers. They'd get this sorted.

Ollie spotted Frankie. 'Van, now. Get your friends in. Wait for us.'

Frankie didn't need to be told twice. She ran past her brothers out into the front garden, hauling the back doors of the van open and urging the dozen or so people left on the lawn and hanging around the drive to jump in. They were silent, in shock, some crying, their phones in their hands. As Frankie helped Issie up, she called into the back, 'Squish up there. Find out where your friends are, see if they have a lift. Tell them to wait for us if they don't, and Ollie will pick them up on the way back into town. We'll head for school and then the town centre so they can get cabs.'

Frankie left the van doors open – there was still space inside – and ran around to the front seat. Jumping in, she looked back at the house as someone yanked open the dining room curtains. It was Cian. Behind him, she could see that all the lights had been turned on inside. The room was still full of boys and a few girls, but it looked like things had calmed down.

Suddenly through the dining room window she could see some sort of scuffle start and Ollie appeared, crossing the room. He'd lifted a lad clean off his feet and was heading towards the living room door with him. Cian and Kai started ushering everyone else out like they were evacuating a burning building.

Twisting in her seat, Frankie watched as a stream of the battle-weary stumbled out of the front door, clothing askew, some of them with bloody noses, shirts wet, some splattered with red, eyes already starting to swell. Frankie recognised a few of them, but she still couldn't see Patrick. The boys looked like a defeated army as they trailed down the drive, some girls Frankie didn't know walking with them. Frankie just hoped the fight had finished now and wouldn't continue out in the road. They needed to get rid of everyone and get back to sort out the mess before Katie's parents heard what had happened.

There was a pause in the flow of people leaving and Frankie realised that somehow her brothers had separated the two warring groups of Kilmurray Manor and Raven's Park College. The fight might have started over Ella Diamond but it looked like it had turned into a pitched inter-school battle, rival team tensions and resentments exploding like a volcano.

Now Raven's Park were coming out, but Frankie still couldn't see Patrick. Had she missed him? She really hoped everyone was okay.

A few minutes later she saw Ollie, Cian and Kai following the last few partygoers out. They'd left all the house lights on but pulled the front door firmly shut behind them.

The twins walked down the drive together as Ollie swung the rear doors of the van closed and jogged around to jump in behind the wheel.

'You okay, Franks?'

Frankie realised she was shivering. She nodded. Ollie rooted behind her seat and hauled out his hoodie. 'Put that on. The twins are going to close the gates and walk home. They have to get back – they've got early study at school in the morning and it'll be quicker than waiting for a cab.'

'Is the house awful? We need to help Katie clear up.'

Ollie looked at her for a moment and then, sighing, put the van into reverse. 'Mum's right, you need to stop trying to solve everyone's problems, Franks. It's adorable, but *sometimes* …' He shook his head, but as he turned the van he patted her knee. 'I know Katie's one of your friends, so this is different. And y'know I've always got your back.' He scraped the van into gear. 'Okay, first job is to get this lot home. Then you can tell me what the hell happened. Those lads have some lip.' He paused. Frankie could tell he was holding onto his temper, but she knew him well enough to know it wasn't her that he was cross with. He shook his head, more to himself than her. 'What a mess.' He looked quickly over his shoulder. 'Right, everyone okay in the back there?' There was a rumble that sounded like it might be a maybe.

'Sorcha is at Jess's – can we pick them up on the way back? We really do need to help Katie.'

Ollie nodded, throwing her an understanding look. 'No probs. It's going to be a big job. When are her parents back?'

'Tomorrow?' Frankie's voice was small.

'Jaysus. Better get moving, so.'

AFTER

NINETEEN

I t had been the perfect party.

Well, it could have been, if all the stuff that had happened *hadn't* happened. If Frankie had woken up this morning with nothing more than the disappointment of not talking to Patrick to worry about.

If Josh Fitzpatrick was still alive.

The words went through her head excruciatingly slowly, somehow whispered as if saying it properly, out loud, would make it true, like it had actually happened.

But it had.

Josh was dead.

Frankie felt herself curl up inside, hiding from the truth. Maybe if she closed her eyes it would all go away. She shut them tight, but it didn't help. *If they'd seen his body sooner, would it have made any difference?*

The thought swirled in Frankie's head like the winds of a gathering storm, mirroring the sick feeling in her stomach.

This was so insane. They didn't know people who stabbed other people. That only happened on TV. Until it didn't. Until it happened in Katie's living room at her seventeenth birthday party. To her boyfriend.

Frankie felt like the image of the knife sticking out of Josh's back was imprinted on the inside of her eyelids.

It had taken her and Sorcha a few minutes to real-ise that the body belonged to Josh. From where she was standing at the end of the sofa, Katie had realised long before them, had stood paralysed, unable to speak. It had only been as Frankie had hauled the sofa further into the room that the true horror had hit her. Josh, lying on his side, one hand clutching a red Solo cup. They hadn't even seen the knife then, just his pale skin and staring eyes, the blood pooling under his shoulder, dark and sticky. Frankie had tried to roll him into the recovery position, sure that he was still alive, that he was just unconscious, that the blood was from ... she didn't even know where, but ... then they'd seen it, the sleek black handle sticking out of his T-shirt.

Frankie felt her stomach contract as she remembered. At least the ambulance had been fast, the paramedics sending them out of the room as Frankie anxiously tried to call Ollie to come back.

Frankie pulled her duvet up to her chin, willing the memories away. If she wished hard enough maybe she could roll time back to the start of the week when the only thing she'd been worried about was what to wear and whether Patrick would talk to her. Perhaps if she went back far enough Katie would decide that going to see a movie for her birthday would be a great idea, or her parents would say no to a party.

Last night Katie's panic attack had been almost as frightening as the pool of blood on the polished floor. Jess had held both her hands, trying to get her to breathe, and then, when the paramedics had arrived for Josh, they'd taken over with Katie too. Frankie and Jess and Sorcha had been hooshed out of the room. Thank God the ambulance had been fast; Katie having a heart attack on top of everything would have been more than Frankie could cope with. It was all too awful already.

'So, what happened, love, can you tell me?'

Curled up in bed, the weight of Katie's slumbering dogs against the backs of her legs, Frankie felt more tears rolling down her cheeks as the Guard's words came back to her: '*The paramedics are doing what they can for him, and your friend will be fine, lass, she's getting some oxygen now. So, this fight, what happened exactly?'*

The Guards had wanted to establish that there were no more victims, and had searched the house and the grounds as the paramedics tried CPR on Josh – at least that's what Frankie assumed they were doing. Even from the stairs she had heard the medics' voices, urgent, professional, trying everything to save him.

Frankie had shrugged in answer to the Guard, taking a deep breath as the memory of the fear she'd felt on the dance floor came flooding back. 'I think one of the Raven's Park guys hit a Kilmurray lad and then it all kicked off.'

'There was alcohol taken?'

She'd looked at him, wrinkling her nose. What sort of a party did he think it was?

The punch had been strong, and everyone had brought bottles with them. Katie had hidden the extra bottles of vodka that she'd bought in the oven so nobody could pinch them and get really sick. She'd sent Frankie a photo of her own bottle of gin in the tumble dryer with a row of laughing emojis.

There was nothing funny about any of this now.

Frankie had cleared her throat. 'Yes, they were all fairly drunk. The fight got really bad really fast, so I called my brothers and they helped break it up. They threw everyone out – a lot of girls had already left, but the boys were wrecking the house.'

'Your brothers didn't think of calling the Guards?'

Frankie had sighed. Like everyone getting arrested would have made things any better? Thank God Katie didn't have any neighbours.

'We thought we had it all sorted. Ollie and the twins threw everyone out, and Ollie had his van so we went and collected up the girls. They scattered when it started getting messy, a lot of them didn't have any money, or ...' Frankie had found herself staring at one of the black marble floor tiles. A wave of exhaustion and despair welled up inside her, her eyes clouding with tears, wishing Ollie would hurry up and get here. After he'd dropped them back at Katie's to clear up, he'd gone to meet his band for the end of their session and hadn't heard his phone when she'd called the first few times.

By then, she'd just wanted to go home and crawl into bed with her Bagpuss hot-water bottle and never leave her room again.

'And what happened next?' The Guard's voice had been gentle. Frankie had blinked and run her hands over her face. She knew these questions were important. Didn't they say in cop shows that the first forty-eight hours after a crime were crucial? But who could have done this? Who would have brought a knife to a party and then pulled it out in the middle of a fight?

'Sorry.' Why did she keep saying sorry? This wasn't her fault, was it? 'We made sure they got home, Ollie did,

I mean. Then we went to fetch Jess and Sorcha to come back and help us clear up.'

It all sounded very calm and organised when you said it like that, even to Frankie. But Snapchat had been pinging with the drama of it all.

And that was before they'd realised what was waiting for them back at Katie's house.

'And then?' The Guard had leaned on the end of the banister where it curled around, writing something in his notebook. When they'd got back, the true devastation of the fight, the smashed TV, the broken glass, had been the first shock.

The Guard had asked the question again and Frankie rubbed her face with her hands. She needed to focus and get through this.

'Ollie dropped us back and went down to his studio while we started clearing up the house, but Marshmallow and Cheesecake were going nuts. They're Katie's dogs. They were locked up during the party but when we got back, she let them out. They went next-level crazy.' Frankie had paused as the Guard nodded. 'I called him to come back straight after I called you, he's on his way ...'

At that moment Ollie had arrived through the front door behind the Guard, and jumping up, she'd run into his arms.

Remembering everything in what felt like freeze frames, Frankie snuggled deeper under her duvet, hugging Bagpuss even closer, the dogs snuffling in their sleep beside her. She didn't think she could cry any more, but the tears kept coming. Rooting under the duvet for a tissue, she wiped her nose again. It was getting sore but she didn't care. She felt like she was broken inside, and she didn't have any idea how to fix it. *It was all so awful.*

Dead.

Josh was *dead*.

Dead didn't happen when you were seventeen.

Dead was something that happened to old people, or people who were sick, or people on the news.

Not to her school friend. Her friend's boyfriend.

The tears came again. It was like she couldn't turn them off. Frankie took a gaspy breath. Ollie had brought Katie home with them, along with Marshmallow and Cheescake. The paramedics had given Katie something to calm her down and eventually she'd fallen into a drug-induced doze, but Frankie had hardly slept. Everything was swirling around in her head like some sort of horror movie – the Amber drama and then the fight, and then … she must have slept a bit because she'd woken up with her heart beating and her mouth feeling like it was full of sand … how could something this terrible have happened?

TWENTY

The tap on Frankie's bedroom door made her jump. Marshmallow and Cheesecake's heads shot up at the end of her bed. They tumbled off, yapping, as Frankie felt a flood of relief. Jess and Sorcha. *Thank goodness.*

'Coming.' It came out as a croak as Frankie pushed her duvet back and swung her legs out of the bed so that she could grab hold of the dogs' pink leather collars. The last thing Katie needed now was her fur babies escaping and getting lost. Holding them back so they didn't dash out through her bedroom door, Frankie called out again, 'Come in.'

The door opened a crack and Sorcha peeped around it. 'It's us. You okay?'

Frankie heaved a shaky sigh, trying not to start crying again. She could see from Sorcha's blotchy face that she was the same.

'Come in quickly. My mum's taken Katie to meet her parents at the airport – these two aren't impressed at being left behind.'

Sorcha slipped inside, followed by Jess, who closed the door behind them firmly. Letting go of the dogs, Frankie put out both her arms for a group hug, a sob catching in her throat. The sound set Sorcha off and they all clung to each other.

Scampering around them, sniffing at the new arrivals, the dogs must have sensed their mood. They started to jump up and paw at the girls' jeans, whimpering.

Jess sniffed loudly and, breaking away, bent down to give them a hug. 'They must be feeling awful too. Animals really pick up on your mood.'

Biting her lip, Sorcha bent to tickle the dogs. 'How is Katie? Did she sleep at all?'

Sighing, Frankie shrugged and rubbed her eyes with her hands, trying to clear away the blur of tears. 'Whatever they gave her knocked her out, or maybe it was exhaustion, but I think she had nightmares.' Frankie took a breath. 'She didn't want me to go with her to meet her parents. I –'

Jess rubbed the top of her arm, interrupting her. 'It's not you. Don't worry. You were amazing last night.' Jess's smile was brave. 'She needs space to grieve. I think she needs to see her parents on her own too. It's such a huge thing to take in, it's probably not even hit her fully yet.'

'It's hit me.' Sorcha pulled Frankie in for another quick hug. 'You don't look like you got much sleep.'

Frankie let out a big sigh, shaking her head. 'I'm not sure I'm ever going to sleep again. It didn't help that Mum kept popping in to check on us every five minutes.'

When she'd got home last night, while Katie had been in the bathroom, Frankie had pulled down the huge photo poster she'd taken on the pier at the start of the summer. Seeing Josh's happy, handsome face smiling out at her was bad enough; for Katie it would be the end. Rolling the poster up carefully, she'd tucked it in beside her bed. Now, as Sorcha dumped her backpack on the floor, and sat down on the end of the bed, she looked up and Frankie could see her realising that the poster was missing.

Sorcha opened her mouth to say something but then, apparently thinking better of it, bent down to tickle the dogs again, saying instead, 'Same. We didn't sleep much either. We were talking all night.'

Jess went to pull out the chair at Frankie's dressing table. She was wearing a black sweatshirt over her jeans and black Vans. The dogs switched their attention to her, jumping up with their front paws on her knees as soon as she sat down.

Sorcha watched them. 'Have you got these two for the foreseeable? Can they go down with the others?'

'Ollie reckoned Wolf and Bear might eat them in the night.' Frankie looked at the two white curly bundles of crazy. They were so different from Ollie's huge, calm Rottweilers it was like they were a different species.

Sorcha sat back on the bed and took a deep breath. 'So, tell us what's happening – anything from the Guards this morning?'

Frankie went to pull out another tissue from the box on her bedside table and climbed back under her duvet, shaking her head. 'They're still at the house, apparently. Mum's got the penthouse suite ready in case Katie's parents can't stay there tonight. I don't know how long the Guards'll be.' She paused, her voice shaking as she continued. 'Me and Katie have to go down to Kilmurray station and make proper statements today. I'm dreading it, but Mum's going to go with me.' Frankie blew her nose and slid back onto her bed, pulling the pillows up behind her. 'She's going to be mad when she hears about everything, and it's not like I even drink.' She let out a sharp breath. 'Ollie and the twins have to go down too.'

'We have to, as well. Jess's gran is coming over and my dad's coming. He can't believe it. Will we meet you after?' Sorcha paused. 'I'm not going to training. I can't concentrate today. I keep bursting into tears.' As if on cue, her eyes filled again.

Frankie reached for a tissue and passed it to her. 'Hopefully it won't take too long.'

'I've called in sick to work. How are you doing with the list of people who were there?' Jess put her elbow on the dressing table as she ran her fingers through her hair. Her normally sparkling eyes were dull and red-rimmed.

Half-heartedly, Frankie reached for the copy book on her bedside table. 'We started last night, making lists of everyone we could remember under the name of each school, but we've only got a fraction of them. The house was packed. There had to have been well over a hundred people there between the different schools and I'm sure there were some Sixth Years too. I mean, I've no idea who those TikTok girls were at all. It's hopeless.'

'That's maybe where we come in.' Sorcha bent down and pulled her iPad from her bag. 'We were talking about it last night. The best way we can help Katie – and the Guards – is to work out exactly who was there.' Having something to focus on seemed to have flicked a switch in Sorcha. Frankie could hear it in the edge in her voice, as if she was suddenly able to see beyond the nightmare of Katie's house. Sorcha might have only just started at Raven's Hill, but Katie and Frankie had been in the same friend group forever and Sorcha knew Katie from birthday parties and sleepovers. She clearly wanted to help.

Jess stood up and came to sit beside Frankie on the bed. 'We were putting together a video for Katie of all the posts and stories from last night as a present, but I reckon if we go through everything we've gathered up, we should be able to get a list together pretty quickly. We'll cross reference with Instagram anyone we don't recognise, then screenshot the faces we're really stuck on so we can ask around to find out who they are.'

Frankie could feel the tears coming again, but this time they were tears of gratitude. This was one way they really could help. She reached for her phone. 'You're right. I've been feeling so useless.' She sighed, a pain beginning to spread across her forehead. 'The bit that's making me feel so sick is *who* did it? I mean, it could be someone we *know*.'

Who? The thought had bounced around her head all night until she felt as if her brain was a pinball machine. Who could have done this? It was the question everyone would be asking when they knew. Josh was one of the most popular boys in school. Everyone loved him. *Didn't they?*

Jess put her arm around Frankie. 'I know, that's the bit that's really awful, but maybe it was someone totally random. There were so many people there and I mean, fights happen. Your friends don't seem to be the types that carry knives.' She paused. 'We were thinking, if we can grab enough footage, between the stories and the posts and Snaps, we might be able to work out where everyone was when it all started. I think if we use the time stamps on the photos and create a diagram of the house …' Jess paused again. 'We might be able to see who could have done it.'

Frankie turned to look at her, hope swirling with the sadness inside her. 'Do you think you could, Jess? Really?'

Sorcha glanced at Frankie, her face serious. 'We already recorded a lot of the stories from our own accounts for Katie's video. There'll be hundreds of posts we can look at. The only thing is, we need to get the ones that are going to disappear off social in the next twenty-four hours.'

Marshmallow jumped up beside Jess as if she was listening. Jess rubbed her ears as she spoke, 'My dad's got a huge whiteboard in his office. He's away until Wednesday now, so we can use it to map everything. I can't face moving into the boarding house after all this, so why don't we use my place as a base to gather everything?'

As she was about to reply, Frankie's phone pipped. Grabbing it, she looked at the screen. It was a message from Katie. Dread seeped into her stomach, making her feel sick. She opened the message.

'It's okay.' She shook her head, part of her had been terrified that Katie might have more bad news, but what could be worse than what had already happened? 'Katie's parents are back.' Frankie paused, reading the text again. 'She says they're really upset. She thought they'd be furious about the house, but they're just devastated – they really liked Josh. The Guards still have the house sealed off – she's not sure if her parents are going to come and stay here or go to her aunt's.'

Jess winced. 'Poor Katie. Poor, poor Katie.'

Frankie sent Katie a heart emoji and looked up from her phone at Jess and Sorcha. 'Do you really think we can work out who did this?'

Jess nodded slowly. 'We can give it a very good try.'

Looking from Jess to Sorcha, Frankie could feel a potent blend of hope and anger filling the spaces inside her that weren't filled with grief. Proving who could have been involved was something solid to focus on, like a life ring in a stormy sea. And Frankie knew she needed something, anything, to help her get through this. They all did. She took a ragged breath. 'I mean, *Josh*? He had everything – captain of the rugby team, dating the prettiest girl in school. How could this have happened? How could he have been *stabbed*?'

TWENTY-ONE

In a small cream-walled interview room in Kilmurray Point Garda Station, Frankie slid her copy book over to the Garda taking her statement, a tissue balled in her hand. She felt like she was teetering on the edge of a cliff, and at any moment she could plunge down it.

She tried to keep her voice level as she spoke: 'The other Guard asked me last night to make a list of everyone at the party. This is as many people as we can remember. Jess and Sorcha are going to go through the social posts and see who else we can add.' Frankie paused. 'When I got there last night, Katie said something about not knowing everyone who had turned up. There were a lot of people I didn't recognise either.'

The Garda nodded knowingly, like she'd been at parties that had been gate-crashed too. She was way younger than Frankie had expected. Her mahogany-brown hair was scraped back into a ponytail, and she had very little make-up on. 'Our team will go through the social media posts from the night, but that list will be very useful too.'

Frankie nodded silently and shifted in the hard chair. She'd realised when she sat down that it was bolted to the floor. Was that to stop it being thrown around? She wasn't sure, but it didn't make her feel any safer.

Frankie's mum put her arm around her shoulder. 'You did a great job already with the list.' She turned to the Guard. 'Frankie wants to help as much as possible. This is really shocking for them all.'

Frankie was so glad her mum was here. Part of her had been dreading her mum finding out all the details of the party, but as Ollie had whispered to Frankie as they were leaving, Mum had survived three boys before Frankie, along with a few weddings and parties at the hotel that had ended up in chaos. And he was right, of course. As mums came, theirs was pretty brilliant. No matter how busy she was, or how late it was at night, she found time to help with the bits of forgotten homework that were due the next day; and she'd been fully supportive of the twins wanting to keep up their extracurricular stuff despite the academic workload to get the points they needed for medicine. She'd drawn the line when Max had wanted to get a chameleon, but she was always there, hovering in the background, and she always listened. She'd made sure Ollie gave his statement first, so he'd been able to explain the procedure to Frankie before they came down to the station.

Her mum squeezed Frankie's shoulder and continued, 'The girls will keep working on it and get a fuller list of names back over to you as soon as they can.'

The Guard smiled her thanks to them both. 'That would be great. This gives us plenty to get started on.' She cleared her throat. 'One last question: tell me, how well do you know Rob Doyle?'

Rob Doyle? According to gossip, he had history – could he be involved this time? Frankie pulled Ollie's hoodie sleeves over her hands and crossed her arms. She'd grabbed it off her chair this morning. She knew he'd want it back, but it made her feel safe.

It took her a moment to answer. Her mind felt like it was moving more slowly today than it ever had before. Even more slowly than when she'd had Covid and had been stuck in bed for ages. As they'd waited outside in the station hallway, Mum had said that it was shock, and that it would take her a while to work through everything. Frankie had closed her eyes and Mum had given her a hug. It felt to Frankie as though her whole life had suddenly lurched onto a different train track, and it wasn't one that she wanted to be on at all.

'I don't really know Rob,' she said at last. 'Just of him. I mean, what people say happened last year. He goes to Kilmurray Manor.'

The Guard nodded slowly. 'But he was at the party? Does he know Katie?'

Frankie's tone was tentative. 'Yes, he was there, he's on the list we made. But I don't think he knows Katie. You'd have to ask her. They wouldn't be in the same sort of circles.'

'Who was he talking to, at the party?'

Frankie shifted in the hard seat. 'Not sure. I only really saw him when I first arrived, at the end of the hall.'

'You didn't see him again?'

Frankie bit her lip, trying to remember. So much had happened. 'He was on the dance floor at one point, at least, maybe, not dancing, but at the edge. He's really tall. I was sitting with Viv and Tara and they were talking about him.'

'And was he anywhere near Ella Diamond when that first punch was thrown?'

Frankie looked at the Guard, puzzled. There was something in her tone, but her face was blank. Frankie was sure they got taught how to question people without giving anything away at training college, but there was something about the way she'd asked. Did they really think this was all to do with Ella? *Could* it be?

'I don't know, it all happened so quickly, there were just people everywhere. I didn't see him specifically, or anyone else. I was trying to keep out the way and then I dropped my phone.' Frankie felt a feeling of panic building inside her as she remembered scrambling for her phone, the fear of someone trampling on it, of being caught up in the fight. She gripped the edges of the sweatshirt again, hugging herself. The Guard paused, as if she could see Frankie was struggling.

Her mum opened her mouth as if she was going to say something, but the Guard continued before she could, 'Ella's popular, is she?'

Frankie wasn't sure how to answer that one.

'She's one of the cool girls?'

'A lot of girls want to be like her.' Frankie paused, then continued carefully, 'She's not always that nice.'

'But the boys like her?'

Frankie shrugged. She didn't want to lead the Guards astray by giving them the answers they seemed to want to hear, but she didn't want to land Ella in it either by telling them about her eventful love life. Frankie only really knew what she'd overheard the other day and a lot of gossip that might not actually be true. 'I guess so. She hangs out at Starbucks after school with the rest of us. The boys from Raven's Park too. But honestly, I've no idea who she knows there. She's not really in my friend group.'

The Guard made a note on her pad.

'And tell me about this site, Rave-fess – what do you know about that?'

Frankie frowned, puzzled. *What did Rave-fess have to do with anything?* 'It appeared over the summer, at the start. You can add comments anonymously through a special portal. It's a confession site.'

Frankie felt her mum shift slightly beside her. The Guard was looking at her hard. 'But someone must run it, someone set it up?'

'Obviously, but I've no idea who – I mean, it could be an ex-pupil or even a teacher.' Frankie shrugged. 'It's all anonymous, that's the whole point.'

Her mum interrupted before the Guard could respond. 'A lot of colleges have them. They aren't unusual. They can be a very good stress reliever, a place to talk – similar to the ones for new mums.' She paused. 'There should be one for hoteliers, in all honesty.'

How did her mum know that? Frankie glanced at her. But the Guard was nodding, half smiling at her mum's last comment. Frankie's head was swirling, trying to figure out why the Guard was asking about Rave-fess. 'It's not connected to all this, it is?'

'We have to explore all the options. We're looking at it to see if it could have had any bearing on what happened. Did you see this post?' The Guard opened a brown manila file she had in front of her. It didn't have a lot in it, just a few pieces of paper. Frankie hoped they had more to go on than this.

The Guard turned one of the pages around so Frankie could read it. It was the post about the person who liked lying. 'Have you any idea who posted that comment?'

Frankie looked at her, confused. 'I've no clue. Like I said, it's anonymous.'

'And how about these?' The Guard ran her finger down a printout of a page of Rave-fess posts. 'There's one here about ex-boyfriends being off-limits.' She paused significantly. 'Do you think there could be some sort of love triangle surrounding Ella or one of her friends – which triggered the fight and perhaps involved Josh?'

Frankie put her hand to her head and ran her fingers into her hair. She really couldn't believe they were asking her about this. Frankie looked down at the posts the Guard indicated and read them again, then looked back at the Guard. She really didn't look that old.

'These are all lines from *Mean Girls*, the movie. We quote it all the time. Like wearing pink on Wednesdays. I don't think they're the reason Josh got stabbed.'

TWENTY-TWO

Jess pushed open the swing door of the Costa on the way back from the Garda station and held it for Sorcha and Frankie as they filed past her.

'I *really* need a coffee.' Frankie pointed to a free table in the back corner.

Meeting up outside the Garda station, they'd been on the way back to Jess's apartment when the decision to get takeaway coffee had morphed into the realisation that they all needed a sugar fix. And a change of scene. It felt normal to hang out here, and they all needed normal right now.

'Sit, I'll order.' Jess made a hooshing motion, urging them all towards a table at the back.

Costa was quieter than Jess had expected for a Saturday afternoon, a definite bonus, but then it was getting late. Her head was so full of questions after talking to the Guards that she only noticed that Matteo, the Italian with the cute curls, was on the counter as he came towards her. With this Costa being so close to home and the charity shop she worked in, Jess came in here far more often than she should. Normally they chatted – Ireland was new for both of them – but today he could obviously sense her mood and looked at her curiously as he took her order.

'Won't be a minute. Are you okay?'

Jess sighed. 'I'll have to tell you next time.'

'You call if I can help?' Glancing over at the girls behind her, he scribbled his number down on a receipt and passed it to her, looking at her intently. 'Please. If I can help.'

'Thank you.' Touched, Jess felt tears pricking her eyes. 'I will.' She nodded quickly. She wasn't up to explaining this right now. It had been bad enough updating her dad on the phone and trying to explain things to her grandmother. She'd text Matteo later.

Jess re-joined the others. Frankie was leaning forwards, her long dark hair hiding her face like a curtain. She was flicking through photos on her phone. Even upside down Jess could see they were pictures of Katie and Josh that Frankie must have taken over the summer. The sea, the beach, smiling faces, ice creams. Their whole future in front of them.

Sorcha put her arm around Frankie's shoulders. Hearing Jess pull out her chair seemed to bring Frankie back to them. Sorcha hugged her. 'How did you do? Was it awful?'

'Terrible. I'm so glad Mum was with me.' Frankie took a shaky breath, turning her phone over as if she couldn't look at the pictures any longer. 'Katie texted to say she'd been there for over an hour before me. I had no idea how long it would take, but it was rotten. I just kept seeing him lying there.' Frankie stopped speaking for a moment and took a shaky breath, then, as if she was focusing on something outside the glass doors, continued. 'They just kept asking me the same things, over and over again. I mean, I would have said if I'd seen anything.'

'Mad things happen during fights.' Jess put her elbows on the table and ran her hands over her face. She was feeling exhausted now. She needed to get some caffeine inside her so she could function at all. When she and Sorcha had got back last night, neither of them had been able to sleep, and they'd both come out of their interviews drained. Then her grandmother had wanted Jess to go back to her house, and it had taken all Jess's powers of persuasion to convince her grandmother that she was fine, that she needed to be with her friends.

Sorcha kept her voice low. 'I think there was so much happening, no one saw anything. I mean from the videos it looked like there were people getting hit and falling all over the place.'

Frankie ran her fingers back into her hair again. 'I still don't understand how it happened – bringing a knife to a party and stabbing someone in a fight, it's completely nuts. Why would you do that?'

Jess ran her pendant along its chain thoughtfully. It had a silver dolphin on it, matching her tiny silver earrings. 'You're right. It makes no sense.'

Sorcha glanced at Frankie. 'Is Katie back at home now? Are they allowed in the house?'

'Not yet. She said they haven't "released the scene" yet.' Frankie wrinkled up her face as if she couldn't quite believe what she was saying. 'But her parents want to stay with family. I think they're worried about the press and Katie wants to be somewhere familiar, but she doesn't want to go anywhere near the living room, so I think it's a good thing if they don't go back for a bit.'

Jess ran her dolphin along its chain again. *This was all so weird. It really felt like they were living in a TV show.*

Frankie continued, 'I told Katie she can stay at ours any time, obviously, but Ollie's gone to drop her dogs over to her now. She's not sure when she'll be back in school. Ms Cooke called her mum – the Guards must have been in touch with her – and Cookie said that she's going to make an announcement to the Fifth Years on Monday. Katie's not sure she can bear it.'

'She should stay out for the week.' Before Jess could continue, Matteo appeared with their order. He slipped their drinks off his tray, his brown eyes meeting hers as a moment of understanding passed between them. She'd explain when she could.

'Hot chocolate, mocha, and toffee hot chocolate?' He delivered each one as they acknowledged it. 'And a flap-jack, lemon drizzle and a chocolate muffin?' He smiled and headed back to the counter.

'Boy, I need this.' Frankie reached for her mocha.

'So, what did the Guards ask you exactly?' Sorcha said, taking a sip, her dark eyes big over the rim of her mug.

Frankie closed her eyes for a minute before she answered, as if she was trying to remember. 'Who was there … loads of questions about Rob Doyle: did I know about his past, who he knew at Raven's Hill. Loads about Ella, about Rave-fess –'

Sorcha looked at her sharply. 'Rave-fess? What's that got to do with anything?'

'They think there might be a post on there that will give them a clue.' Frankie rolled her eyes. 'But honestly, they don't seem to have any idea. They kept asking about Ella and a love triangle. I mean, they would think that, wouldn't they? Dead boy, fight over a girl. They have to be connected. That's like teen drama central.'

Jess let out an impatient breath. 'With Rob Doyle in the middle because he's the one with the criminal record?'

'Yep, that's about it ...' Frankie muttered, sarcasm on max. She shook her head as she continued. 'It's like they had the whole solution right there. I mean, I know Rob was in trouble before but –'

'It was pretty heavy trouble – didn't he attack someone? There are, like, parallels.' Sorcha looked at her, one eyebrow raised.

'If he's back at school now, the rumours must be a bit exaggerated?' Jess looked at them both. 'I mean, surely he'd still be locked up if it was really serious?' She paused. 'He might have been nowhere near what happened at Katie's and now he's going to have to prove he *didn't* do something while they are set on proving he did.' Jess paused. 'There's so much wrong with focusing on just one person. I mean, if it wasn't this Rob Doyle guy, while they're busy looking at him, the *real* killer could be covering their tracks ...' Jess trailed off. 'Don't even get me started on wrongful convictions. This is exactly why I want to do Law – the justice system is broken.'

Frankie grimaced. 'The Guards thought going through social media to get an idea of who was there was a really good idea, so there's that.'

Jess stirred her hot chocolate thoughtfully. 'You know, if the Guards have already decided who did this, then we really *do* have to double-check everything. I mean, they really might go after the wrong person. We don't know Rob Doyle, but if it's not him, then it's someone else, and that person could end up getting away with murder. It's possible they could be in our friend group.' Jess paused and looked at them both. 'And what's to say that it couldn't happen again?'

Frankie shook her head, her eyes closed. 'Don't even say it.'

Beside Jess, Sorcha pursed her lips, obviously thinking hard. 'She's right. We need to gather all the photos and videos, I mean *all* of them. We'll go through every single one to work out where everyone was from the start of the night to the end.'

Frankie took a sip of her drink. 'Surely the Guards will be doing that too, though? They've got a whole cyber team. How much difference can we make?'

Jess cupped her hands around her mug. 'We'll be looking with different eyes. And we'll look in the background of the photos. If we can get hold of the extra pictures, the ones people didn't mean to take, we might see even more. We know who should or shouldn't be talking to who. And –' Jess paused '– we'll have open minds.'

Frankie frowned. 'How are we going to get all the

bad pictures, though? No one shares photos of themselves looking terrible.'

'I was thinking about that.' Sorcha sat forwards in her chair as she spoke. 'If you make a new Fifth Year WhatsApp group and ask everyone for photos – say it's because you've been asked to make a list of who was there – I think people will want to help. We'll leave Katie out of the group, obviously, so she won't have to see anything.'

Frankie took a deep breath and held it for a moment. 'People always want to share when there's a crisis. You're right, it'll help with the list and then we can look at everything. Someone who was there last night knows what happened – even if they don't know that they know.'

TWENTY-THREE

'Is that you, Frankie?' Ollie thundered down the stairs and into the family kitchen as Frankie walked in, blowing her nose.

'Obviously.' She felt exhausted and deflated. Like the good had gone out of everything. She flopped down on the sofa at the opposite end of the room to the breakfast table. The tears were threatening again.

'How were Sorcha and Jess?'

Frankie turned her head to look at him over the back of the chair. 'Still shocked. It's just so unreal, all of it.'

He didn't answer for a moment. 'I've got to take the dogs out, do you fancy a walk? It's a lovely evening. Mum's picking Max up from a party, Sinéad's on reception and Dad's … not sure where he is but he was wearing his boiler suit when I got back from dropping those two mad dogs, so he's probably up a ladder.'

Frankie closed her eyes. Part of her actually wanted to close her bedroom door and never leave her room again, but she knew if she was on her own for too long her thoughts would start to spiral.

As if Ollie was reading her mind, he said, 'You don't have to go into school on Monday if you don't want to, you know. Mum and Dad would understand. I'd say it would be grand to take the whole week off. You're not going to miss much at the start of term.' He paused. 'As soon as it gets out that it was you and your friends who found him, you're going to get lots of questions. It might be an idea to let that die down, or wait until you're ready to talk about it.'

Frankie looked at him, her eyebrows raised. 'Die down?'

He grimaced. 'Bad choice of words.'

She sighed. 'I was thinking about that, but I think I actually need to go in and see everyone. It's like the whole night is on some sort of loop in my head – I keep going over and over it, trying to see what I'm missing. I need to hit stop and refresh somehow.'

'You're not missing anything. Sometimes things happen that we have no power over. Come on. I was going to take the dogs down to the beach, and a bit of sea air will help loads. Really, it might sound like a bad idea now, but you'll feel better after.'

Frankie scowled at him. 'You sound like Mum.'

Ollie threw her a grin. 'I'm going to get a hoodie while you decide. A bit of fresh air will help you sleep too.' He held up both his hands as if he was stopping traffic. 'Don't say it. I don't sound like Mum!'

Turning around, Ollie disappeared out of the kitchen door just as Frankie's phone pipped with a string of texts. She pulled it out of her jacket pocket, expecting it to be Katie, or Jess or Sorcha. It wasn't. It was Patrick. She almost dropped the phone. Why was he texting now? She opened the messages.

> **Hi Frankie, I heard what happened. Are you okay?**
> **Katie said you'd been to the guards today.**
> **It's just so awful. Patrick xx**

Two kisses. He'd put two kisses at the end of the messages.

Frankie looked at the texts blankly. She would have given anything to have got them yesterday – well, almost anything. And now she didn't know how she felt. It was like all her emotions had been wrung out of her.

What should she say in reply? He must be feeling terrible. Josh had been his friend too. But she couldn't spend ages thinking about it; he'd know she'd read the messages.

Frankie took a deep breath. She just needed to be supportive. And he must have spoken to Katie, which was lovely of him. A lot of people wouldn't know what to say.

> **Thanks for checking on Katie. Big shock.**
> **Guards not too bad.**
> **Still can't believe it happened. x**

Frankie looked at her response for a few minutes and then hit Send. There wasn't a guidebook on texting when your friend had just been killed; she couldn't make too much of an eejit of herself. Why was she even worrying about that now? Everything was so mixed up in her head.

A second later he replied.

> **If you feel like meeting, text me.**
> **Sometimes it helps to talk x**

Deep inside, Frankie felt a warm glow beginning to build. You got to really know who your friends were when awful things happened. And she was sure Patrick needed someone to talk to too. He must have known Josh really well if they were in the same team: Patrick had been Josh's vice-captain.

Frankie flicked to the folder of screenshots she'd made of Patrick, to the ones she'd taken from Katie's Insta – the photos Katie had posted before the party of her, Conor and Patrick messing about putting up lights and making punch. They all looked so happy.

Frankie fired off texts to Sorcha and Jess to update them.

TWENTY-FOUR

By the time Frankie got back from the pier with Ollie, Cian and Kai had appeared in the kitchen, lolling back in their chairs, phones in hand, pizza boxes open between them on the table. Sometimes, when they dressed identically, they looked like some sort of optical illusion, the only difference between them a nick on Kai's ear where he'd fallen off a rock at the beach when he was five. Both dark-eyed, with thick curly hair that needed a cut, they sat up as the dogs clattered into the kitchen, making straight for the food.

'Hey, you brute, get down.' Cian pushed Wolf away

from his knee. He was wearing trackie bottoms and the dog's claws dragged at the fabric. They didn't have a uniform at their school; it was more like an intensive college, with classes and study in the evenings, and at weekends if they needed it. They both wanted to study medicine and needed huge points to get their places at university. 'We ordered extra for you two. Max is on his way back with Mum and already fed.'

'I bet he's hyper too.' Ollie came into the kitchen properly, hanging the dog leads up in the passageway and clicking his fingers to take the two Rottweilers outside to the yard and their kennels. He left the door open, and Frankie could hear the dogs lapping their water noisily.

'Here you go, Franks, we got pineapple on yours.' Pushing a box towards her, Kai looked at Frankie from the opposite side of the table, his face creased in a frown. 'How are you doing?'

Frankie took a deep breath and let it out shakily. 'Well, I'm alive, which is more than you can say for Josh.'

The twins nodded in unison. 'We went down to the Garda station when we got out of study this morning. I don't know how none of us saw him behind that sofa.'

Ollie came back in as he spoke. 'I've been thinking about that. We didn't look there at all. Everyone was in the living room and we fecked them all out. I locked the patio doors and checked through the kitchen when I closed the garden doors, but I went in from the hall.' He shook his head sadly. 'Just one of those things, I guess.' He paused. 'I'm going down to the bar. Is one of you doing the glasses tonight?'

Cian held his hand up. 'Me. I'll be down in a minute. Kai's got a physics test on Monday. We'll put your pizza in the fridge?'

'I'll clean up and get changed, and then grab a slice. It's quiet enough tonight, no hurry.'

Cian pulled out the chair next to him for Frankie. 'Here, eat, you need to keep your strength up.'

She sat down with a sigh. 'I still can't believe it. I mean, getting stabbed in a fight at your girlfriend's birthday party. It's not what you expect, is it?' Frankie took a bite of pizza. It tasted like cardboard. 'Did the Guards ask you both loads of questions?'

Across the table Kai raised his eyebrows as he reached for a slice of pizza. 'What makes you think he was stabbed in the fight?'

Frankie looked at him, frowning, as she finished her mouthful. 'There was a fight. Josh was stabbed. In the same room. I mean?' She made an exaggerated shrug, her hands open. 'How could they not be connected?'

Cian sat forwards in his chair. 'The thing is ...' He paused, frowning. 'We were thinking that if he'd been attacked during the fight, it would have been more logical for him to have been stabbed in the chest or stomach.

From what Ollie told us, he had his back to whoever did it. Which meant he was no threat.'

Frankie's mouth dropped open. The twins both did martial arts, understood attack and defence. Were they right?

Cian glanced at her. 'We told the Guards, but we reckon it's what they suspect anyway. Think about it. If you're waving a knife around, you're going to be facing someone.'

'When Ollie said it was in his shoulder,' Kai cut in, 'we knew it had to have been deliberate, not just part of the drama.'

Frankie looked at them aghast. 'You mean someone stabbed Josh on purpose? Like, murdered him. That's mad, I mean ...?'

Kai nodded slowly. 'Looks that way to us. Whoever stabbed him had to be behind him, obviously. We reckon he was coming out of the kitchen – maybe because he heard the fight starting – and it happened then. That was such a weird place to fall, too. The sofa was pulled out from the wall because of those speakers Katie's got, but we reckon he must have started to turn to see whoever was behind him, and maybe grabbed for the door frame as he fell.'

Frankie looked at them blankly, trying to compute what they were saying. Kai stood up. 'Look, we'll show you.'

Standing with his back to her, Kai gestured for his twin to get up. Wiping his hands down his trackie bottoms, Cian went to stand behind his brother. They were both slimmer than Josh, but around his height.

Cian took a step towards Kai. 'See, if I've got a knife in my right hand, and I stab Kai in his right shoulder …'

Frankie's voice wasn't much more than a whisper. 'It was lower down, a bit more in the middle of his back.'

Cian glanced back at her. 'Here?' He put his hand on Kai's back, between his shoulder blade and his spine.

'A bit higher.' She watched as Cian moved his hand. 'That's right.'

'If I hit him here,' Cian lifted his hand in a stabbing motion, 'look what happens to him.'

Kai glanced back at her. 'I'm not expecting it, so I stagger forwards, but then I begin to turn to see who did it. Was Josh left- or right-handed?'

Frankie screwed up her nose trying to think. 'Left, I think? I'm pretty sure he was left-handed.'

'Thought so, like us. I would naturally turn to the left. If I grabbed the back of the sofa to steady myself, I'd probably fall onto it, but if I was in the doorway when the knife hit me, then I might grab the door frame.' Frankie nodded wordlessly as Kai continued. 'So I'm reaching out with my left hand. But then I'm starting to feel faint.' Kai pivoted towards his left, his attempt to turn and look behind him carrying him around. 'So, when I fall … it's like this.'

As if he was moving in slow motion, he replicated Josh's fall, landing on his shoulder on the kitchen floor, facing the kitchen table. 'Which is how you found him, right?'

'Yes, that's exactly how he was, like half on his back. I pulled the sofa out and tried to roll him into the recovery position, and that's when I saw the knife.'

Standing over Kai, Cian looked back at her. 'And the knife was sort of under him before you moved him?'

Frankie nodded wordlessly.

Cian put his hands on his hips and looked down at his brother on the floor, then back at Frankie. 'We're pretty certain whoever stabbed him had to be in the kitchen. It might have happened at the same time as the fight, which was why no one was looking his way, but it wasn't part of it … This was deliberate.'

TWENTY-FIVE

By the time Frankie got to Jess's apartment on Sunday she'd rolled Cian and Kai's re-enactment of Josh's stabbing around her head a thousand times.

And every time it made the black hole in her stomach spin even faster. The twins had said they'd told the Guards, and the nods and expressions they'd got had made them sure that they were right. And then the Guards had started asking them about Rob Doyle.

Now it was time to tell Jess and Sorcha their theory. Sorcha answered the door and, giving her a hug, led

Frankie through Jess's modern open-plan living room to the office. They had obviously been working hard on compiling the information as it came in. Since Frankie had formed the new Fifth Year group chat yesterday afternoon, all their phones had been going mad with video and photos.

And they'd organised everything with military precision, Sorcha printing off key photos so Jess could stick them on the whiteboard, adding names and times. The two of them had drawn a map of Katie's house on the left-hand side of the board and had a timeline worked out down the right-hand side, divided into columns for each room. It looked like an FBI investigation room.

Jess started filling Frankie in before she could share her own news. 'Building on the list you started, these are all the people we think were at the party. Anyone we don't recognise we've given a number and a photo reference.'

Frankie scanned the list on the flip chart. She could see a bunch of names she didn't know. 'You've way more names than me and Katie managed.'

Jess looked over her shoulder. 'That's Sorcha – she's been cross-referencing all the tagged photos with other social media accounts. There's a few we're not sure about but we think we're almost there.'

Frankie looked around, her eyes wide. 'Wow, this is amazing.'

Jess stood back from the board, marker in hand, and grinned at her.

'Thanks. It's keeping us busy.' She paused. 'So, this is what we know so far.' Jess pointed to a flip chart set up beside the window. 'Using the time stamps on the photos and videos we have, we think the fight started around 12.06. It escalates really fast and at 12.07 someone turns off the music.'

Sorcha tapped the board. 'You said you called Ollie at 12.11. Rolling back, we've got video showing Josh on the patio up to about 11.40. He goes inside across the dance floor and then we lose him at 11.45.'

'Maybe he went to the bathroom?' Frankie scanned the photos on the board.

'Maybe. The hall's a bit of a blind spot – the pictures we have are mainly selfies and taken close up.' Jess picked up where Sorcha had left off. 'There's not much video from out there, apart from Georgia's account. We do know, though, that Patrick was out on the patio for ages.'

Sorcha cut in before Jess could continue. 'Has he texted you again?'

Frankie shook her head. 'Not since yesterday. Jess, keep going.'

'So, there was a gang out on the patio chatting and smoking, and we pretty much know who they were. But there could still be people we're missing. From our friend group, we definitely lose Maeve and Caitriona – and

Ruth, if you can count her – after Josh goes inside. So there could be others.'

Frankie's phone pinged with a text, but she was too absorbed to check it.

Jess frowned at the board as she spoke. 'We'll see if we can get more photos of the hall area. I think this could be Rob Doyle.' Jess went up to the board and tapped a square image of the dance floor that she'd printed off. It looked packed, the dim lighting making it hard to see anyone clearly, but there was a tall shadowy figure visible near the edge of the dance floor. 'This is a bit before it all went mad. Whoever this is has their back to us, but from the height it seems likely it's Rob.'

The figure in the photo was a head taller than everyone else. Frankie could see exactly what she meant. 'Can we tell if he was involved in the fight?'

Jess bit her lip. 'We've got a good bit of footage of the actual fight but it's pretty bad quality. It was so dark and everyone was moving so fast, it's hard to see who was involved. There are some bits of video that caught the start. Here's what Viv and Tara took.' Jess pointed to a row of stills at the top of the board. 'We can watch the full video on the TV with the others we've got, in a minute.'

'They were sitting on the sofa in the living room, near the double doors.' Frankie bit her lip as the memories came back. 'I was talking to them before Amber appeared.'

'Which explains the angles that their photos are taken from. And Ella's obviously on the dance floor. Her dress is so bright you can see her in their video even with the bad light.' Jess took a step back, her eyes narrowed. 'Basically, we're working on the assumption that everyone is a suspect unless we can definitively rule them out. Maybe Josh was trying to stop the fight? To protect Ella? It's possible, but … I don't know.'

Frankie ran her hand into her hair. As if they sensed she had something important to say, Jess and Sorcha turned to look at her expectantly. 'What?' Sorcha put the lid on the marker she was holding.

'I was talking to Cian and Kai last night. They both do martial arts, they understand fights.'

'And?' Sorcha rolled her hands, urging Frankie on.

'Well, it's really obvious when someone says it, but they don't think Josh was stabbed in the fight. They reckon if someone had pulled out a knife in the middle of it, they would have attacked from the front. Josh would have got stabbed in the chest or stomach. But he was stabbed in his back, high up near his shoulder, so whoever did it was behind him. He had to have had his back to them. The boys showed me last night. Neither of them think it could have been to do with the fight itself.'

Jess and Sorcha looked at her, trying to compute what she was saying. Frankie knew it would take them a few minutes; she still couldn't believe it herself. They'd all assumed the stabbing had to be related to the fight, but if it wasn't …

Sorcha responded first, her voice not much more than a whisper: 'So the twins think someone did this on purpose? As in murdered him?' She looked from Jess to Frankie, her face pale.

Turning around, Frankie pulled over an office chair that they'd pushed out of the way. She needed to sit down. 'They do, and I've been thinking about it all night and I think they're right.'

'The Guards *have* been asking about love triangles. Maybe they think it was some sort of jealous row, or revenge?' Sorcha took a step closer to the board, her face screwed up in thought. 'I think we need to try and work out who is most likely to have been involved, and then we might be able to work out the why and the how.'

While she'd been speaking, Frankie remembered her phone and checked her texts. She glanced up at them.

'It looks like we know the how.' Frankie held up her screen. 'Katie says the Guards have been asking about the kitchen knife she was using to cut up the fruit for the punch. It's part of a set.'

Jess tapped the end of the marker off her teeth thoughtfully. 'Which could confirm, going on what the twins said, and where he was found, that this actually happened in the kitchen.'

Frankie nodded. 'I think you're right. I mean, you'd

hardly be able to wander around a crowded party with a huge kitchen knife without someone noticing. The knife she was using for the fruit was massive.'

Frankie shuddered, images from Friday night jostling for attention in her head. The blood, the blue lights, the dispatcher's voice. *Which service do you require?*

Jess's voice cut thought her thoughts. 'Very true. And presumably the knife, the one that was used, is going to have fingerprints on it?'

'Unless whoever it was wore gloves.' Sorcha frowned.

Frankie's phone pipped with another text. But it wasn't Katie this time. 'It's Ollie – he's in the bar covering lunches. Oh … my goodness.'

'What, what?' Jess and Sorcha echoed each other.

'He says some off-duty Guards have just been in and he overheard them saying that Rob Doyle's gone missing.'

TWENTY-SIX

Frankie sat down heavily on the sofa in Jess's living room. Seeing all the photos of Katie's house had taken her right back there and she needed some headspace for a few minutes. Jess and Sorcha followed her in.

This was all so big.

Josh had been *murdered*, and now Rob Doyle had disappeared.

Frankie could feel an even greater sadness welling up inside her. She'd been texting Katie almost hourly but it didn't make anything better. All she could do was be there for her. It just didn't feel like enough.

Jess put a side-light on, making the room immediately cosy as Sorcha came and sat on the end of the sofa, balancing on the arm and looking out the glass doors that opened onto the balcony. 'Looks like there's a storm coming.'

Frankie was barely listening. She looked at them both. 'Why would Rob Doyle vanish? Doesn't that make him look really guilty?'

Jess sat down in the armchair across from the sofa and pulled her knees up. She was wearing pink fluffy socks under her jeans. 'Yes, but maybe it's because he knows the Guards will look straight at him because of his past.'

Sorcha looked out at the sea and the gathering clouds, saying half to herself, 'That would certainly freak me out if I was in his position.'

Frankie leaned her head on the back of the sofa as Jess sighed, her face creased with worry. 'Disappearing makes him look like he's got something to hide,' Jess pointed out, 'and it means the Guards are definitely going to spend all their time looking for him now, and not for someone else who might have done it.'

Frankie rubbed her face. 'We can't rule Rob out either, though, can we? Not until we've got something that proves that he couldn't have done it. Though I can't see what problem he could possibly have had with Josh. I mean, did they even know each other?

'I suppose it's possible –' Sorcha said it like she didn't believe it herself '– that the Guards are onto something and Rob's in some kind of complicated entanglement with Ella … or Katie. I mean, maybe?'

Frankie shook her head. 'Not Katie. She is –' Frankie corrected herself '– *was* … mad about Josh. I don't think this can be about her. But Sorcha, you saw Rob talking to Ruth at the station? And then Ruth talking to Josh on the train?'

'Sure did.'

Jess leaned forwards in the chair. 'So, *she's* a link to them both. Sort of. I mean, if we're looking for connections. Maybe she could shed some light on all this – *and* she's someone else we've lost track of at the party.'

Frankie looked across at Jess. 'She couldn't have done it, could she? Ruth?'

Sorcha suddenly looked at them both, her eyes wide. 'She's tall enough. Think about it – Josh was over six foot, and the knife was in his shoulder. So that means it had to be someone tall. I could never have reached that high, unless I jumped, maybe, or was attacking him standing on a table or something …'

Suddenly alert, Frankie leaned forwards on the sofa. 'You're so right. Height narrows down our pool of suspects significantly.'

Jess pulled the cushion out from behind her and hugged it. 'But that brings Rob Doyle right back in as a possibility.'

'As well as most of the rest of the guys from Kilmurray Manor and Raven's Park College. *Everyone* has to stay in the mix until we can prove they couldn't possibly have done it.' Frankie sounded surer than she felt. But working on this was helping her focus, which at least held the sadness back from overwhelming her for a few moments.

Sorcha drew a breath in through her teeth, as if it helped her think. 'That's true. And some of the tall girls. Viv's tall as well, she's the same height as Ruth.'

Frankie ran her hand into her fringe, pulling at it. 'I can't believe we're looking at our friends as suspects in a *murder*, I mean …'

Sorcha nodded slowly. 'I know, it's horrible.' She paused. 'But we're looking at everyone through the same lens. We're not suggesting someone is guilty, we're trying to establish the likelihood that they could be involved. Think of it as statistics. Maths, not people.'

Sighing, Frankie could see what she meant, but it didn't make it any easier. 'Why don't we just ask Ruth where she was when it happened? We don't have to tell her she was seen at the DART station, but we can ask her how well she knows Rob.'

Sorcha looked doubtful. 'If it *was* her who stabbed Josh, she's hardly going to tell us. And who's going to ask her? She's not very user-friendly, is she?'

'No, but she might say something that gives her away if we could just get her talking about it. She doesn't know that we're piecing together the story from the photos.' Frankie pursed her lips. 'There could have been a whole lot going on that we can't see yet.'

'There must have been, or Josh would be at home with a hangover, not lying in the morgue.' Sorcha slid off the arm to sit on the sofa properly as she spoke.

Frankie glanced across at Sorcha. 'There *are* rumours that Rob sells drugs.' She turned to Jess. 'I know you were saying that the Guards could be jumping to conclusions because of his record but ...'

Jess shook her head emphatically. 'I didn't just say it. Really, there's so much evidence now of miscarriages of justice because the obvious suspect was made to fit the picture. We, at least, have to keep an open mind. Just because he's got a record doesn't make him guilty of this.'

Frankie sighed again. 'But Jess, what if Ruth was talking to him at the station because she was buying drugs? Or maybe Josh was buying steroids or something from him? We don't really know him, do we, only what we've heard. Maybe this *is* all about Rob?'

TWENTY-SEVEN

Frankie was just through the hotel entrance gates when her phone buzzed in her pocket. She'd walked back from Jess's, needing the fresh air to clear her head. Everything felt like it was spiralling – so much was happening so fast. Pulling her phone out of her pocket, she saw the caller was Katie.

'How are you doing?' Pausing on the pavement that wrapped around the side of the building, Frankie leaned back on the white pillar signposting the car park. At least there was nobody here to overhear their conversation.

Katie's voice was husky. 'I'm doing okay. Marsh-mallow and Cheesecake are going a bit nuts in my aunt's garden, but they'll calm down when they're worn out.'

'They missed you.'

'I think they're a bit confused. They can't understand why we're not at home. The Guards said it's probably going to be tomorrow morning before we can go back. A bit of me just wants to be in my own room, but the rest of me is dreading it.' Katie's sigh was ragged. 'Thanks for minding them, though, Franks, they love you.' She paused. 'I'm not going to go in tomorrow. Can you text me any news?'

Frankie leaned back and looked up at the roof of the hotel. Above it the clouds were dark, threatening rain. There was no way she was going to tell Katie the twins' theory about what happened. Knowing it might not have been an accident would eat Katie up. 'Of course. Did you hear that Rob Doyle has disappeared?'

At the other end of the phone, Frankie heard Katie closing a door. 'Conor just texted me. I knew the Guards wanted to talk to him, but honestly, Josh really liked Rob. It just seems so unlikely that it could have had anything to do with him.'

'Wait, Josh and Rob were friends?'

'Josh has been giving Rob maths grinds for ages, I think he really enjoys it.' Katie's voice broke. '*Had*, I mean. Oh God.'

Frankie own eyes filled up with tears as she tried to focus on what Katie was saying. *If Rob and Josh had been friends, maybe Jess was right about the Guards jumping to conclusions.* Right before she'd left Jess's, Sorcha had pointed out that if Rob *had* wanted to kill Josh, it would have made a lot more sense to have done it down a dark alley – anywhere, in fact, where there weren't over a hundred potential witnesses. Particularly given that he already had a conviction for stabbing someone at a party.

And now Katie was telling her Rob and Josh were studying together – that Josh had been helping Rob. Which made Frankie feel that Jess really was right. The more they knew, the less and less likely it felt that this could have been Rob Doyle.

'This is so awful.' Frankie shifted and leaned her shoulder on the pillar, one eye on the road into the car park. Under the eaves of the hotel, she could see the black casing of a fisheye security camera. It always made her think of *Doctor Who*. They could all do with a time machine right now, one that would take them back to Friday morning when none of this had happened.

Frankie cleared her throat. 'We're going through all the socials – me, Sorcha and Jess, I mean – to get a list of everyone who was there, but we also want to see if we can work out where everyone was when … when it happened.' She sighed. Even though they'd been texting constantly, saying it was still hard.

Katie was silent for a moment. Finally she said, 'That's a brilliant idea, Frankie, thank you. I just can't see how it could have been Rob, and if he was somewhere totally different when everything happened, the Guards will have to listen. I just want to find out who hurt Josh.'

Her words trailed off as she started softly crying again.

'I'm so sorry, Katie,' Frankie said quietly. 'We loved Josh too and we'll do anything we can to help find who did this.' Her eye went back to the security camera as a thought suddenly formed in her head. 'Katie, have the Guards got your security camera footage from the party?'

'Yes, they asked for everything. Thank goodness I had the cameras on. I was going to turn them off and I totally forgot.'

An idea was bubbling up in Frankie's head. 'Are they all digital, like the camera on your gates?' Katie's electric gates were connected to her phone and she'd been buzzed constantly over the summer when her parents were away, opening the gates for delivery drivers and pool cleaners. It had driven her mad.

'Yep, it's all recorded in the cloud.'

'And the recordings are still there from Friday night?'

'Yes, do you want to look at them? I can send you the passwords.'

'Would you? Could you send them now?'

✗ ✗ ✗

Up in her room, Frankie grabbed her iPad from her dressing table and clicked on the link Katie had sent her. As the portal opened, she could see that there were four cameras on the house: at the main gate, the front door, the side passage covering the double garage, and one that took in the back garden, patio and swimming pool.

Sitting on her bed, Frankie found Friday's recordings and clicked through them all, looking to see how much of the grounds each camera covered.

The camera that was focused on the patio seemed to be positioned at the dining room end and covered the whole area down to the kitchen, where Frankie could see the garden doors had been pushed open. Moving the recording on, she found the start of the party and fast forwarded it through to midnight, stopping every now and again to check what was happening. At 12.06, she could see from the reactions of everyone on the patio that the fight had started. The angle meant that the camera didn't quite cover the whole area, but she could see everyone turning, reacting, and some rushing inside.

Her neck suddenly stiff with tension, Frankie kicked off her trainers and wriggled up the bed, pulling her pillows up behind her and resting the iPad on her knee.

Re-running the video, she watched carefully, trying to work out who was on the patio. Perhaps Rob Doyle had been out there and not been caught in anyone's selfies.

But the lighting was terrible, only the candles and the LEDs giving any definition to the dark shapes that formed the crowd, the occasional glow of a cigarette punctuating the darkness. Katie had obviously switched off the security lights in the garden. The only one that was working was a fairly weak one over the kitchen doors.

Frankie sighed. So much for that brilliant idea. It was hopeless.

Sitting back, she rubbed her nose. She'd thought this would be the answer to everything, helping them pinpoint who had been outside during the evening. She rewound the video to 11.57 and hit Play again, scanning the screen, this time looking around the edges of the frame. At 12.03, at the far end of the patio, the kitchen light came on.

This time Frankie watched that corner of the screen carefully as the dark figures of two girls almost fell out of the kitchen doors. She rolled the video back to check again.

Laughing uncontrollably, half obscured by the open glazed door, they dived into the bushes in the flowerbed on the far side of the garden. Frankie strained her eyes to see the details. Even though their faces were turned away from the camera, Caitriona's wild red curls and Maeve's platinum-blonde bob were unmistakable. What on earth were they up to?

TWENTY-EIGHT

'Girls, can I have your attention, please?' Ms Cooke clapped her hands as she tried to call everyone to order in the Fifth Year common room. Flanked by two Sixth Years, who stood with their hands behind their backs, concerned expressions in place, Ms Cooke looked around to check to see everyone was listening.

It took a few minutes for everyone to stop talking – they all knew what had happened by now. Frankie's mum and Ollie had tried to persuade her to stay at home today, but that would have just made coming back in the next time twice as hard, and after the last few days Frankie felt she just needed a bit of normality.

Some hope. Things would never be normal again.

When she, Jess and Sorcha had walked in earlier, they'd been besieged with questions. Frankie didn't think it was possible to be all hugged out, but really it was. Katie had made the right decision about not coming in.

Frankie couldn't see Ruth either. Ella and Georgia were leaning on the kitchenette counter talking to Amber, but there was no sign of their blonde ringleader.

Ms Cooke clapped her hands again. 'Girls, please. I know how distressing this is for you.' She paused before continuing, her voice serious. 'Many of you will have heard by now that there was an incident at Katie Cipriani's birthday party on Friday night. Josh Fitzpatrick, who I understand a lot of you know, and who was Katie's boyfriend, was stabbed and unfortunately died before he could be treated in hospital.' She paused. The room had gone so quiet you could hear the footsteps in the corridor outside.

'Katie won't be in today for obvious reasons, and perhaps not for the rest of the week. I want to make sure you respect her boundaries and give her some space to grieve.' She looked around the room, making her point with her small dark eyes. 'It's an unspeakable tragedy, but it's vital that we find out what happened and who did this. The Guards need to speak to everyone who was at the party. They are working off a list of names that has been compiled. I'm going to put it on the board here, but if you were at the party and your name isn't on the list, please make yourself known. Equally, if you know someone from another school who was there, please tell us so the Guards can compile a full list of attendees. I know Frankie O'Sullivan is helping them with that.'

Jess elbowed Frankie sharply in the ribs, and muttered under her breath, 'The Guards can't talk to us on our own, so how's that going to work?'

As if Ms Cooke had heard her, she continued, 'Obviously if you are under eighteen …'

'Like *all* of us.' Jess kept her voice low.

'… you can arrange to call down to the Garda station with your parents. If you prefer not to do that, with your parents' permission, myself and the school nurse are available to be your appropriate adult so that you can speak to the Guards here. They will have all the required protocols in place and I emphasise that neither myself nor Nurse are here to judge you. This will be completely confidential. Getting to the truth is paramount. The Sixth Year are here to support you too, if you are worried about anything. The Guards just want to know what everyone saw.' She paused, clasping her hands together. 'The Head will be along to see you a little later. Classes will run as normal today, but the school garden will be open exclusively for you all week, if any of you feel you need some space. If you see that any of your friends are struggling, please let someone know. It's not always easy to ask for help.'

Ms Cooke looked around the room, trying to look positive and together. But the room felt flattened by grief, like all the energy had been sucked out of it.

'Obviously we'll organise a proper assembly to support Katie in due course, but for now let's all just try to get through this week. If you need me for anything, I'll be in my office – just come and knock on my door.'

Ms Cooke took another glance around the room, her eyes alighting on Frankie. She smiled sympathetically. Frankie could feel herself blushing. *Please don't let her come over.* But as Ms Cooke turned to leave, she paused beside the sofa. 'I heard what you did, Frankie,' she said quietly. 'How you helped everyone get home safely and then went back to support Katie. Well done. It must have been very frightening. You know where I am if you want to talk.'

Frankie forced a smile. 'Thanks, Ms Cooke.' What else could she say? She shuffled to the edge of the squishy sofa as the girls began to move again, some heading for the door, nobody really speaking. Someone put the radio on, breaking the tension. It felt like there was a collective sigh.

Frankie stood up, turning around to face Jess and Sorcha. 'I don't know about you two but I'm not going to be able to concentrate on maths now.'

Jess stood up next to her. 'Me neither. I think I'll go to the library. You coming?' As she spoke, Frankie caught Maeve's eye over the top of the sofa. Maeve blushed and looked away quickly.

Puzzled, Frankie looked at her again, but she seemed to be very involved in tidying her locker. Frankie had been planning to quietly ask her about the security camera footage this morning. But why would she turn away like that? She looked worried.

Frankie looked at Jess and Sorcha. 'Sorry, yes. I'll catch you up?' They looked confused for a moment, but Sorcha must have assumed Frankie needed to be on her own. She grabbed hold of Jess's sleeve. 'Come on, we can look at the magazines. And I need some help with my *Macbeth* quotes. I read it over the summer but I've no idea which the important ones are.'

Jess looked at Sorcha, one eyebrow raised, but Sorcha pulled her sleeve again. '*Come on.* They'll be chasing us to get back to lessons tomorrow and if I don't get these worked out Miss McNally won't believe I've read it at all.'

As Sorcha spoke, Frankie glanced back at Maeve. She was really spending a very long time sorting out her locker, deliberately not looking in Frankie's direction. Something was definitely wrong.

Maeve had no idea that Frankie had seen her on the security camera footage, so it must be something to do with what Ms Cooke had said. Had she heard or seen something?

A moment later Frankie was standing behind her. She put a hand gently on Maeve's arm. 'Have you got a minute?'

Maeve froze, not turning around as Frankie continued, 'In the garden, maybe?'

TWENTY-NINE

Frankie had half expected Maeve to come up with an excuse for not joining her in the garden. She hadn't turned around to look at Frankie, but had just nodded wordlessly, pulling her sweater out of her locker and tying it around her waist before heading towards the door. Frankie had never seen her so jumpy. As she crossed the common room, Maeve kept glancing nervously at Caitriona.

The corridor was quiet, but Maeve didn't speak. Instead, she walked slightly ahead of Frankie, biting the skin on her thumb. It only took them a few moments to go through the swing doors and down the corridor to the entrance leading to the walled garden, preserved from when the main part of the school was a grand home. Now sturdy wooden benches had been placed around a small central fountain, the flower beds packed with herbs. Close to the entrance, rows of plant labels and crayoned-in flags marked where the primary school were cultivating something. Gravelled paths led from the central fountain, like the points on a compass, to more benches concealed in among the fragrant plants, dense thick-leaved bushes providing privacy. Maeve skirted around the edge of the garden, heading for a bench buried deep in the foliage.

Curiosity growing inside her, Frankie followed.

Reaching the bench, Maeve sat down, pushing her hands underneath her legs and rocking forwards slightly. Frankie sat down beside her. Should she mention the security footage now? Before she could say anything, Maeve glanced sideways at her. 'You can't tell anyone what I'm about to tell you. Anyone. Promise me.'

Frankie pushed her hair back behind her ear. 'Is it about the party?'

Maeve bit her lip, nodding. 'Tara said you were asking for photos on the group chat. She sent a load of pictures that she and Viv took.'

Frankie nodded. 'They were sitting right beside the dance floor.'

'I know.' Maeve pulled her hand out from under her and started to chew on her thumb again. 'It's just ... well, Tara thinks I was dancing and then went to the loo and there was a queue upstairs, so you can't breathe a word of this to her.'

Frankie felt her stomach lurch. Maeve was really wound up about something, that was for sure. 'Okay,' she said slowly, 'what's "this"?'

'So, I *did* go to the loo, but the downstairs one was busy, so I went upstairs and I met Caitriona coming out. She waited for me.' Maeve looked at Frankie sideways again. 'Ruth was in the hall when we were coming downstairs.' Frankie looked at her encouragingly as she continued. 'Neither of us like Ruth very much – you know what she's like. And Caitriona was a bit drunk. I was too. That punch was powerful and we'd been smoking a bit as well.' Maeve stopped speaking and put her hands under her thighs again as if she was trying to keep them still. Her eyes locked on the paving stones at her feet. It was as if she was somewhere else for a moment. Frankie recognised that feeling.

Frankie kept quiet. It seemed to work. After a moment Maeve screwed up her eyes as if she was wincing and started talking again.

'We were having a giggle about Ruth, like for ages, and we sort of ...' She stopped. 'We ...' She stopped speaking, then started again: 'Caitriona was messing about, filming, and it was really hot inside so she said we should go outside.' Maeve drew in a nervous breath. 'But we didn't want anyone to see us, so we slipped into the kitchen from the hall.'

The kitchen? The knife had been in the kitchen. *Could Maeve and Caitriona have seen who picked it up?* Trying to hide her reaction, Frankie said casually, 'Was there anyone in there?'

Maeve glanced at her sideways again. 'Just Josh. All the lights were off – I don't think Katie wanted anyone in there. But I think he was getting a drink for her, because he had two cups in front of him and was pouring vodka into them.'

'Did he say anything?'

Maeve shook her head. 'No, nothing, he just like glanced at us, and I saw a can of Coke on the sideboard so I grabbed it. We were looking around for cups to share it, but we couldn't see any, so we went out into the garden. The security light came on but we didn't want Tara to see us, so we sort of dived into the flower bed.' Frankie frowned as she continued. 'We were both really drunk, and we sort of kissed a bit and then, well, a bit more.'

'Oh. I *see*.' *Now* it was starting to make sense. Frankie suddenly felt incredibly stupid. With everything else going on in her head, and Maeve and Tara almost being like two halves of the same person, it hadn't even *occurred* to her that Maeve could have been messing about with Caitriona. Frankie rubbed her eyes. *If she could miss something this obvious, what else was she missing?* She kept her tone light: 'Did you see Josh again?'

Maeve shook her head. 'We were a bit hyper. We didn't even realise Caitriona's phone was still recording, and the next thing we knew everyone was shouting about the fight.'

'What happened then?' Frankie realised she was holding her breath and let it out slowly.

'I got out of the flowerbed and scooted over to the patio to look in the living room through the glass doors. It was really bad. I didn't know what to do. I don't think I've ever sobered up so fast. We'd left Tara in the living room and I was so frightened she'd get dragged into it. But we couldn't go back together, and the only way in was through the kitchen, and we didn't want to go that way in case Tara saw us through the door or coming out into the hall or something. I know it makes no sense now, but I wasn't thinking straight.' Maeve let out a shaky sigh, closing her eyes as if she was reliving her panic.

'Did anyone come out of the kitchen?' Had Frankie missed something on the security tape? The images had been so poor, she'd clicked it off just after the start of the fight. Which must have been right before Maeve had emerged from the flowerbed.

Maeve shook her head and, pulling her hand out from under her thigh, hooked her platinum hair behind her ear.

'So, what did you do?'

Maeve bit her lip. 'I thought I was going to have to go through the fight. It was so scary, all the noise and the stuff being thrown about, and then there was this huge crash. It was so awful.' She took a deep breath. 'I went back to tell Caitriona, we were in a total panic. We'd got totally trapped. Then she realised the patio doors into the dining room might be unlocked. I mean, thank God. We went to try them, and they were.' She shook her head, brushing away a tear. 'We vowed we'd never say anything. I mean, we were both drunk, it wasn't a real thing. I went in first. It was carnage, and Tara wasn't where I'd left her on the sofa. I realised there was another set of doors into the hall from the dining room, they come out by the stairs, so I went out through those.'

Maeve shuddered as she relived the moment and turned to look at Frankie, her voice shaky. 'Tara was at the top of the hall. We were both crying. She'd thought I'd gone back to look for her and was stuck in the fight. It was all so awful.' Maeve shook her head again. 'There were so many people in the hall, when Caitriona appeared Tara just grabbed her and we all left together.' Maeve hesitated, clearing her throat. 'The thing is, I can't tell anybody, but I think we might have been the last people to see Josh alive.'

THIRTY

'So she said that she saw him in the kitchen and he was *definitely* on his own?' Jess drew the word out as Frankie glanced anxiously back between the book stacks to make sure no one could hear them. They were in a corner of the library miles away from the librarian's desk, between classical languages and the reference section, where it was always quiet.

'Yes, and it was right before the fight started. Maeve's terrified that Tara will find out she was there with Caitriona, so this is super top secret. She told Tara and Viv that she'd gone up to the loo and there was a huge queue.'

'Lied to Tara, you mean.' Sorcha folded her arms. She had the sleeves of her honey-coloured shirt rolled back and her sweater tied around her waist.

'Exactly. I think she and Caitriona got such a shock they just want to forget it, but the important thing is that she said Josh was in the kitchen. She can't quite remember if the knife was there, but she thinks it was on the chopping board on the counter.'

'And he was on his own.' Sorcha wrinkled up her nose, obviously deep in thought.

'Yes. Exactly.' Frankie looked at them both.

Jess nodded her head slowly, taking it in. She looked how Frankie felt. Just a bit stunned. 'And he was making a drink for Katie?'

'That's what Maeve said; he had two cups on the counter and a bottle of vodka in his hand.'

Sorcha's brows knitted. 'If Caitriona's phone kept recording, it would be really good to get the video, even if it's just all of them messing about. Everything helps build the picture.'

'I've asked Maeve for it. I said Caitriona could send it straight to me. She won't put it in the group chat. She's terrified Tara is going to find out about them.'

Jess ducked her head to look through the bookshelves and double-check that there was nobody near them. 'She needs to talk to the Guards. Did she say if she saw Rob anywhere?'

Frankie shook her head. 'She doesn't know that the Guards are looking for him. I didn't want to ask, in case I put an idea into her head.'

Jess pursed her lips, frowning. 'You're right. But if we can get hold of that video, we can have a look to be sure. The two of them may have picked something up in the background they aren't aware of.'

Frankie bit her lip. 'It may have been too dark outside – that security video was practically useless. But you're right, we need to look at their video just to be sure.' She paused. 'This gives us a clearer window on the timing, though, doesn't it? It sounds like the twins are right about Josh maybe coming out to see what was happening in the living room.'

Sorcha leaned back on the shelving. 'And in the process he turned his back on someone who had gone into the kitchen right after Maeve and Caitriona headed into the garden. I can't wait to get this all on the board. When is she going to send you the video?'

'Today, I guess.' As Frankie was speaking her phone pinged with an incoming text. She felt her heart rate increase for a moment in anticipation. 'Oh, it's Katie.' Frankie read the message. Then read it again.

Sorcha nudged her. 'What does she say? C'mon, don't keep us in suspense.'

'She's seen Rob Doyle. The Guards have all gone and she's home again. He was in her pool house. He said he just wanted to see if she was okay and to say he was sorry.'

Jess's eyes opened wide. 'Sorry for stabbing Josh?'

Frankie held her breath as she scanned Katie's text again. 'No, just sorry. He said he liked Josh – that he'd helped him so much with the grinds and that he wouldn't have hurt him.' She paused. 'Katie says he only stayed a few minutes and then went into the woods through the back gate. She warned him that the Guards were looking for him.' Frankie paused, sighing. 'Josh and Rob Doyle just still seems like such a weird combination.'

Sorcha looked thoughtful. 'Presumably Rob was paying him?'

Frankie nodded. Before she could speak, her phone pinged again. Expecting it to be Katie, Frankie glanced at it. And caught her breath.

Patrick.

Starbucks tomorrow? xx

Frankie felt dizzy for a second, her head whirling with grief and anxiety and the tiniest dash of hope.

Two kisses.

THIRTY-ONE

'How are you doing? I heard your party was a bit of a drama.'

Danny leaned over the reception desk of the Berwick Castle Hotel and looked at Frankie with concern, his thick blond fringe falling into his eyes, his face full of questions. The hall was quiet now – when Frankie had arrived it had been filled with noisy American tourists, their tour guide, bus driver and many bags. She'd jumped in beside Sinéad to help check them all in. Thankfully they'd gone up to their rooms now, while Sinéad slipped off for a much-needed break.

Frankie felt her lip wobble as emotion suddenly rose up inside her, tears pricking her eyes. She couldn't cry *again*. She put her elbows on the counter and rubbed her face, trying to get herself together. She had thought she'd got a grip of things but telling anyone new brought it all back. She rubbed her face again and looked up at Danny, his eyes meeting hers, full of concern.

'That's the understatement of the year. Let's just say it was as bad as it sounds plus about a million per cent. Were you talking to Ollie?'

Danny nodded. 'And listening in on the chat in the restaurant. Two motorbike cops dropped in for an early breakfast when their shift finished.'

There were always Guards in the hotel; her parents gave them a special discount to encourage them to come in for their breaks. There was always a good Irish fry-up or a pint of Guinness available, and their presence guaranteed that the Berwick Castle Hotel rarely had trouble in the bar or at weddings.

'Really?' She looked at him reproachfully. 'What were you doing here so early? Shouldn't you have been in school?'

'I was, I came in at six to help get the conference room set up for those tech heads. They started at eight.'

'And *then* you went to school?' Frankie knew she sounded incredulous, but who *did* that?

'Yes indeed, and here I am again. I need the overtime – I want to buy new editing software and a camera.'

Danny smiled his half cheeky, half shy grin.

'For filming the cat documentary?'

His face crinkled into a smile. 'Not just the cats. You know how I want to get into news? I'm doing local stuff on my TikTok channel. It'll be good practice.' He paused. 'But it sounds like you're the one in the middle of the biggest local story for years. It was on the RTÉ news. There was a reporter outside your friend's house.'

Frankie put her elbow on the desk and ran her hand through her fringe. Her mind suddenly jerked back to Katie's hallway and the paramedics wheeling Josh out of the front door on a trolley. They must have known then that he wasn't going to make it, but she'd still been praying he'd be okay, that the pallor of his face and his blue lips had just been down to shock. She cleared her throat. 'It's awful, all of it. I still can't believe it. And poor Katie.'

'I heard the Guards this morning saying they had a strong suspect?'

Frankie felt a surge of annoyance. Jess was so right about the dangers of looking at only one person. Why weren't they questioning everyone properly? The Guards were supposed to be the experts, she knew, but sometimes adults got things so wrong, particularly when it came to teenagers. She sighed. 'They keep asking about this one lad, Rob Doyle. He was convicted of attacking a guy at a party last year. I don't know exactly what happened but it feels like they're only looking at him. I mean it *could* have been him, but there had to be over a hundred people at Katie's party – at least.' She paused. Should she tell him? Did it sound totally stupid, like they thought they were detectives? But he wanted to get into news: perhaps he could help. She cleared her throat. 'We – me, Jess and Sorcha – have been going through everyone's posts trying to work out where everyone was when it happened.'

'D'you know when it all went down?' Keeping his voice low, Danny shifted on the other side of the desk, leaning in a bit closer, immediately interested.

'Well,' Frankie lowered her own voice, relief flowing through her, *at least he didn't think they were being ridiculous*, 'two of our other friends went through the kitchen on their way out to the garden and Josh was in there making a drink, and that was right before the fight started.'

'So he was alive and well then.' Danny looked at her intently.

'Exactly. They were going into the garden to mess about with their phones, taking photos and video. They shared it this afternoon – we've been trying to see if Rob was anywhere nearby when it all started.'

'Did you find him?'

Frankie stood up and checked the hallway to make sure there was no one lurking before she spoke. 'It's hard to see on their video, but we *think* he was on the grass near the patio for a bit, on the other side of the pool from where Maeve and Caitriona were. You can see everyone on the patio in the background. The only problem is that they dropped the phone right before the fight started, so most of the footage is of the sky.'

Looking at Danny, Frankie's mind clicked through everything Maeve had told her. 'Could you take a look at the video? See if you can enhance some frames with your fancy editing kit? If Rob was in the garden when Maeve and Caitriona were outside, I can't see how he *could* have got into the kitchen to stab Josh. He'd have had to pass them, or to go through the fight to get to the other kitchen door. Everyone would have seen him. The timing might be off, but that video could be his alibi.'

Danny raised his eyebrows. 'I can indeed. I can look tonight if you can send it over.'

Frankie smiled at him. 'That would be amazing. We've set up mission control at Jess's apartment cos her dad's away – he's a journalist. Jess has this huge white-board and we're collating everything, trying to get it organised by time and location to work out where every-one was.'

'WhatsApp the video over to me. And I'd love to see mission control – it sounds very cool.' He paused. 'So, if this guy Doyle was arrested before, then the cops must have his fingerprints on file?'

Frankie nodded. 'I guess so.'

'It's just I heard the Guards who were here for break-fast say that there were a few different sets of fingerprints on the knife that was used to kill Josh.'

Frankie screwed up her nose. 'That doesn't help a whole lot, though, given how many people were in the kitchen. I mean, you can't put a time on a fingerprint, can you? Lots of people were using the knife.'

'True. If Rob did use it, he's going to have to explain that, but if his fingerprints aren't there, they can eliminate him as a suspect. And unless the killer thought of putting on gloves, his or hers *will* be there.'

Frankie nodded slowly. *His or hers.* Could it be a her? They still didn't know where Ruth had been when Josh had been stabbed. Could she have been involved?

THIRTY-TWO

'Frankie, are you awake?'

Frankie turned over and looked at her alarm clock, the red digits taking a moment to form into something she could read.

3 a.m.

She felt like she was surfacing from somewhere deep under the sea, struggling through layers of heavy water. Her hand had automatically reached for her phone when it had rung and answered it, but it was taking a while for the rest of her to catch up. She still wasn't totally sure that she was awake and not dreaming.

'Sorry, did I wake you up? You've got your video on.'

'I've what …' Frankie pulled the phone away from her ear and looked at the screen to see Jess staring intently back at her. Wide awake.

She groaned. 'Why are you up, Jess? Has something happened?' The part of Frankie's brain prone to panic about her friends was kicking in before the sensible part caught up.

'I couldn't sleep. Something was bugging me, so I came back into the office and went through everything again.' As Jess spoke Frankie could see her carrying her phone to the desk. She propped it up, the whiteboard behind her. She was wearing pink-and-white striped pyjamas. 'The thing is, I think I've found something.'

Frankie levered herself up on to one elbow and pushed her hair out of her face. 'What?'

'It's one of your photos. You need to open it on your iPad.'

One of her photos? Only half-awake, Frankie looked across the room for her iPad. She was going to have to get out of bed. She winced at the thought. Where even was her iPad? She scanned the room. 'Okay, just a minute, it's on my desk.'

Swinging her legs out of bed, she crossed the room to collect it. What on earth had Jess found?

Frankie climbed back into bed and pulled the duvet up around her, flipping open the cover and resting her iPad on her knees, her phone beside it. She logged in. 'Good to go.'

'Open your email, I just sent it.'

Frankie clicked through and opened the attachment Jess had sent. It was one of the shots she'd taken by accident right before the fight had begun, the image itself lurched sideways. Frankie peered at it. It had been taken at 12.07, just as the fight was starting. But it wasn't even a clear photo: she'd been walking and fiddling with the settings when the camera had fired.

Frankie turned her iPad around to look at it better.

'What am I looking at? I was changing the settings, to get everyone dancing, but I got a load of random shots on the way.' Moments later she'd been swept into the fight and the phone had been knocked out of her hand.

'Don't worry about that. Look to the left of the shot and zoom in as much as you can. The glare from the strip lights around the fireplace is making that whole area look really dark, but look hard.'

Frankie opened up the image with her fingers, enlarging it on the screen. The left-hand side was murky and black, but in the middle of it, something was catching a ray of light and reflecting it back out of the darkness.

Frankie peered at it. 'What am I looking for?'

'Just keep looking at the dark bit.'

A moment later Frankie realised what was bothering Jess. 'Oh, I see it.'

'I'm right, aren't I? That's Josh? I think that little glow is his Saint Christopher catching the light. We'll have to enhance the photo but I've zoomed in here and I think he's standing in the doorway of the kitchen. He's got a red Solo in each hand – you can just see the white edges on the rim if you really look.'

Jess was right. The kitchen lights were all off so the doorway behind Josh was dark too, and his black T-shirt and jeans merged him even more deeply into the shadows. Frankie tried to make the image even bigger, looking at his face. It was incredibly hard to see, his features grainy, but it looked like his mouth was open, his eyes wide. 'Look at the time, that's literally when the fight started, right after the music was turned off.'

'Exactly. I think he came out of the kitchen to see what was happening and collapsed seconds after this was taken. All hell was breaking loose on the dance floor and no one saw him.'

'My God, if someone *had* seen him, he might still be alive.'

Jess let out a sigh. 'If I'm right, I *think* he might just have been stabbed. Look at his face – that could be surprise at the fight starting ... but it could also be the pain of being stabbed. He looks shocked. '

'So that means his killer was still in the kitchen and I was right there?' Frankie's voice wasn't much more than a whisper. Was this the last photo of Josh alive?

She suddenly felt very sick. 'If I'd been looking up and not fiddling with my phone I would have seen him … I might have been able to save him …'

She'd been there, *right there*, just looking in totally the wrong direction.

'I think whoever did it would have left pretty fast, but this photo makes perfect sense when you know he was stabbed with that kitchen knife.' Jess paused and Frankie heard her moving at the other end. 'There are three doors into the kitchen – the one that comes in from the hall, this one connecting with the living room, and then the patio doors at the end that Maeve and Caitriona went through into the garden. Whoever stabbed him could have left by the hall or the garden.'

'But if they went out into the garden, I'd have seen them on the security recording and surely Maeve and Caitriona would have seen them too? So that means we need to look at all the photos of the hall again.' Frankie shifted on her pillow. She was wide awake now.

She could almost hear Jess nodding. 'For sure.'

Frankie looked at the image hard again. 'If Josh turned his back on his killer, he couldn't have been expecting to get stabbed. Do you think that means it was someone he knew, rather than a gate-crasher?'

'I was thinking about that, that maybe he knew them. That's how it feels to me. If he'd had a row with someone, a big enough row where he felt threatened, he wouldn't have picked up the two drinks and just walked out, would he? He was a big guy, you'd sort of expect him to have tried to defend himself if he saw it coming?'

Frankie found herself nodding in agreement. 'This all fits in with what Maeve and Caitriona said.' Then something suddenly hit her. 'You know what's weird? Katie doesn't drink vodka. She had her own stash of gin for the party. Surely Josh would know that?'

On her phone screen, Jess looked surprised. 'Seriously?'

Frankie rubbed her face. Katie had even told her where she'd hidden her gin – why hadn't she thought of that before?

'I'm sure he'd know, they've been dating for ages.' Frankie closed her eyes for a moment, then opened them again. 'So who was that other drink for, if he wasn't getting it for Katie?'

THIRTY-THREE

Ruth Meaney heard the sound of something hitting her bedroom window before she realised that it was a shower of pebbles. She'd gone back to bed and curled up after her mum had gone to work at 7.30 a.m. and right now really couldn't face the thought of leaving the house for a few days at least. That was assuming she could override the part of her that felt a desperate need to go into school to find out exactly what was happening. She'd got the details from Ella yesterday morning about the Guards wanting to talk to everyone, but not much on what they thought might have happened. And that was the bit she really needed to know.

Ruth knew she had to work out exactly what her story was before she spoke to anyone.

Another shower of stones hit the window and Ruth turned over. The curtains were closed but her bedroom looked out over her family's tiny back garden. Who the hell could be out there, this early in the morning? There was another bang and she realised that whoever it was wasn't going to stop until she opened the window. *They must really want something.*

Her mouth was suddenly bone-dry. Who was it? And, more to the point, what did they want? She felt her stomach churn, although she'd barely eaten since she'd left Katie's house.

The realisation of the mess she was in had hit her hard, and there had only been one thing to do – get out. Thank God everyone had been focused on the action in the living room and hadn't noticed her exit.

Pushing back the duvet, she slipped from the bed and peeked through the curtains. Below her, standing on the patio, was Rob.

Ruth turned and grabbed her dressing gown off her chair. Pulling it on, she flew down the stairs, panic rising like bile. There was no way anyone could know he was here. And the side gate was locked. How had he even got in?

In the kitchen she pulled open a drawer and found the back door key. He'd seen her come in and was standing on the other side of the frosted glass, a looming dark shape. Hurriedly she flipped the key in the lock and flung open the door, pulling him inside before she slammed it shut. She looked a wreck, she knew; she'd barely slept and she felt like she hadn't stopped crying for days. Her eyes were sore and puffy, but she couldn't care less right now.

'What the hell?' She looked at him aghast.

It took him a moment to find the words. 'Any chance of a cup of tea?'

She looked around wildly at the kettle. *Tea?* Was he joking? 'Where have you been? You do know the Guards are looking for you?'

'Obviously, why do you think I've been at my brother's mate's?'

His tone was so cool that it made her feel worse. Fighting her rising panic, she shot back at him, 'How did you get in? Did anyone see you?'

Rob raised his eyebrows. 'Is that what you're worried about? I came over your fence from next door. You really need to talk to them about that rabbit hutch.' Moving over to the kitchen table, he pulled out a chair and sat down, pushing the hood of his sweatshirt back. He looked at her, his blue eyes hard. 'I thought you'd have given yourself up by now.'

Ruth's mouth dropped open. 'Me? Why would I?' She put her hand on her chest, shaking her head in disbelief.

'Because of your texts. Did you think he was deleting them?'

'What?' she almost shrieked.

'How long do you think it'll be before the Guards check the number they came from? He might have had your name disguised, but I bet you didn't think of using a burner phone.'

Ruth looked at him, fear biting at her like a wild animal. How did he know about her texts to Josh?

As if Rob could read her mind, he shook his head slowly. 'You really are a bitch, Ruth. I thought everyone else was just jealous when they talked about you, but actually, they were right. Just as well we broke up, I've got enough problems as it is.'

'You broke up with me by *text*! Why the hell should I care what you think?' Ruth felt like slapping him. She was angry now, but she'd been pretty upset at the time. His timing had been terrible too – she'd been trapped waiting to go in to see Ms Cooke to sort out dropping Chemistry. Who even did that? Break-up by text was the ultimate humiliation. How dare he even consider it, let alone do it to *her*, Ruth Meaney?

But he hadn't said anything about her and Josh then. *What did he know?*

He looked at her accusingly. 'I saw your texts, Ruth.

I guessed straight away they were from you. We were doing grinds and Josh left his phone on the desk when he went to the door. You can thank Sports Direct for your secret coming out. If he hadn't had a delivery, I'd never have known.'

Grinds? Rob was getting grinds from Josh? He'd never mentioned that before. Not that they'd exactly had a lot of conversations about school.

Her mind was darting now, trying to get a grip on what Rob was saying. Maybe if he only saw one message, two tops, then he didn't know *everything*. But the Guards …

She knew he was waiting for an answer, but her head was flying, trying to take in everything. If the Guards looked at Josh's phone records, it was inevitable that her texts would come to light. *Why hadn't she thought of that before?* Ruth kept her face straight as her mind frantically reached for solutions.

The most important thing was that the real story didn't come out.

But if Rob knew, that meant – as the thought arrived in her head Ruth felt a bolt of electricity shoot up her spine like someone had plugged her in – *that meant* that Rob was someone who had a motive. Maybe he was her solution. If the Guards found out about her and Josh, she'd tell them about Rob, and on top of his record, he'd become a very credible suspect. Maybe their fling hadn't been a waste of time after all?

Ruth looked at him accusingly. 'Ella said the Guards kept asking her about love triangles. And they already think *you* were involved. Means, motive, opportunity, isn't that the lethal combination?'

Rob glared back at her, his eyebrows raised. 'I liked Josh, he was my ticket to getting the Leaving. Why would I stab him?' He paused, his eyes cold. 'You've got a much stronger motive than I have.' He shook his head. 'You sucked me in, but I know you now, Ruth, I know about your random lies to stir shit up, about how you can't bear to lose and how you'll do anything to get what you want. About your temper, how you fly off the handle when something doesn't go your way. It's a shame the pretty face doesn't match what's inside, isn't it?'

Ruth suddenly felt weak, as if she was really about to faint. She leaned back on the kitchen counter for support. She'd only got involved with Rob because he'd ignored her one day on the DART; the fun for her was always in the challenge, in the chase. But then she'd quite liked him. He was different from the boys she normally hung out with. Obviously she'd had to keep the fact that she was seeing him a secret, because she didn't want people to know that she was dating someone like him – which was quite apart from the fact that she had other areas of romantic interest and it really wouldn't have been good if they'd found out about each other.

Ruth tried to process everything, but it was all

getting overridden by the feeling of panic building inside her. If Rob suspected she'd stabbed Josh, did anyone else? And where was Josh's phone? She'd told him to delete their messages, but what if he hadn't? Part of her prayed that the Guards had his phone and Katie hadn't seen their texts. There were lots of them. And some photos ... She cringed inwardly. 'You know running has made you look as guilty as hell, Rob. Can you prove you didn't do it?'

Rob's face clouded. 'I ran because I'm the first person they're going to look at, amn't I? I got locked up before. For a stabbing, at a party. I'm the easy solution. And I was smoking a joint in the garden when the fight broke out, so if I don't get done for murder, I'll probably get done for possession.' He stood up. 'Anyway, I came to warn you that if the Guards have Josh's phone then they're going to be asking you a lot of difficult questions.' She could hear the satisfaction in his voice. He paused. 'You're the one with means, motive and opportunity, Ruth, think about it. Although stabbing someone is a bit of an extreme reaction just because they wouldn't dump their girlfriend. But nothing would surprise me when it comes to you.'

Ruth stared at him. He was enjoying this, enjoying watching her panic. He hadn't needed to come here but this was revenge for her cheating on him, she was sure. She couldn't let the truth get out, she just couldn't. Nobody would ever speak to her again; she'd have to change schools.

'And I want my bracelet back too. Now would be good.'

His bracelet. Could this get any worse? 'I ... I ...'

How stupid was she for wearing it to the party? After he'd dumped her, she'd kept it on out of meanness, knowing it was valuable and that he'd want it back. She'd had it on for so long before that, that she'd forgotten to take it off, and by the time she'd realised she was wearing it at the party, she didn't have anywhere safe to put it.

She started stuttering. 'I haven't got it, I ... I'll get it for you.' What the hell was she going to do now? She'd only noticed that she'd lost it when she got home from the party. What if it had fallen off at Katie's?

THIRTY-FOUR

It had taken Frankie ages to fall back to sleep last night after Jess had called, and she really didn't feel like going into school this morning. She was exhausted.

She had a free period first thing at least, but she was going to need a serious amount of caffeine just to get to her classes, never mind stay awake in them.

And meeting Patrick was weighing on her mind. She didn't know if she wanted to see him. He'd want to talk about the party and Frankie wasn't completely sure she could face that.

Ruth hadn't come in at all yesterday and, as Frankie

pulled her backpack onto her shoulder, she wondered if she would be in today. She paused for a moment, mentally running through the contents of her backpack to make sure she had everything: phone, iPad, locker key …

On her dressing table.

Frankie slipped her backpack off her shoulder, dumping it on the end of the sofa as she headed out of the kitchen and back up to her room to collect it. If she couldn't even get her stuff organised enough to get out of the front door, how was she going to concentrate at school today? Jess's latest discovery was filling every corner of her mind. Josh's shocked face, murky in the darkness of the photo, was imprinted on her memory and she was finding it very hard to focus on anything else.

Upstairs she glanced in the mirror as she grabbed the key on its soft lanyard and pulled it over her head. Dark shadows were starting to form under her eyes. Not a good look at all. She grabbed a tube of foundation and her mascara from the dressing table. If she hadn't got a bit more colour after her walk up the hill, she was going to need them both.

Frankie headed back downstairs. Patrick had arranged to meet her in Starbucks during her free period, but should she send him a 'good morning' sort of text? Maybe just a 'how are you doing' to show she was thinking of him? It felt wrong to be messaging him in the middle of all of this, but perhaps he needed friends too.

Josh had been his team captain. Boys were rubbish at showing their emotions, and keeping everything bottled up wasn't good for anyone.

Frankie was hovering in the kitchen doorway, trying to decide what to do, when her phone rang. *Sorcha.* Frankie could hear the noise of the common room buzzing in the background as she answered.

'Hiya, are you coming in late?'

Frankie put her phone on speaker as she checked she had everything one last time. 'Yep, free period first thing, what's happening there?'

The sound died down, and Frankie guessed Sorcha was moving into the corridor where she wouldn't be overheard. Frankie heard a door close. Sorcha kept her voice low.

'Ella's with Amber. Being dramatic. Georgia's talking to Jess about something to do with the play. I think Ella's got the hump because she isn't the centre of the news at the moment. She keeps talking about the fight starting over her.'

Frankie sighed. That sounded about right. 'And Ruth?'

'No sign yet. Ella said she's hardly been in touch. She's answering some of her texts but hasn't said if she'll be in.' Sorcha changed the subject: 'Jess sent me the photo. We're going to take it to the Guards after school – are you coming?'

Frankie felt her chest tense. She knew they'd probably want to question her again about what she'd seen when she'd taken it, but right now she'd be quite happy if she never saw the inside of that Garda station ever again. 'Do you really need me?' Frankie paused. 'We can talk when I get in. But listen, I'm going to drop into Starbucks on the way. If I'm not there by Irish can you tell them I've got a headache?' She could feel herself blushing.

Sorcha must have heard something in her voice. She paused before answering. 'There's obviously more, come on, spit it out.'

Frankie sighed. Sometimes being so close to your cousin was a curse: Sorcha seemed to know what she was thinking half the time. Although it never seemed to work the other way around. 'I got a text.'

'You sound like you're on *Love Island*.' Sorcha's voice was expectant. 'Come on, you can't keep me in suspense.'

Frankie cleared her throat. 'Another one from Patrick.'

'Seriously? How is he? Has he heard anything from the boys about what happened?' The questions were like machine-gun fire, typical Sorcha.

'I've no idea yet. I'll ask. He wants to meet me for a coffee.' Frankie felt herself blush again, heat flooding her cheeks. It was just as well Sorcha couldn't see her.

THIRTY-FIVE

When Frankie got to Starbucks, Patrick wasn't there, but Ruth Meaney was.

Frankie could see her through the glass door, huddled in a corner over what looked like a hot chocolate. Her backpack was on the chair opposite, making a statement that she didn't want company. She was wearing her red sports hoodie instead of the regulation V-neck sweater, her kilt shortened to micro-mini. It looked like she was heading to school but hadn't quite made it. Frankie could understand that. Seeing everyone was like reliving Friday night all over again.

Ruth didn't react as Frankie pushed the door open. She seemed to be in a world of her own, her long blonde hair pulled back in an uncharacteristically messy pony-tail, her face pale despite her make-up.

Frankie hesitated. Should she go and say hello? Would she be intruding? It felt weird not saying anything after everything that had happened. They were somehow bonded now, connected by the trauma of Josh's death – everyone who had been at the party was.

It was as if a cloud of sadness hung over Ruth, dark, like a storm about to break. Letting the door fall closed behind her, Frankie checked her phone. Patrick had said he'd try to slip out of school and walk over, but he'd be a few more minutes at least. Butterflies did an anxious dance in her stomach as she glanced behind her out of the door and then back to Ruth. There was no sign of him yet, but she didn't really like the idea of Ruth listening in on their conversation, which no doubt she'd make a huge deal of and tell everyone about. Frankie might as well put it up on Instagram.

Frankie went to the counter and ordered. Out of the corner of her eye she could see Ruth wiping the back of her hand across her cheek as if she was wiping away a tear. There were dark circles under her eyes and her mascara was smudged. Everything about the way she was sitting said she didn't want to talk to anyone, but Frankie couldn't just ignore her, especially if she was upset.

Picking up her mocha, Frankie made her decision and went over to Ruth's table.

'Hey there, how are you doing?'

Ruth looked up at her with a default scowl, and then, registering who it was, her face hardened. Frankie recoiled mentally. Despite Ruth's track record with others, she'd never been openly mean to Frankie, apart from the usual snide and smart comments, but this felt different.

'About as good as I look.'

Trying to pretend she hadn't noticed the hostility on Ruth's face, Frankie took a sip of her mocha. 'Everyone's devastated. Katie's going to be out all week.'

'I bet.'

Her tone was curt, dismissive.

Frankie kept her face straight, hiding her surprise. Whatever about being horrible to Frankie, why would Ruth be bitchy about Katie, when her boyfriend had just been murdered? Everyone called Ruth and her groupies the Mean Girls, but this was next-level nasty.

Why had she even bothered trying to speak to Ruth at all? Frankie glanced out through the door again. The last thing she needed now was for Patrick to walk in and Ruth to see that they were meeting. Could she just walk away without looking rude?

'Did Ella and Amber tell you – Cookie announced yesterday that the Guards want to talk to everyone who was there –' Frankie left the sentence hanging.

Ruth didn't answer, her eyes locked on her empty mug. Then she looked up as if she hadn't heard Frankie. 'I heard you've been down talking to the Guards. What do they think happened?'

Ruth had tried to sound nonchalant, but to Frankie she sounded fake. Like she wasn't just making conversation but really wanted to know. Frankie shrugged. She wasn't about to share anything with Ruth Meaney; they weren't exactly friends.

'They don't seem to know yet.'

As if Ruth immediately picked up on Frankie's caginess, she stared at her hard. 'Really? I hope they're looking at your brothers wading in. I heard they smacked a few heads. How much did they have to do with it? If they hadn't arrived, Josh could still be alive.' Ruth's tone dripped contempt.

Frankie looked at her in astonishment. What on earth was she talking about? 'They broke up a fight that stopped more people getting injured and Katie's house getting wrecked … I don't –' Frankie felt a surge of anger. Did Ruth really think Josh had been stabbed during the fight while Ollie and the twins were breaking it up? That they had somehow made things worse? Her brothers had risked getting beaten up themselves to calm things down, and then Ollie had spent half the night dropping everyone home. *How could she?* 'The fight started because of Ella. My brothers stopped it.'

Ruth looked up at her sharply as Frankie paused, wanting to choose her words carefully. She wasn't about to tell Ruth that they were working on the photos. Especially if she was a possible suspect. Right now Frankie felt like Ruth was looking for someone to blame, which was weird. Josh wasn't her boyfriend *and* she hadn't even asked how Katie was.

Cradling the hot mug, Frankie took a slow sip of her mocha, trying to stay calm, but there was no way she was going to let anyone say anything bad about Ollie or the twins. 'Josh wasn't even near the fight when it started. He was in the kitchen getting someone a vodka.'

'Vodka?' Ruth sounded surprised.

Why was that odd? What did she think people were drinking? This conversation was getting stranger and stranger.

'Apparently. It must have been right before it happened.'

As Frankie said it, she realised Ruth must have left the party ahead of Ella and Georgia; she hadn't been out on the front lawn or in the van. Frankie had seen them heading down the lane when she drove past with Ollie – they hadn't wanted a lift. She had called out the window to tell them about Amber and assumed they were walking back to Georgia's. But Ruth wasn't with them. And she wasn't back at the house.

Where had Ruth been when the fight had started? Was she lashing out trying to blame it on Ollie and the twins because she was involved somehow? Before the thought could form itself more fully in Frankie's head, Ruth stood up, towering over her.

'I'm going home. Don't ever speak to me again, Frankie O'Sullivan, or you'll regret it.'

Frankie took a step backwards, her mouth open.

It was just as well the door of Starbucks was reinforced glass, or it could have broken with the force Ruth used to push it open. Even the barista looked up from his phone to see what the noise was.

What on earth had got into her?

THIRTY-SIX

rankie was still trying to calm down when Patrick appeared a few minutes later. She'd gone to the opposite corner of the café, beside the window, as far away from Ruth's table as she could get, still reeling from Ruth's nastiness. Just wait till she told Ollie what had happened.

What was wrong with Ruth? It wasn't Frankie's brothers' fault. Frankie had actually found Josh's body and called the Guards, and *she* wasn't falling apart – well, not completely. Not until now, anyway. Ruth's outburst had really shaken her. She felt as if the shock of the last few days was bubbling up, overflowing like lava and threatening to overwhelm her.

Ruth was behaving like she had a right to be more upset than anyone. They were *all* upset. What made her a special case? Frankie was starting to get a creeping feeling that Ruth meeting Josh on the DART had been a lot more significant than they'd all thought. She'd been flirting with him, and now she was *really* upset.

But Josh and Ruth? The idea was just so ridiculous. He couldn't possibly have been interested in Ruth when he had Katie – could he? It had to be all in Ruth's head.

'Are you okay?' Patrick's voice cut though Frankie's thoughts, but gripping her mug, staring at her coffee, she was so caught up in everything that she didn't quite register him. Finally realising someone was standing beside her, she looked up, her eyes filled with tears.

'Hey, you're not okay, come here.' Pulling up a chair, Patrick sat down and put his arm around her shoulder. 'You need a hug.'

Frankie leaned into him. She closed her eyes, everything swirling in her head. He was wearing his team fleece over his uniform and it was soft against her cheek, the scent of Dior Sauvage enveloping her. He felt warm and safe, and for a moment she wished she could stay like this forever.

'Better?' Patrick pulled away, his eyebrows knitted in a frown of concern.

Sitting back, she blushed hard. 'Thank you. Sorry. I had a run-in with Ruth. She was ...' Frankie stopped, the words tripping over themselves. She wasn't ready to relive Ruth's poison yet. *Patrick had just hugged her.*

This morning was getting weirder by the minute. She took a deep breath, trying to stop her heart racing. 'But how are you? You must be devastated.'

Patrick's eyes dropped. 'He was our captain and now I am, so I have to get the team through this. We've got a really important match this weekend – they were going to cancel it, but I want us to go out there and win it for Josh.' His eyes filled as he spoke, overcome for a second. He cleared his throat. 'Can I get you another coffee?'

Frankie looked at the one she'd been nursing. 'Please. A mocha would be amazing. I need a sugar hit.' He smiled and stood up, rubbing her shoulder, and for a moment she felt like she'd known him forever.

A few minutes later he was back beside her. 'So, what was the story with Ruth?'

Frankie closed her eyes for a moment and sighed. 'She basically said my brothers caused everything. I mean, how ridiculous is that? It's like she missed the whole fight thing.'

Patrick shook his head, his forehead creasing in a frown as if he was annoyed with Ruth. 'Sounds like she's looking for someone to blame.'

Frankie nodded, played with the spoon in her mug, Ruth's accusations still stinging. 'What happened to you?

I couldn't find you when I got there and then …'

He sighed. 'I was out on the patio for most of the time, just talking. It was so hot in the house.'

'I was on my way to the patio when it all started.' Frankie paused. 'Do you know what happened?'

'Apparently Ella was dancing with Conor and a couple of the guys from our team and this lad from Kilmurray Manor tried to cut in. Conor loves dancing, he doesn't care who with, but this Kilmurray guy had his eye on Ella. He put his arm around her.'

'And tried to kiss her.'

'Yeah, she sort of yelped apparently. Conor wasn't sure what the lad did, but from the way Ella reacted, he could see it wasn't good. He gave the Kilmurray lad a shove, and then doesn't the dude try and square up to him.' Patrick paused. 'It's like so stupid, Conor's there with the whole team around him. So anyway, one of our boys took a pop at this Kilmurray dude.' Patrick shook his head. 'And that was it. Our boys don't let something like that go. Then Kilmurray Manor weighed in and it all went a bit mad. I don't even know who the lad who grabbed her was, but apparently he was out of his tree. I don't think it was just from the drink, either.'

'I saw him get hit, but I missed the bit in between. There were so many people crowded around it was hard to see. Everyone was pretty out of it and the whole place stank of weed.'

'That's parties for you. ' He paused. 'What are the Guards saying? What do they think happened to Josh? It's horrible that you found him.'

Frankie took in a shaky breath. 'Me and Katie.'

'I heard. Frankie, that's awful.'

'Jess and Sorcha were there too. They came to help clear up.' She sighed, her eyes on her mug. 'We didn't even know he was there at the start, or that he'd been stabbed. He'd sort of fallen sideways onto the knife. It was in his shoulder. But he landed right behind the sofa, which was why no one realised.'

She could feel Patrick looking at her. 'Who brings a knife to a party? I mean ...'

'I don't think they did – the Guards said it was one of Katie's kitchen knives. It was really big, too.' Suddenly feeling a chill, Frankie put her hands around her mug.

'Seriously?'

Frankie sighed, glancing at him. 'Katie said it was on the sideboard – it was the one you guys were using for the fruit.'

'So mine and Conor's fingerprints are all over it. That's just great.'

'Have you spoken to the Guards yet?'

Patrick shook his head. 'I'll go down there and explain. There's no point in them trying to track us down.'

'They want to talk to everyone. But Katie posted pictures of you both using the knife before the party, so at least there's that.'

He raised his eyebrows. 'Too right. Do the Guards have any idea who it could have been?'

Frankie grimaced. 'When I was at the station, they were asking lots of questions about Rob Doyle. It sounded like they were thinking it might be him.'

'Weird. I didn't know Josh was into pills.' Patrick leaned in closer, his voice low. 'Rob does a bit of dealing, apparently. He can get anything you want. Maybe Josh owed him money?'

Frankie shook her head. 'I know Rob's meant to be a dealer, but I heard Josh was giving him maths grinds. Do you really think he'd be selling to Josh at the same time?'

'When drugs are involved, anything can happen. Maybe that's what's up with Ruth – perhaps she was buying stuff from him too and is snarky because she doesn't want the Guards to find out? She'd know by now that you've been talking to them.'

'Yeah, maybe.' Frankie had been about to say that Ruth didn't seem the type to take drugs, but honestly, who knew what was going through Ruth Meaney's head? Perhaps he was right.

Patrick shrugged. 'Maybe Doyle was trying to black-mail Josh or something and they had a row.'

THIRTY-SEVEN

lackmail. The word stuck in Frankie's head as she headed into school. Could Rob Doyle have tried to blackmail Josh? Surely if he was supplying Josh, he couldn't expose Josh's drug use without revealing his own part in it?

None of this made sense. And like Sorcha had said, Rob Doyle stabbing someone at a party *really* didn't make sense, given his track record.

It was almost lunchtime. She'd missed Irish while she'd been talking to Patrick but it had been worth it. He'd given her another hug as they'd parted.

And a lot to think about.

The part of Frankie that wanted to focus on Patrick, on how he'd skipped school to meet her, hugged her twice, and been so lovely, was also being overwhelmed by questions.

Why *had* Ruth reacted like that? Maybe Patrick was right and she had been buying drugs from Rob and was terrified people would find out. But what had that got to do with Josh?

Sorcha *had* seen her talking to Rob at the station. Not that she'd known it was Rob at the time, but Frankie had recognised him the minute Sorcha had shown her the photo she'd taken.

Had Ruth met him at the station that afternoon so she could buy drugs from him?

Heading down the corridor towards the lunchroom, Frankie could smell food and hear a babble of voices as the lower years queued up. When Sorcha had seen Ruth on the DART, she'd said Ruth had got up and deliberately looked out of the door for Josh, like she'd been expecting him.

What had that been about? Had she been buying pills *for* Josh, so no one would see him talking to Doyle? Steroids, perhaps, to help improve his game? He'd be kicked out of the team if anyone found out. But that didn't make sense if Josh and Rob saw each other for grinds anyway. Why would he need to go through Ruth?

Perhaps Ruth and Josh were old friends. Had Ruth been in school with him like Katie had been to junior school with Conor? It was a possibility. And it might explain why she was so upset about his death. Frankie decided she'd try to find out.

She was desperate to know if the Guards had already been in touch with Ruth. When Danny had overheard those two motorcycle cops, they'd said that they had a few sets of fingerprints – could Ruth's be among them?

Pushing through the doors of the lunchroom, Frankie looked around for Jess and Sorcha. Her mind was starting to roll like a runaway train, jumping to conclusions. But *was* she jumping to conclusions, or just making connections?

Jess and Sorcha were already on the Fifth Year table, Ella and Amber at the far end, sitting in a huddle with Georgia. Closer to Jess, Maeve and Tara were sitting next to each other, Viv and Caitriona opposite them. Maeve glanced up anxiously in Frankie's direction as she arrived, looking relieved when Frankie threw her a reassuring smile.

'You look pleased with yourself.' The diamond in Jess's nose caught the light as she pushed her tray across the table and offered Frankie a chip. 'Not eating?'

'I had a muffin.' Frankie felt herself blushing hard. She tried to sound offhand. 'I'm only just back from meeting Patrick.'

Sorcha leaned forwards. 'Ooh, spill, you were ages. I said you had a headache at the start of Irish, you owe me one.'

Frankie kept her voice low. 'Thanks, Sorch. But listen, I got to Starbucks first, and when I went in, Ruth was there and she was acting really weird. She said it was Ollie and the twins' fault that Josh was attacked.'

'Well, that's ridiculous and you know it.' Jess shook her head despairingly.

'I know, but she was so adamant, and she was really upset. Like, and I know this sounds mad, but *too* upset, somehow. I mean, it wasn't like she was dating Josh.'

'Maybe he was giving her grinds too?' Sorcha raised her eyebrows suggestively. 'They were definitely very comfortable with each other when I saw them on the DART.'

'Stop, Sorcha.' Frankie let out an impatient breath, 'This is Josh, Josh and Katie, remember. Whatever Ruth thought she was doing, you didn't see him flirting back, did you? Or anything else.'

Sorcha held her hands up. 'Sorry. Just saying. Maybe he *was* giving her grinds – like, actually, I mean. Properly. She's not that bright, is she? Maybe she needs them.'

Frankie rolled her eyes, 'Don't be so mean, Sorch. Just because you're brilliant at maths and coding and would never have needed Josh's help in your life.' Frankie paused; she didn't have the energy for an argument with

Sorcha now – and she was actually right, Ruth was always saying she hated maths. 'Amber or Ella would know if Ruth was having grinds, wouldn't they?'

Jess popped a chip in her mouth, talking as she chewed. 'You'd expect so. But they probably won't tell us, secrets among witches and all that. *But* I've got drama club with Georgia after school, so I'll ask.' Jess paused. 'Did Ruth say where she was during the party?' she asked, in such an offhand way that it made Frankie look at her.

'She didn't really. It made me wonder if she saw something ...'

Jess frowned, as if she was weighing up something that was bothering her. 'I've found footage of her going upstairs, but I can't find any of her coming back down.'

Frankie wrinkled her nose 'She must have come back down. Maybe she was outside?'

Jess shook her head. 'She went up a bit before the fight started but then I can't find her downstairs again. I went back over everything last night and there are only a few gaps in the timeline – we've pretty much pieced together everything.'

Sorcha had been eating and listening while they talked. 'If Ruth *didn't* come down before the fight, that would explain why she didn't know how it started and what actually happened.'

Frankie reached for one of Jess's chips. 'So if Ruth was upstairs, and the other people we were trying to account for were in the garden,' Frankie kept her voice down, making sure no one could hear her, 'we just need to confirm where Rob was.'

Jess's voice was matter of fact. 'Patio, I'm pretty sure, almost all evening, apart from when he was on the edge of the dance floor that one time.'

'Patrick said he was outside most of the time too. It was so hot inside.'

Jess picked up a chip herself. 'Perhaps Rob was selling drugs on the patio, and Ruth bought some then went upstairs to use them?'

THIRTY-EIGHT

Frankie was exhausted when she got home after school. The others were going to call into the Garda station with the photo of Josh coming out of the kitchen at the start of the fight, but she couldn't face it. As she threw her backpack on the end of the sofa in the family kitchen, Ollie appeared from the yard with Wolf and Bear straining on their leads.

'You look like you need an ice cream.'

She threw him a withering look. 'Bring me one back?'

'No chance, you need some air. Come on, you'll love it when you get out there.'

Frankie looked at him for a moment, about to protest, but he was actually right. She did need some air. And ice cream was a definite bonus. After the events of the day, a walk beside the sea, away from everything, sounded very attractive.

When they got there, the pier was busy, dog walkers and couples taking the opportunity for a stroll while the weather was still fine. Seagulls circled, crying for attention.

As they reached the lifeboat slip, Ollie let the dogs off their leads, giving them space to run.

Walking beside him, Frankie felt like her head was full of Patrick and Ruth.

'You okay?'

She sighed 'Ish. Today has been a bit mad. I had a run-in with Ruth Meaney earlier – she was really horrible, said Josh getting stabbed was because you and the twins came to break up the party.'

Ollie looked at her and shook his head. 'You know that's nonsense. Mean by name and mean by nature.'

'Yep, I know.' She sighed. 'And the Guards are looking for Rob Doyle. There are loads of posts on Rave-fess about him selling drugs and asking if something went wrong with a deal.'

'That's why people think he stabbed Fitzpatrick? They think he was selling?' Ollie frowned.

Frankie sighed. 'The Guards think this is all down to Rob. He was arrested before for assault, and everyone says that had something to do with drugs.'

'Well, it was, but not like you're thinking.' Ollie glanced at her and then looked off down the pier at the dogs as they followed scents, zig-zagging backwards and forwards. 'He did get caught up in a stabbing before and it *was* to do with drugs, but I heard he was defending a girl from her junkie boyfriend. He didn't exactly attack the guy.' Ollie paused. 'Maybe that's where the drugs rumours started.'

Frankie looked at him hard. 'How do you know that? I mean, how true is it?'

Ollie shrugged again. 'I'm sure it's in the court records, but the sister of someone in my year was at the party when it all went down.'

'I heard he stabbed the guy with a screwdriver.'

Ollie drew in his breath. 'He did, but it was the other lad's screwdriver and he was getting stroppy with his girlfriend. I heard he was high and when Rob stepped in to ask him to lay off her, he goes mad and produces the screwdriver. There was a fight and he got stuck in the side of his chest.'

'And Rob got convicted.'

'Yep. I mean, he did stab the guy, but the judge was only listening to the other lad. Rich kid from Raven's Park College, father was some bigshot banker.'

Frankie looked out to sea. Was history repeating itself? Was Rob about to be falsely accused again? 'That's not nice.'

'It really isn't. Rob ended up missing a load of school, and that's why he's back resitting.'

'Someone said Josh was giving him grinds.'

Ollie raised his eyebrows. 'That's hardly a reason to stab someone, is it? I think the drug stuff is all rumours tied up with the original story. The other guy was the main supplier in Raven's Park, Taylor someone. I've forgotten.'

'So the Guards think it was Rob again because of that?' A half-remembered quote shot through Frankie's head: *'The right thing to do and the hard thing to do are usually the same.'* Had Rob Doyle been doing the right thing, defending this guy's girlfriend, and now it might land him in jail for a second time? Frankie sighed, looking out to sea as Ollie whistled for the dogs.

'Maybe they didn't believe it was self-defence the first time,' he continued. 'It was a party and there was a stabbing, so you can see why they might think there are parallels.'

Frankie looked at her brother. 'Yeah, right. Assuming you're looking at what's at the end of your nose and no further.'

'Bit of that. But look, Frankie, you don't know what happened. You need to be careful.'

'Why?'

'Because someone is potentially guilty of murder if the twins are right, and they haven't been caught. They might have had it all planned. Someone like that is dangerous. If you girls start sniffing around, they could get desperate. You don't want anything nasty happening.'

Frankie looked at him, too shocked to speak. She hadn't even considered that.

THIRTY-NINE

'Katie darling, Conor's here.' Katie rolled over at the sound of her mum's voice calling up the stairs. 'Will I send him up?'

Slipping off the bed, Katie pushed her feet into her fluffy slippers and went out to the landing, leaning over the banisters to look down into the hall. Conor was on the doorstep, talking to her mum in a low voice.

All this creeping around was starting to get on Katie's nerves. It was like her parents had wrapped her up in cotton wool since they'd got home, tiptoeing around the house and whispering as if any sudden movement or loud noise might upset her even more.

When actually she just wanted to scream.

Katie watched them for a moment, her mum putting her hand on Conor's shoulder. Then he looked up, and his face cracked into a smile, his eyes connecting with hers.

Conor understood her better than anyone. They'd known each other forever. Thank goodness he was here.

She gestured for him to come upstairs, waiting as he took the stairs two at a time. At the top, Conor threw his arms around her.

'Kates, this is all so bad. I'm so sorry.'

Hugging him back, hard, Katie felt a wave of thanks that he was her friend. She'd missed him and his silliness in the past few days. Whatever life threw at him, Conor seemed to bob to the surface, like a bubble trapped in a bottle. Now she needed him more than ever.

Struggling out of the hug, she pulled him towards her room.

'Come on. I've got hundreds of chocolates that need eating. I didn't know people sent chocolates when someone dies, but apparently they do. Or maybe they were just an option with the flowers.'

'Clickety click, add to cart. Everyone just wants to cheer you up, babes.'

Katie looked at him as she pushed the door open. 'I think it's going to take a bit more than chocolate.'

Back in her pale pink room, Katie kicked off her slippers and sat cross-legged on her four-poster bed, pulling a huge white teddy bear onto her knee. Conor sat down on the end, shoving the mountain of white cushions piled up against the brass bed rail behind him to get comfortable. Outside, Marshmallow and Cheesecake were yapping again. They'd been put in the back garden to work off some energy after being cooped up in Katie's aunt's townhouse, but they got bored very quickly on their own. Exactly like Conor did.

'God, I've missed you. Everything's been so intense.' Katie took a shaky breath. 'I just feel so hollow, like I'm empty inside. And I keep bursting into tears.' She could feel her lip trembling.

Conor jumped up and moved to sit beside her, shunting her up and putting his arm around her for another hug. 'I came as quick as I could. I couldn't believe it when you texted to say you were back home already.'

'I didn't think I could face it at first, but then I just needed to get back into my own bed.' She bit her lip. 'I haven't been in the living room yet, but Mum and Dad are going to get the decorators in and change it all. I really thought they'd be so mad, but my mum's just really upset. She loved Josh.'

'Have the Guards said anything yet?'

Katie shook her head. It was so good to see Conor, but she still couldn't talk about what had happened the other night without feeling like she was suffocating. It was like someone had pulled a thick black curtain over her life and she was trapped here until they allowed it to open.

'Was it awful?' He pulled her close and rested his head on top of hers. 'That's a stupid question. It couldn't really be worse, could it?'

Tears in her eyes, Katie smiled weakly at him. He was so lovely and had been trying so hard since Saturday morning, when she'd messaged him to say what had happened. He'd texted at least as often as Frankie had, sending her memes and goats doing silly things on TikTok. She wasn't really in the mood for laughter, but he was trying his best.

Her therapist had said there wasn't a handbook for this, that they would all find their own ways to cope. But it was coping that was the problem. Right now, Katie couldn't imagine life without Josh. Every single thing she saw and touched reminded her of him or of something he'd said, from the shells they'd collected on the beach together that she kept on her dressing table to the peacock feather he'd picked up at the zoo for her and stuck behind her mirror. She'd asked her mum to take down the photos Frankie had taken, blown up to poster size. She'd loved that group shot so much, but she wasn't ready to see Josh's face smiling back at her yet. She welled up again.

A tiny part of her felt like he'd just gone on holiday, or gone to college early, that she'd see him again soon. Every time the phone rang, she thought it might be him. And then it wasn't and a wave of emotion would engulf her.

She took another shaky breath, trying to answer Conor properly. 'The Guards asked so many questions. I really don't know who was here, not really. There must have been a hundred at least between Raven's Hill and Raven's Park, and there were lots from Kilmurray Manor and ...' Katie stopped, suddenly exhausted. She ran her hand over her eyes. 'There were other schools too, and some Sixth Years.' Her voice cracked. 'I've no idea. I keep thinking if I hadn't invited so many people, it wouldn't have happened. I couldn't even find Josh for half the night, the house was so packed.'

'He thought he had all night to talk to you, Kates.' Conor squeezed her hand, then wiped away the tears springing up in his own eyes. 'It all just went so bad so fast. I'm sorry we left, I looked everywhere for you, but Patrick just wanted to get out of there. He'd already got blood on him from someone getting punched and he couldn't afford to get injured before the match. A couple of the Kilmurray Manor team hate his guts. When he gets wound up he can be pretty brutal on the pitch and they've been looking for a chance to get back at him.'

'It's okay, you couldn't have done anything. It took all Frankie's brothers to calm everything down.'

Conor sighed, shaking his head. 'What time did you get back home?'

Katie cleared her throat. 'Just after lunch yesterday, when I texted you. Mum got industrial cleaners in the minute the Guards left. As soon as they were finished, we came home.' Katie sighed. She'd barely spoken to anyone for the last few days and now she was babbling. 'The worst thing is that I can't even remember most of the evening. I was so shocked after the fight, I drank the best part of a bottle of gin. By the time Frankie got back here to help clear up I was pretty well on.'

'I think we were all a bit like that. Patrick said the same thing – he's got big gaps for most of the night too. I sobered up pretty quickly when everything kicked off, to be honest. Kudos to Frankie's brothers.'

'I know, but I feel so, so bad. If I'd drunk less, would I have seen something? I mean, I was useless, I could barely answer any of the Guard's questions.' Katie could feel the tears coming again, hot on her cheeks. 'Frankie had to make the guest list from everyone's socials.'

'Did they ask about Rob Doyle? Patrick said they were looking for him. There's loads of stuff on Rave-fess now. But do NOT look at it – there's nothing you need to see and it's all malicious gossip.'

Katie shook her head, unable to speak. Everyone was talking about them on Rave-fess? Conor wrapped his arms around her more tightly. 'You've had enough questions to last you a lifetime. You know we've got this big game on Saturday?'

Katie pulled back from him in surprise. 'Are you still playing? I thought it would be cancelled.'

Conor bit his lip. 'A bit of me did too, but it's going to be a tribute match. We're all going to wear black arm-bands and have a minute's silence.' His phone pipped with a text as he spoke, and he pulled it out. 'It's Patrick, I'll just tell him I'm here.'

Katie hardly heard him. It seemed a bit soon for the team to be playing. But she knew it was a big game. It all felt so unfair. Josh had been so good at everything. Now his talent would never be realised.

FORTY

oming in from their walk, Ollie took the dogs back to the yard and vanished to get changed for his shift. They'd got a burrito each on the way back, and then ice cream. Frankie went straight up to her room, picking up her backpack in the kitchen on the way. Upstairs, she leaned back on her bedroom door, deep in thought.

She had a lot to process.

Even after talking it through with Ollie, the Ruth incident had left her seething, Ruth's words churning in her head all afternoon. Frankie wished she'd known about Ruth being upstairs at the party when they'd met in Starbucks: she could have countered her ridiculous accusations with a few questions of her own.

And on top of that, meeting Patrick had felt like a glimmer of light in a very dark few days. It was as if they'd gone straight past that awkward stage and into serious chats without passing Go. They'd had coffee and then muffins and then Patrick had told her all about the team and the match and how important it was to celebrate Josh on the pitch. Frankie had been a little bit mesmerised by his passion for the game. He was planning to study sports science and wanted to play rugby professionally. Apparently there were international scouts coming to the match too. Despite the situation, he'd made her laugh with some silly rugby stories and she'd felt relaxed for the first time since she couldn't remember when.

It had been a pretty meteoric meeting.

Frankie was jolted out of her thoughts by the sound of her phone. Anticipation balled in her stomach. Was it Patrick again?

Are you busy? Need to talk.

Danny.
She texted back.

Free now, where are you?

The reply was instant:

Look out your window.

Pulling back her curtain, she spotted Danny standing in the middle of the service area below, looking up. He gesticulated for her to open the window. She leaned out so he could hear her: 'Come around to the back door and I'll let you in.'

He waved and disappeared. Pulling the window closed, she left her bedroom and ran downstairs. He was waiting for her as she opened the door.

'Come in. Are you on your break?'

Everyone was out, except Ollie, who was running the bar tonight. As usual, the O'Sullivans were off in opposite directions: the twins were still at school studying, her mum was at Pilates and Max was at a playdate, and her dad had some dinner with the tour bus operators in Dublin. The family schedule on the kitchen wall looked like an air traffic control chart some days.

Ushering Danny into the kitchen, Frankie watched as he sat down at the glass table and ran a hand over his face. 'Yes, I've only got fifteen minutes, I've been looking out for you.'

'Will I put the kettle on? I'll make you some toast?' Frankie pulled a couple of slices of bread from a bag on the counter and popped them into the toaster.

'Only if you're having some.' He pulled his phone out of his trouser pocket. 'I need to show you something.'

Frankie flicked the switch on the kettle and turned around, her eyebrows raised.

Danny leaned his forearms on the table and spun his phone on its end as if he was trying to find the right words. 'You know that video you asked me to look at? The one with the two girls?'

'Caitriona's video from the party?' Suddenly excited, Frankie pulled a chair out beside him and sat down. 'Did you find something?'

'Yep, I think so. Something big.'

'Come on, don't keep me in suspense.'

'I ran the video through the editing software I use. It enables you to look at each frame of the video. But it also allows you to isolate the audio. The girls were messing about videoing each other, so about half the shots pick up the pool and the patio area in the background. The other half is mainly flowerbed, and like you said, the sky.' The kettle came to the boil as he continued. 'I've emailed you all the stills I could get of the patio. I enhanced them as much as possible. You should be able to recognise some people.'

'Wow, that's brilliant, thanks so much. The shots we've got so far are all quite narrow, there's not a lot of background.'

Danny's face creased into a frown. Frankie had never seen him look this serious before. 'So then I thought I'd take a look at the audio. It's mainly those two giggling, to be honest, but then they stop talking and I'm guessing they're kissing. The thing is, the video keeps rolling.'

'But that's not going to be much use if they weren't filming anything?'

'Well, not the visuals. But the phone has a really good microphone. It's picked up two lads having an argument relatively close by. It's a bit muffled, I think the Garda tech guys will be able to do more with it, but do you want to hear it?'

FORTY-ONE

Jess was heading out of school after drama club when she saw Georgia walking ahead of her, her eyes glued to her phone. Jess had been trying to work out a way to speak to her as they'd gone through the *Macbeth* auditions, but there hadn't been a moment. Now Jess lengthened her stride to catch up with her.

'Hiya, how are you doing?' Georgia looked up at her blindly for a second. Jess wasn't too sure if it was because her mind was busy with her phone or because she didn't recognise her. Or perhaps she was just shy. Georgia had seemed lovely when Jess had spoken to her very briefly at the first drama club meeting last week, but a lot meeker than Jess had expected for one of the 'Mean Girls'.

'I really liked your audition.' Jess paused. 'I'm a bit surprised about them keeping going with *Macbeth*, after Josh and everything.'

Georgia shrugged. 'I suppose it's because it's the set play for this year. We could have switched to *Philadelphia, Here I Come!* but they always do Shakespeare. It means everyone gets to see it, so even if they hate English they might remember the bits their friends were in when they get to the exam.'

'That's very true.' Jess nodded and was silent for a minute. 'I hope they give you Lady Macbeth. You'd be amazing.'

Georgia blushed. 'Thanks. Your audition was brilliant too.' She smiled as if she didn't know what to say next. She reminded Jess of a timid baby bunny. It was strange, because she'd shone on stage, as if being someone else was easier than being herself.

'I played Lady M before, in London, I was in this amateur dramatics society, but I'd love it if you got it. I really want to be stage manager this time.'

Georgia looked at her in admiration. 'It would be so great to join a proper theatre company. I adore Shakespeare, but really I'm just mad about acting.'

Jess grinned. 'I love all his plays – some of the comic scenes are hilarious. And there's loads of drama.

Although there seems to be plenty of that in real life right now too. I thought London was bad, but ...' Jess glanced at Georgia with her eyes wide. 'Woah, this whole thing with Josh ...'

'It's so terrible, isn't it? I don't know how Katie is coping.'

Jess sighed, shaking her head. 'I wasn't at the party but Sorcha and I went round afterwards to help Katie clean up.' She grimaced. 'It was awful.' Jess paused. 'Did you go with Ella and Amber ... and Ruth?'

Georgia glanced at her. 'Ells and Amber came over to mine to get ready. We weren't really *with* Ruth, she'd had her make-up and everything done by the time she got to my house. Then she went off on her own when we were dancing. I hardly saw her.'

She said it like she'd rehearsed it. Immediately Jess felt her bullshit detector warning system going off. She'd moved schools a few times as her dad's job had changed, and one of the things about being a newbie was a learned ability to get the measure of people pretty quickly. You needed to know who was plastic and who was genuine in a new school.

From Georgia's tone, it sounded like she knew exactly where Ruth had been, and she didn't want to tell Jess.

Georgia continued hastily, 'I was in the loo when the fight started – I came out into the hall and everyone was just screaming.'

They reached the school gate. Georgia hesitated. 'My bus stop is up here.' She indicated left. 'Which way do you go?'

Jess's usual route took her right and down towards the town, but she didn't want to end this conversation right now. 'I live down by the sea so I can go either way.' She kept pace with Georgia as they both turned out of the gate. 'How's Ella now? She must have been terrified when the fight started around her. Boys can be such prats.' Jess pulled her backpack further onto her shoulder as she spoke. She didn't want to push on Ruth any more – not just yet.

Georgia's face mirrored her emotions, as if she was reliving the whole episode in her head. 'She was really shaken, so we left super-fast. Amber had already gone – she wasn't feeling well and her mum came to get her. Ella just wanted to get out of there. We went straight to my house.'

'That sounds like the best decision. She must have been relieved to have you there.' Jess said it with conviction and Georgia glanced at her shyly. Jess suddenly got the feeling that not many people complimented Georgia. She was always in Ruth, Amber and Ella's shadow, the eternal foot soldier. 'So, what happened to Ruth? Didn't she come to find you both when everything kicked off?' Jess made it sound offhand, like she hadn't picked anything up in Georgia's tone previously.

Georgia paused, obviously thinking. It was almost as if she'd just realised that Ruth coming to find them to make sure they were okay would have been the one thing a friend would do in a situation like that. Jess glanced sideways at her, but she looked like she was turning something over, finding the right words.

'I think Ruth was upstairs. She and …' Georgia paused again, as if she was weighing up what to say next. 'You can't say this to *anyone*. It's totally secret.' She glanced nervously at Jess.

'I won't, I really don't know anyone here to say anything to, so you're safe.'

Georgia took a deep breath. 'She had a bit of a thing with Josh over the summer. I think she was planning on meeting him upstairs. Ella went off and was dancing and I was sort of watching to see where he was.'

Jess almost stopped walking, as she fought back the questions flying around her head. She couldn't spook Georgia now. *Ruth had an actual thing with Josh?* Shit, was that why she'd been so horrible to Frankie in Starbucks?

'Where was Josh during the party? Frankie said she didn't see him.'

'On the patio for a bit, and then he came out to the hall. I could see he was looking for someone and Katie had just gone the other way. He sort of passed Ruth by and then he went into the kitchen, and she followed him a few minutes later.' Georgia bit her lip. 'She wasn't in there long. She came out smiling, then went upstairs. He came out after a few minutes but he kept checking his watch. Then he went back in.'

'Someone saw him in the kitchen, getting a couple of vodkas. Do you think one was for Ruth?'

Georgia's eyebrows shot up. 'It might have been if she was expecting him; it looked like he told her to go upstairs and wait for him.' Georgia frowned, her face puzzled. 'But Ruth's on medication that means she can't drink. Even a mouthful and she goes really weird, like totally drunk. She tried round at Ella's once when she switched tablets and she started seeing things, and her heart rate went mad. It was really scary.'

'You'd think he would have known that, if they were seeing each other.'

'Yes, so perhaps he wasn't meeting her and I've got it all wrong. I mean, I could have done.' Georgia didn't sound at all sure.

'Or perhaps he *wanted* to get her drunk.' Jess said it half to herself. They'd almost reached Georgia's bus stop. 'I think you might need to tell the Guards about Ruth, or she needs to. If Josh was seeing her, him getting stabbed could have had something to do with that. Ruth wasn't dating anyone else who could have found out that she was cheating on them?'

Georgia looked unsure for a moment. 'She was hanging out a lot over the summer with that guy Rob from Kilmurray Manor. Nobody knew except us, and she swore us to secrecy. But I know she was really mad about Josh. He'd kept telling her he was going to finish with Katie.' Georgia lowered her voice. 'Apparently Katie wouldn't sleep with him.'

'But Ruth would?'

Georgia shrugged. 'She wanted to. I think that's why she went upstairs.'

FORTY-TWO

The moment she was out of sight of Georgia, Jess's thumbs flew over her phone as she texted Sorcha.

Call me STRAIGHT AWAY. Can't get hold of F.

She had given Georgia a hug and left her at the bus stop, heading down towards the sea. She'd loop around past Frankie's parents' hotel on the route home so she could call in and find her. She wasn't going to believe this.

Jess waited until she was around the next corner to look at her phone, her heart beating fast. But Frankie still wasn't answering.

She stopped for a moment to catch her breath. Leaning back on a high granite garden wall, she tapped the phone on her teeth. This whole thing was such a mess. They'd all thought Josh was the innocent victim of an attack, but how could he even have considered sleeping with Ruth at Katie's house on her birthday?

This confirmed why they hadn't been able to find any pictures of Ruth after she'd gone upstairs. But if Georgia was right – and it sounded like she'd been watching everything pretty closely – it also ruled Ruth out as a potential killer.

Had Katie somehow found out and got mad with Josh? Or had Rob Doyle discovered something was going on and had it out with him? Jess thought back to the photographs on their board. They thought they knew where Rob was, but they hadn't tracked Katie's movements; they'd all just made the assumption that she couldn't have been involved.

But Katie was tall, almost the same height as Ruth. If she'd pulled her arm back with the knife in her hand, could she have got it into Josh's shoulder? Jess would have to think about that, to work out the maths, but it was a possibility. The thought ricocheted around Jess's head, her shock growing as it gathered momentum.

*Could the one person none of them had even consid-
ered be Josh's assailant?* Jess was pretty sure that if she
found out her boyfriend was going to sleep with one of
her classmates, in her own house, at her own birthday
party, she'd be pretty close to stabbing him too.

You really couldn't make it up. And Jess was totally
sure Georgia *hadn't* made it up.

What a secret to keep. Jess could see how Ruth had
earned her name as head of the Mean Girls: it wasn't just
a play on her name and the film. Georgia had looked
terrified as she'd told her.

She had to tell Frankie. This explained so much about
why Ruth had reacted the way she did when Frankie had
met her in Starbucks. Jess was sure it was because Ruth
was looking to deflect attention away from what she'd
been up to that night. And Ruth knew Frankie had been
helping the Guards. Perhaps lashing out at her had been
a way to stop Frankie asking any awkward questions.

Suddenly Jess's phone vibrated with a text. It was
Sorcha.

**What's up? Will call. Meltdown on Rave-
fess. Take a look.**

Rave-fess? Jess opened the app on her phone. What
had happened now?

FORTY-THREE

In the family kitchen, Frankie looked at Danny, her mouth open.

'You've really picked up an argument on the video soundtrack?'

'That's what it sounds like. Here, have a listen. From what you said about how close the kitchen is to the pool and the patio, and where Caitriona and – Maeve, is it? – were, I'm guessing it must have happened close to or inside the kitchen.'

Forgetting about the toast she'd put in when Danny had sat down, Frankie fixed her eyes on him as he found the recording on the phone.

'Here you go. Right, this is the whole track. It's a bit muffled, so I've turned it right up.'

Frankie leaned forwards.

Maeve's voice came first: '*Careful, get my good side.*' There was a lot of giggling. In the background Frankie could hear the music from the party.

'*Mind my glasses ... I want to kiss you.*' Caitriona now, slurring; she sounded very drunk. '*Ouch, my hair's caught.*'

'*Is that better?*' Maeve's voice. '*Put that down ...*'

There was a scraping sound like the phone was spinning across concrete.

'*Careful, I ... oh ... damn.*'

Frankie opened her eyes wide. Danny's face twitched as he put his fingers to his lips.

'*Got enough vodka there, have you?*' The new voice was male, but it was further away than the girls', only just clear enough to decipher.

'*Mind your own fucking business.*' The second voice was raised, clearer.

Danny stopped the recording. 'When I heard that, I did some work on the voices. You ready to hear the rest?'

Frankie nodded in disbelief as he picked up the phone and started to look for the cleaned-up recording. The toast popped behind her and she jumped.

'Oh my God, my heart.' Frankie jumped up and grabbed a plate and a knife from the drainer. The butter had been left on the sideboard and she flipped the toast onto the plate, hurriedly returning to the table. Frankie put it down in front of Danny, but neither of them was thinking about eating right now. He looked up at her, his eyebrows raised.

'Okay, I'm ready.'

Danny hit the play button on his phone, taking the conversation from the beginning again. The voices were clearer this time.

'Got enough vodka there, have you?'

'Mind your own fucking business.'

'Oh, I think it is my business when the captain of the team is a lying cheat.'

Without realising what she was doing, Frankie reached out and grabbed Danny's arm.

'What are you talking about?'

'You and Ruth Meaney. She's waiting for you now, isn't she, upstairs? I saw you in the hall. Got her kit off already, has she? What will Katie think about that?'

'Don't talk crap.'

'It's not crap. If I go upstairs now, who will I find in Katie's guest bedroom? You planning to have some private time with her, are you?'

'Fuck off, it's none of your business.'

Frankie was getting a horrible feeling. Would Josh say the name of the person he was speaking to?

'But it is Katie's business, and I'm sure she'd want to know.'

'What the hell? Don't you dare breathe a word, you little shit.'

'Why not? I think she should know.' There was a pause. 'Although maybe I could be persuaded.'

'What are you talking about?'

'Maybe if you called in sick for the next game, I could be persuaded to keep quiet.'

'What?' Another pause. Frankie looked at Danny, her eyes wide. Then the voice that had to be Josh's continued, 'Because the scouts will be there, is that it?'

'Sounds like a plan to me. You've already got your scholarship sorted.'

'No fucking way.' Josh again.

'You really want Katie to know? I'll go and find her, will I?'

'Don't you dare. You keep well clear of both of them, or your dad might get to hear about you and Conor.'

'What?' The retort was sharp, shocked.

'You think I don't know? You play it straight but you're as gay as he is.'

'That's crap and you know it. I'm not some gay-boy fag.'

'Really? You sure? What'll your ultra-right-wing father think about his son screwing boys, hey? He doesn't really do gay, does he? Didn't he defend that restaurant that was taken to the high court for discrimination?'

'Shut your face. You're talking bollocks.'

'Photos don't lie, and I've got one of you and Conor kissing in the showers. You think nobody wonders why you two always take so long to get out of the changing rooms?'

'You wouldn't bloody dare.'

'I think I would, because nobody wants a snake on the team. When I tell O'Reilly you tried to blackmail me into throwing the game, you'll be lucky to be playing next week. And Conor deserves a lot *better.'*

Danny paused the recording. 'I've taken out the background noise so we can hear the voices, but in the original, at this point the music stops outside and there's a load of screaming. This is what comes next.' He hit Play again.

'Don't you turn your back on me.' It came out as a snarl.

Danny tapped the phone. 'That's where it stops. I can't get any more, there's a load of roaring that drowns everything out.'

'The fight starting?' Frankie's voice was little more than a whisper.

Whoever had stabbed Josh was dating Conor and keeping it a secret. Plus, they knew that something was going on between Josh and Ruth – and had tried to use that to blackmail Josh to pull out of the match. It was all whirling in her head, making her feel very sick.

'I guess so. I'd also guess that whoever it was then flipped when Josh turned away from them. Josh's accusation made them really mad and at that point they grabbed the knife. If Josh was injured, he wouldn't be able to play in the match, would he? And maybe outshine whoever this is, in front of the scouts. Maybe they never meant to kill him.'

Frankie winced as Danny spoke. It all made sense now – well, sense was the wrong word. None of it made sense, but it fitted with what they'd discovered.

'You think the noise of the fight starting was what made him go and look in the living room?'

'Yep, I reckon he heard the music go off and all the screaming and went to have a look. Turning your back on someone in a row is a real signal that you think you've got the upper hand. Whoever he was arguing with must have just seen red.'

FORTY-FOUR

I t took a moment for the Rave-fess page to load, so Jess started walking down the hill towards the sea, her eyes on the screen. If she kept moving the reception might improve.

Suddenly the loading symbol disappeared and the page opened. She scrolled down.

> **NGL getting the LC nightmares already. How will I do revision when I can't even concentrate when I'm trying to write an essay?**

That can't have been the post Sorcha meant. Scrolling down further, Jess spotted another post. Just five words had kicked off over fifty comments.

Josh Fitzpatrick was no angel.

What on earth did that mean? And who had posted it?

Jess scanned the comments. There were loads saying that he *was* an angel with loads of angel emojis, then one about seeing Rob Doyle going to Josh's house. That had started of a bunch of speculative comments about Josh and steroids and how Rob Doyle knew where to get stuff.

Before she could read more, Jess's phone rang. Sorcha. *At last.*

'What's happening?' Sorcha sounded like she was at the pool, her voice echoing off hard surfaces, the sound of water in the background.

Jess kept her voice low. 'Can anyone hear you?'

'No, everyone else is still in the pool. I'm finished early.'

Jess drew in a breath. Where did she even start? 'It seems that that Rave-fess post is true.'

'What now?' Sorcha sounded like she'd gone into the changing room.

'I've just been talking to Georgia. You won't believe this, but when you saw Josh on the DART with Ruth,

271

you were right – he did have a thing with her. He's been cheating on Katie *all summer.*'

'And Katie didn't know?'

'Apparently not. Nobody knew except Amber, Georgia and Ella. But listen, you know how we couldn't find Ruth in the photos?'

'Uh-huh.' It sounded like Sorcha was drying herself now. Jess wished she'd just stop and listen.

'It's because she was upstairs waiting for Josh. I think the second drink he was carrying was for her.'

'That's *so* not good.'

'Worse, he was bringing her vodka and she can't drink at the moment with the meds she's on. I don't know if he knew or was planning on getting her pissed.'

'Maybe he forgot.'

'Yeah, maybe. But I was thinking, what if … Oh, there's another call coming in – it's Frankie.' Jess put Sorcha on hold. 'Hiya, I've been trying to call you.'

Frankie cut across her. 'I need you both down here right now. Come as soon as you can. There's been a development, a big one.'

Jess looked at her phone in astonishment. There was something about the seriousness of Frankie's tone that jolted her. Jess clicked back to the call with Sorcha but she'd been put on hold in her turn. Frankie must be calling her too.

What had she found out?

FORTY-FIVE

Jess got to Frankie's first, jogging down the hill to the hotel. It only took a moment for Frankie to answer the kitchen door.

She looked deathly white.

'My God, are you okay? You look like you're going to be sick.'

Frankie let out a shaky breath. She was close to tears. 'Come in. Is Sorcha on her way?'

'She was swimming, but she's just finished.'

Frankie showed Jess into the kitchen. 'Everyone's still out, thank goodness, we'll be okay here for a bit. This is Danny.'

Jess almost did a double take. Tanned, with thick blond hair falling over his deep brown eyes, Danny was drop-dead gorgeous. He stood up as she walked in. 'I have to get back. Keep me in the loop?' As he passed Frankie, heading for the door, he rubbed her arm. 'It'll be okay, honestly.'

Jess watched their interaction, her curiosity more than piqued. Where had Frankie been hiding *him*?

'Thanks.' Frankie smiled at him gratefully. 'Don't say anything to anyone until we've worked this out. What time do you finish?'

'Eight. I'll call you then?'

Frankie nodded. He rubbed her arm again and vanished out of the door.

Jess slipped her backpack off her shoulder onto one of the kitchen chairs, her eyes wide. 'You kept him quiet.'

'Who, Danny?' Frankie looked back at her, confused, like she wasn't really concentrating.

'Er, *yes*, he's like, super-hot.'

Frankie clearly couldn't focus on what Jess was saying, so she just nodded. 'Sit down and we'll wait for Sorcha. You won't believe what he's found out.'

Jess sat down. 'I've found out something else *you* won't believe.'

Frankie looked at her, startled. 'What?'

'Josh was cheating on Katie with Ruth Meaney all summer.' Jess paused for a moment to let it sink in. 'The reason that we lost her in the photos was because she'd gone upstairs to wait for him. I think the drink Maeve saw him making was for her.'

'Oh my God.' Frankie's face paled even more, if that was possible. Jess looked at her, surprised. She'd expected Frankie to be excited, to see that this could be the piece of information they'd been missing. Frankie swallowed hard. 'That sort of confirms the thing I need to talk to you guys about.'

As she spoke there was a banging on the outside door.

Frankie went to open it and Sorcha came barrelling down the short corridor into the kitchen, obviously out of breath.

'I got a lift and ran the rest of the way. Did Jess tell you about Ruth?' Before anyone could reply, Sorcha continued. 'And listen, Rob Doyle's been arrested. They caught him. He's down at Kilmurray Garda Station being questioned.'

'How? I mean, seriously?' Frankie looked at her incredulously. 'How do you know?'

'One of the girls on the swim team's dad is a legal aid solicitor. He does all the criminal work around here. He was supposed to be picking her up after practice and couldn't make it because he'd gone down to the Garda station. She wasn't supposed to tell anyone, obviously, but you know …'

'But what evidence can they possibly have?' Frankie stood with her arms wrapped around herself as Sorcha put her bag down on the sofa.

Sorcha shrugged. 'His previous conviction and the fact that he was there at all probably doesn't help. And there's been loads of talk on Rave-fess about drugs. Look.' Sorcha pulled out her phone to show them. 'And they don't even know about a possible love triangle between Ruth, him and Josh ...'

Frankie bit her lip. 'But the drugs thing is all just gossip. They need evidence to charge someone, surely.'

'That's what everyone is saying. People are freaking out – not in Rob's favour, though. Wait till they hear he's been arrested.' Sorcha pulled a chair out from the table and sat down opposite Jess, looking at the cold toast in the middle of the table. 'Have you got any proper food? I'm starving.'

Jess put her elbows onto the table and rubbed her face. 'I bet his prints were on that knife. I *bet* that's what it is.'

Frankie looked at her, still dazed. 'But we know lots of people's prints were on that knife.'

Sorcha nodded. 'They must have something on him if they've arrested him. Is it okay if I put some more toast on?'

Jess tapped her nails on the table as Sorcha headed across the kitchen for the toaster. 'It has to be solid to get to court. He can't be convicted unless there's proper evidence.'

Frankie looked from one of them to the other. 'But they've got it wrong.'

FORTY-SIX

'How can you be so sure Rob Doyle didn't do it, Franks? I know we don't think he did, but they're the Guards. Like Jess says, they must have real evidence.' Sorcha leaned back on the counter as she spoke, her arms folded.

From the moment she'd heard the voice on the recording, Frankie's stomach had been spiralling out of control, and now the smell of toast was making it worse. She'd been stalling telling them what Danny had found – explaining it made it all the more horribly real – but now she had to.

'Sorch, come and sit down. I need you and Jess to listen to something.'

Frankie picked up her phone. Danny had WhatsApped her the track he'd separated from Maeve and Caitriona's video. She found his message and opened it.

As she hit Play, Frankie took a deep breath. Part of her was dreading hearing it again. Glancing at her, both frowning, Jess and Sorcha leaned into the phone to listen.

Re-running it made Frankie even more sure she knew who was arguing with Josh.

'Oh. My. God.' Sorcha's hand shot to her mouth as it played.

Jess glanced at her, then back at Frankie. 'Who do you think it is? It must be someone on the rugby team?'

Frankie took a deep breath. 'It's not Rob Doyle, that's for sure. Whoever this is has a posh accent. Rob's is much more Dublin.'

'We have to give it to the Guards. They'll be able to find out who it is.'

Behind them the toast popped, but nobody moved.

Frankie looked at Jess. 'Will they, though? Or will they just say that this had nothing to do with the stabbing, that Rob was there too but his voice wasn't picked up, or he didn't say anything? There's nothing in this recording that says that this person actually stabbed Josh. They had an argument and the timing seems to make sense, but they're bound to say that they left Josh alive and well.'

Jess and Sorcha looked back at her. They knew she was right. She could see it in their faces.

Jess shook her head slowly. 'But who is it? If we can find *that* out, the Guards could question them.'

Sorcha frowned. 'Frankie's right, they'll just deny it. This proves this person had an argument with Josh, which gives a motive perhaps, and they maybe had the opportunity – but that's all. We'd need some solid evidence, like a confession or something, to prove Rob really didn't do it.'

Jess looked at her like she was being ridiculous. 'We'd need to know who it was to get a confession.'

Frankie looked at them. 'I think I know who it is.' She'd said it. She felt like she was literally about to throw up.

Jess and Sorcha's mouths fell open. 'Who?'

Frankie cleared her throat. 'When I met Patrick, he mentioned those scouts were coming to watch their next game. He's taken over as captain. He kept saying they hadn't cancelled the match because they wanted to play in Josh's memory.' She paused. 'But if something happened to Josh, all eyes would be on him. And that's exactly what the person on this tape wanted. For Josh to call in sick.'

Jess and Sorcha looked at her for a moment, still frowning, processing what she was saying.

'And,' Frankie continued, 'Patrick's always with Conor. I thought it was because they were best friends.'

She shook her head. 'But what if they were secretly dating?'

'Surely Katie would know. Wouldn't she have said something to you?' Sorcha frowned.

'Not if Patrick had sworn Conor to secrecy. And I never really said anything to her about Patrick. I mean, it's pretty obvious I fancy him, but remember how I said she kept changing the subject whenever I brought him up? Maybe it was because she knew he and Conor were a thing but couldn't say.'

Jess let out a sharp breath. 'There could be a lot about Patrick we don't know. Are you sure?'

Frankie nodded. 'It really sounds like him. He has that exact same accent and tone of voice. I was only talking to him this morning. I'm almost sure it's him.'

FORTY-SEVEN

By the time Jess and Sorcha left, Danny was just finishing his shift.

Frankie had been keeping an eye on the time and texted him to meet her in the hotel garden. It was starting to get chilly now. She hadn't had a chance to get changed so was still in her school uniform, but she'd thrown a jacket around her shoulders. Now she sat on the bench in the middle of the walled scent garden, one of her mum's 'features' for a relaxing stay.

She heard Danny's footsteps before she saw him. He appeared, pushing aside the purple flowering creeper which grew over the curved gateway to this section of the garden. It was a lot more private than anywhere inside, where someone could appear at any minute.

'Hiya, how are you doing?'

He sat down heavily next to her. 'Shattered. I think I've peeled about five hundred spuds tonight. But those Americans in 202 left and gave me a whopping tip, so I'm all good.'

Frankie smiled. 'You deserve that. Sinéad said they were high maintenance.'

Danny smiled. 'They were nice, just old. Travelling's hard work when you can't get about very easily.' He turned to look at her. 'What did the girls think of the recording – any idea who it is?'

Frankie pulled the jacket around her and looked back at him. Even though she'd shared it with Jess and Sorcha, she felt like she and Danny were bonded somehow by the discovery of this terrible secret. She took a shaky breath. 'I think I do. The problem is proving it.'

Danny's eyebrows shot up. 'Go on.'

'It's the voice, the accent, but also what he says. I'm *sure* it's Patrick Kelly. He's vice-captain of the Raven's Park College rugby team. But the Guards have arrested someone else – that guy Rob Doyle I was telling you about.'

'They must have evidence to arrest him. So the recording can't be what we think.'

Frankie shook her head. It only took her a few minutes to explain Rob Doyle's history.

Danny let out a sigh. 'Okay, I get it.' He paused. 'The thing is, even if they *do* enhance that audio, I'm not sure whether they'll be able to identify the speaker without a voice match. Maybe there's one on social, but like you said, even if they did match it, it's not conclusive, is it?' Danny paused. 'Unless you can get him to admit it, on the record, of course.' His brow furrowed and Frankie could almost see the cogs whirring in his head.

'But how can we get him to do that?' Frankie felt her eyes filling up. This was suddenly all too much. Josh had been murdered. He'd had his whole life in front of him.

And she'd really thought she could have something with Patrick, but he'd totally deceived her. He must have wanted to meet her in Starbucks to get information, not to see if she was okay.

Before she realised it, Danny had moved up next to her and put his arm around her shoulders. 'Cry if you need to, don't hold it in. This whole thing is terrible.'

Danny suddenly felt warm and safe, and Frankie felt the tears hot on her cheeks as they started to flow, the shock and emotion from the past few days gushing out again. She turned into his shoulder and he held her tighter as she started to sob.

'I don't know how you've held it together at all. What a total mess.' Frankie felt him stroke her hair. 'Let it out, you're safe here.'

As he spoke, Frankie heard her phone pip with a text. She ignored it but then another one came, and another.

'I think someone wants you.'

Oh, why now? She could smell the comforting scent of washing powder from his shirt. She didn't ever want to move.

The phone pipped again.

'Oh feck, I better look.'

Pulling away from him, she wiped her face with the back of her hand as she glanced at the screen. 'It's all right, it's only Sorcha.' Frankie scanned the first text. 'She says not to say a word in school. She wants to talk tomorrow, back here. She's had an idea about how to prove it wasn't Rob Doyle.' Frankie looked at Danny, excitement bubbling up inside her as she flicked to the next message. 'She wants you there too. Will I add you to our group chat?'

FORTY-EIGHT

The next day went so slowly Frankie almost screamed. Every time she tried to talk to Sorcha or Jess about anything, they changed the subject to random topics like maths homework and make-up. She could understand that they were paranoid that someone would overhear them and could leak their suspicions, but it was so frustrating.

Around them, Frankie could hear everyone talking about the Rave-fess post about Josh, and Rob Doyle, and whether Josh was buying steroids from him, or worse, cocaine. The Guards had arrested Rob so fast, everyone was convinced they must have a solid case against him.

When the final bell went, Frankie couldn't get home quickly enough. Glancing over her shoulder on the way out of the school gate, she could see Jess and Sorcha deliberately sauntering down the drive as if they weren't in a hurry to get anywhere. Nobody knew what they were planning but they'd agreed it was important to act relaxed, even if their hearts were racing.

Watching for them out of her bedroom window, Frankie saw Danny emerge through the staff entrance to the kitchen to meet them. It didn't take the three of them long to get upstairs to her.

She opened the door and they all filed in, Sorcha and Jess plonking down on her bed and Danny sitting on the armchair opposite it. Closing the door behind her, Frankie leaned back against it.

'So, what's up? Spill.'

Sorcha slid forwards on the bed, getting straight to the point. 'So we're pretty sure it's Patrick Kelly on the recording. But you're right in thinking that he could easily worm his way out of it. And I checked up on his dad – he's one of the biggest criminal defence lawyers in the country, never mind Dublin.'

'So Rob Doyle doesn't have a hope.' Frankie rolled her eyes.

'Not if we take this to the Guards, but if we can get a confession, or at least something more conclusive that would be harder to get out of, and take *that* to the Guards as well, he'd have a much better chance.' Sorcha looked around at them all.

'That's basically what Danny said, but how do we do that?' Frankie rested her head back on the door. She'd been thinking about the whole situation since chatting to Danny, but it seemed an impossible task to get Patrick to confess: he was too clever. Stabbing Josh sounded like it could have been a spur-of-the-moment thing, a flash of temper, but she was damn sure he'd have been thinking of ways to prove that he wasn't involved since the moment it had happened.

'We play him the tape. And then we film his reaction.'

Frankie let out a sigh and shook her head. 'Sorcha, really? How are we going to set that up? He'll see it coming a mile off and just deny that it's him.'

Jess had been frowning while Sorcha was talking, her elbow on her knee, her chin resting on her hand. 'She's actually right. If someone he trusted was there and asked him about it, he could let something slip.'

'That's assuming he reacts the way we expect.' Ollie's words about how trying to catch a murderer could be dangerous, flew into Frankie's head. 'We'd have to be careful. This could go really, really wrong.'

As she spoke, Danny sat forwards in the chair. 'The key here, is who we get to challenge him. It needs to be someone he doesn't think is trying to trap him.'

Jess looked at Frankie. 'Katie? She and Conor have been friends for years – maybe she could ask Patrick?'

Frankie weighed up the idea. Jess was right: if anyone had a vested interest in finding out who Josh's killer was, it was Katie. And she went back forever with Conor. 'We'd need to try and keep the bit about Ruth quiet. I don't think she could cope with that too.'

Danny nodded. 'Agreed. But this Conor dude's loyalties might be stronger to Katie than they are to Patrick. I mean, I know you said Conor's out, and Patrick isn't, but Patrick denying their relationship like that has got to hurt. And if Conor finds out Patrick's responsible for stabbing his best friend's boyfriend …'

Jess pulled her necklace out from her collar as if playing with it helped her think. 'We'd need somewhere for all this to happen, somewhere that it would be natural for Patrick to meet Conor and Katie.'

'Here at the hotel?' Danny narrowed his eyes. 'We could use the conference room?'

Jess looked at Danny, confused. 'Why here? It's not exactly a normal place to hang out.'

'It is for Frankie – and for me, and it's kitted out for recording, audio and video, live-streaming – the whole lot. If we can get him in there, we could record everything really easily.' He paused. Jess still didn't look convinced. 'I don't see how else we could set it up. He's going to notice someone just filming on their phone, isn't he?'

Jess nodded slowly, taking his point, as Sorcha leaned forwards. 'Could you invite Patrick over, Frankie? Then we get Katie and Conor to come here too? Patrick would think he was meeting you, and there'd be no need to mention them.'

Jess ran her chain over her nose. 'That sounds like it could work. Patrick thinks you're a hotline to the Gardaí, Frankie, so he'll want to come down and find out what you know if you drop enough hints.'

The part of Frankie that found the whole idea terrifying was getting overruled by the part that was getting angrier and angrier that Patrick had stabbed Josh – and then thought he could lead her on and try to use her to get information. Not to mention that he'd tried to blackmail Josh in the first place. 'When, though? We need to check the conference room is free.'

Danny looked up. 'Friday evening? There was something booked in for Saturday but they cancelled at the last minute. I was supposed to be helping with the set-up.' He played his phone through his fingers on the arm of the chair. 'And that trad band are booked for the bar on Friday evening. They're starting early, so there'll be plenty of noise and no one will have any reason to be on the conferencing side of the hotel.'

Frankie nodded slowly. 'And if we do it here, we'll have Ollie and the twins nearby as back-up.' She looked around the room at them all. 'I'm going to need to talk to Katie.'

FORTY-NINE

Frankie could feel her stomach churning as she stood on Katie's doorstep and waited for her to answer the doorbell. She'd had a horrible feeling walking back down Katie's drive, like it was all going to happen again. Ollie had dropped her off, saying something about PTSD and to call him the minute she wanted collecting. Last night, after dinner, she'd had a big chat with her mum about therapy and counselling. Ms Cooke had been talking about it in school too, and had pinned up numbers to call on the noticeboard, but her mum was going to find someone for her to talk to in Dublin. Frankie didn't know why, but the thought of bumping into someone from Fifth Year at a therapist's office stressed her out more than the thought of having to talk about everything in the first place.

Now, standing on Katie's doorstep, all Frankie could see was Josh's body lying behind the sofa, a pool of blood soaking into the wooden floor. *The sooner her mum could get a counsellor organised, the better.*

Frankie jumped as Katie pulled back the chain and opened the door. Marshmallow and Cheesecake hurtled out, leaping up at her. It was just as well she'd changed into her jeans; she could feel their claws through the thick fabric.

Katie looked terrible, pale and red-eyed, her face bare of make-up. She held out her arms for a hug. 'It's so good to see you, Frankie. Thank you for being my friend and being there for me.'

She took a step backwards to allow Frankie over the doorstep. The house looked completely different from the last time Frankie had been here, the black-and-white marble floor tiles gleaming after their industrial polish, all the tea lights and flashing LEDs gone. The hall smelled faintly of lavender.

'Here, come upstairs. I can't go into the living room yet. Mum and Dad are getting a new floor put down and changing the sofas. Maybe I'll be able to then, but …' She stopped as if she'd run out of words.

'Don't worry, upstairs will be fab. I love your room.'

Katie smiled weakly and turned to call the dogs in. They were racing around the front lawn in tight concentric circles. 'Mum and Dad are out and the dogs are desperate for a proper walk.'

Both dogs came bounding in the front door when she called them.

Frankie put her hand on Katie's arm as she closed the door. 'We'll take them out, me, Jess and Sorcha. Ollie can drop us.'

Katie sighed and smiled. 'That's so lovely of you. They'd love that. Come on up. Excuse the mess.'

Frankie knew 'mess' was a relative term in Katie's world. Her family had a cleaner who tidied and did all the laundry – a housekeeper would be a better name for her. In Frankie's house everyone had to keep their own space organised, and if you didn't get your washing down to the washing basket, it didn't get done. And as for cleaning, there was a hoover on the landing for everyone. Even Max knew how it worked.

Marshmallow and Cheesecake came belting past them on the stairs as soon as they saw Frankie was going up. Katie's room was definitely untidier than the last time Frankie had seen it, but still nothing compared to the peak chaos Frankie's occasionally reached. Katie's clothes were draped over the padded chair at her dressing table, and her make-up was spread everywhere.

As Frankie closed the door, Katie jumped onto the bed and pulled her huge white teddy bear onto her knee.

Frankie sat down at the end, leaning back on the brass bed post. Nerves were playing a tune in her head, all high notes, giving her a headache.

'How've you been?' Frankie could feel anxiety clutching at her stomach as she spoke.

Katie closed her eyes by way of an answer. 'Terrible. The worst thing is ...' Katie took a deep breath. 'I haven't told this to anybody, not even Conor, but we had this stupid row before the party,' she opened her eyes again and looked at Frankie, 'about whether I should do party food or not. It was just so ... *stupid*,' she sniffed. 'Josh's been a bit off for ages. I felt like we'd been drifting. He started seeing me on WhatsApp and ...' Katie shook her head. 'I don't know. I thought he might need some space or something, but we never got to have a proper conversation about it. Which makes it all worse, somehow.' Her sigh was ragged as she continued, 'That's why I didn't totally panic when he didn't answer my texts when you guys left with Ollie. I thought he'd taken some of the Raven's Park guys home and would come back afterwards.' She sniffed again. 'Honestly, I was a bit traumatised by the whole fight thing. I pretty much hit the gin. I can barely remember waiting for you to get back.'

Frankie reached out and hugged her. 'What have the Guards said?'

'You heard about Rob Doyle?' Frankie nodded as Katie continued. 'I can't see how he could have done it. I mean, Josh was the one who was going to get him through his Leaving. He was going to give him grinds in physics too this term. Rob needed him.'

Frankie felt like all the reasons why Rob wouldn't have stabbed Josh were piling up. Which just strengthened their whole Patrick theory.

She took a deep breath. They'd worked out what she should say, but actually being here and saying it was very different.

'Katie, how well do you know Patrick ...?'

Katie looked surprised. 'Not that well, he's Conor's friend. They've been hanging out a lot recently.' She paused. 'Josh didn't like him at all, so I haven't seen Conor as often as I did before ... why?'

Frankie bit her lip. 'It's just someone heard him arguing with Josh in the kitchen that night. I, well, me, Jess and Sorcha, think ...'

'That Patrick stabbed him?' It came out as a whisper. Katie had paled, but rather than telling Frankie that it sounded like nonsense, as she'd half expected, Katie closed her eyes and sighed deeply. It was as if she was processing what Frankie had said, joining the dots. 'Josh *really* didn't like Patrick. He said he couldn't trust him. Patrick was desperate to be captain, was totally convinced he was a better player. He was so jealous when he heard that Josh had got the offer from Stanford.' Katie paused. 'It was really awkward with Conor and me being so close. And Josh couldn't say anything, they had to play as a team, so he pretended everything was fine. Josh said Patrick has a terrible temper – it came out during matches and caused them loads of trouble.' Katie's face hardened. 'What did Patrick say?'

Any respect Frankie had left for Patrick was evaporating like spilled perfume. She took a shaky breath. 'Apparently, during this argument, Josh said Patrick was hiding that he was gay, that he had a photo of him kissing Conor. Patrick denied it, said there was nothing between them and that he wasn't "a fag".' She cringed at the slur.

'That's so nasty. I don't get why myself, but Conor's crazy about Patrick. It had to be a total secret though because of Patrick's family. Patrick said he'd literally get thrown out and disowned if his dad found out.' She bit her lip. 'But he still didn't have to say *that*.'

'So they *are* an item?'

Katie sighed. 'Yes, but I was sworn to *total* secrecy, I couldn't even tell Josh. That's why I couldn't say anything when you hinted that you liked him. I mean, Patrick could be bi, but even so it would have been complicated if you'd got involved.' She paused. 'And really, he's not your type. From what I've heard, he's completely obsessed with himself and his success. I know he's gorgeous to look at, but apart from looks I can't understand what

Conor sees in him.' Katie shook her head, anger flashing in her eyes. 'Conor will be devastated with all of this. He and Josh had a real laugh, and he knew me and Josh were planning on going to college together. We can't let Patrick get away with it – or let Rob Doyle end up in court again because of him.'

Frankie sat forwards on the bed. 'We had an idea about that. But we need your help. Could you talk to Conor for us?'

FIFTY

On her bed, Katie pulled her bear in closer to her and buried her face in its fur. Frankie slipped off the end and moved up to sit next to her. She could see that Katie needed a moment to take it all in. She reached for Katie's arm and rubbed it. At last Katie looked up, tears gathering in her red-rimmed eyes. 'You're absolutely certain it was Patrick who was arguing with Josh?'

Frankie nodded. 'We've got a recording of them in the background of a video someone took. It's a bit fuzzy, but we're sure it's him. What we're worried about is Patrick and his dad coming up with some reason why he was in the kitchen having that conversation and twisting it. He doesn't actually say that he's going to stab Josh, obviously.'

'Can I hear it?'

Frankie squirmed inside. They'd anticipated this question. 'I think it could be a bit too horrible for you to hear right now.' Frankie had her fingers crossed under her sweatshirt. There was no way she wanted Katie listening to the recording and finding out about Ruth this soon. They'd agreed that when they got Patrick into the conference room, they'd only play part of it. Danny was going to record copies he could edit so that Katie didn't have to hear that Ruth had been waiting upstairs for Josh at her own party. It sounded a lot like Katie knew *something* was going on, but it would never be easy to hear that Josh had been cheating on her – and with Ruth Meaney, of all people.

As Frankie spoke, Marshmallow jumped on the bed beside Katie and rolled over to have her tummy tickled. Cheesecake had curled up on Katie's pure white sheepskin rug and was snoring gently.

Katie rubbed the dog's belly. 'So, what do you want me to say to Conor?'

'We wondered …' Frankie hesitated – she didn't want it to sound like they'd all been plotting, even though they had – 'we wondered, if I invited Patrick down to the hotel, whether Conor could come too. Then we can play the tape and see how Patrick reacts. He can't pretend it's someone else Josh was talking to if Conor's there.'

'Conor will want to kill him. Patrick knows how close me and Conor are, he's like my brother. And he knows how important Josh is to me. *Was* ...' Katie hesitated, biting her lip. 'It's all making sense now. When Conor came over yesterday, Patrick texted him while he was here. Conor said he was talking to me, that he wouldn't be long and he could meet him after. But the next thing, Patrick's there at the front door being all concerned. I didn't really want to see him but Mum had let him in by then, so he came up.' Katie paused as if she was piecing things together in her head. 'They were talking about the match. Patrick said Josh would have wanted them to win, that they were going to play for him, but then he asked so many questions about what the Guards were doing and what was happening that I got upset. Conor was really pissed off with him. It was just too much too soon.' Tears sprang up in her eyes again. 'I know me and Josh had an argument before the party, but I never thought we wouldn't work it out.' Frankie leaned forwards and rubbed Katie's arm as she fought back tears. 'That's the worst of it. I know everyone says death's final, but when it actually happens ... you just don't expect never to see that person again.'

Jess had said exactly the same thing about her mum.

'Come here.' Frankie gave Katie a hug and turned around to reach for a tissue in the pretty pink floral box on the bedside table. As she plucked one out, Frankie spotted a chunky gold chain bracelet snaking around Katie's silk eye mask and a pot of Vaseline. It had a gold letter R charm on it. *Odd.* It didn't look like it belonged to Katie.

'Unusual bracelet.' Frankie handed Katie the tissue.

'Our housekeeper found it in the spare room after the party. Do you know whose it is?'

Frankie shook her head as Katie took a shaky breath, tears falling down her cheeks, suddenly overwhelmed. Frankie pulled her in for a hug as Katie started to sob. 'It's just so horrible, Frankie, I can't go anywhere in the house where I don't see it all over again. I mean, Josh is *gone.*'

'Are you mad, Franks, I mean really?' Ollie looked at her like she'd gone completely bonkers. 'You have to take this to the Guards.' He kept his voice low. Frankie had come to find him in the bar as soon as she'd got back from Katie's. She'd decided to walk back. It was a fair distance, but she'd needed time to clear her head, and it was still early. Thankfully there was a lull in trade and the bar was empty. She'd been going over how to tell Ollie what they were planning all the way home. She knew what his reaction would be, but she needed him to be there for them, just in case.

'I'm not, honestly. Just listen.' Frankie outlined all the reasons why they thought it was Patrick and all the ways he could get away with it, ticking each one off on her fingers as she explained.

Ollie glanced at the main door to make sure there was no one coming in as he replied. 'Okay, I see your point, but getting him to admit it like this sounds like a long shot to me. I mean, would you?'

Frankie shuffled forwards on the stool she was sitting on. 'It's not so much *what* he says, it's his reaction we're after. That's what we need on film. What have we got to lose?'

Ollie looked dubious. 'Let's hope he doesn't bring a knife with him, will we?'

Frankie rubbed her face with her hand. 'If you've got any better ideas, do share. But seriously, Ollie, listen to the tape. It's Patrick, I'm absolutely sure of it, and with the way he's been behaving, it all makes sense. He's been asking loads about the investigation. And Sorcha thinks that maybe he's the one who started putting the posts up about Josh buying drugs from Rob Doyle on Rave-fess.'

'How can she possibly know that?' Ollie picked up a cloth from behind the bar and gave the polished mahogany a wipe. 'Is she still here? It's a bit late for her to go home now.'

'She's upstairs – she wanted to do something online. She's staying over tonight and tomorrow. She's got swim training in the morning.'

Ollie threw the cloth in the sink under the bar. They were all used to Sorcha staying whenever she could. He looked at Frankie thoughtfully for a moment. 'Okay, I'm in. I'll talk to the twins too, and Danny. Film it, get what you can and then take it to the Guards. When's all this happening?'

'Friday evening, we hope. As soon as we know Conor's up for it. I'll need to convince one of the twins to do my Max-minding. They'll be done before anything happens, but I'll need to get ready.'

'And Katie's talking to Conor tonight?'

Frankie opened her mouth to answer, but a text came in before she could speak. She looked at the phone lying on the bar beside her.

It was from Patrick. This time she didn't get butter-flies; instead she felt anger rising inside her like boiling oil.

Awesome to see you. Free tomorrow?

Frankie drummed her fingers on the bar. She needed to work out how to respond. This was the opportunity she needed to invite him over.

303

Before she had a chance to reply, another message came through.

This time from Katie.

Conor v v upset. He says yes.

They were on.

FIFTY-ONE

Upstairs in the hotel, neither Frankie nor Sorcha felt like going to bed. There was too much happening for sleep.

Sorcha lay across Frankie's silver-grey duvet in a pile of lilac cushions, her phone in her hand. 'I wish I got taken out for dinner like Jess. I could seriously do with something to take my mind off all of this.'

Frankie looked at her from across the room. She was trying to sort out her clothes before tomorrow night, although she was pretty sure she was going to wear her jeans. This time she didn't feel the need to impress

Patrick one little bit. But she still needed to look like she thought they were on a date. She tried to tune into what Sorcha was saying.

'I think Jess's pretty lucky when her dad gets home in one piece, to be honest, though dinner is obviously a bonus.' Frankie paused, looking back at her clothes. 'Sometimes I really wish we had a housekeeper who did all the cooking and sorted out our laundry like Katie's.'

Sorcha rolled her eyes. 'Yeah, but you wouldn't swap for the rest of Katie's life right now. Or for her parents. I mean, mine are away a lot, but hers are really bad. She should board with me and Jess.'

'She doesn't want to, she couldn't bring Marshmallow and Cheesecake.' Frankie paused. 'So you're definitely moving into the boarding house next week?'

'Yep. Can't wait.'

Frankie turned back to the pile of tops she'd collected and spread across her armchair. Behind her she could hear Sorcha tapping at her screen.

'You know, there might be another way to catch Patrick. I mean, instead of the whole conference room showdown thing.'

Frankie turned around to look at Sorcha, her eyes narrowed. 'We've come a bit far to change the plan now. Patrick's coming over tomorrow evening at seven, and is "really looking forwards to it", apparently.' The words almost stuck in her throat. 'And Conor's all set. What other way can we do it?'

'Well …' Sorcha drew out the word. 'I was wondering about using Rave-fess. I just haven't quite worked out what sort of post we'd need. But from what we suspect, I think Patrick's the sort to lose his temper fast, so if we could rile him, he might respond with something that ties into the information we have.'

Frankie sighed, looking at her cousin witheringly. 'There are two very big problems with making that work, Sorch.' She ticked them off on her fingers as she spoke: 'Number one, coming up with something that doesn't get us sued by Patrick and his father, but gets him to react. And number two, coming up with something the mysterious admin will actually publish. I mean, I guess they don't publish everything that they get sent, whoever they are – there must be some mad stuff. And a post that's designed to unmask a murderer is likely to send up red flags.'

Sorcha screwed up her face as if she was thinking. 'I'm pretty sure they publish most things.'

Frankie turned back to her tidying, shaking her head. She felt a surge of impatience that Sorcha was coming up with a new plan at the final hour. Honestly, what was she like? Danny had already worked out a minute-by-minute breakdown of how tomorrow evening would – hopefully – run and had sent it to them all to debug. 'How on earth can you know that, Sorch? You aren't an admin.'

It was a statement rather than a question, but as Frankie said it, she froze, a red T-shirt in her hand. She turned around slowly. *Was* Sorcha involved in Rave-fess? She was a brilliant swimmer, but she was also a total tech nerd, planning on doing Computer Science and going into cyber security after the Leaving. Rave-fess was just the sort of thing she'd dream up.

Sorcha was looking back at her screen.

'You *are* involved, aren't you?' The penny had suddenly dropped and was rolling along at high speed in Frankie's head. 'Rave-fess appeared in the summer just after you'd had your place confirmed at Raven's Hill. Sorcha?'

Sorcha looked up at her, deliberately, innocently. 'I might know a bit about it. But don't you breathe a word, Frankie O'Sullivan. It only works when no one knows who the admins are.'

'But why?' Stunned, as much by how long it had taken her to realise as by how obvious it was when she thought about it, Frankie looked at Sorcha, her eyes wide.

'You know how hard it is to move into a school where you've all been together forever – since like Montessori for some of you. Jess has done it loads of times, but I haven't, and I wanted to find out who everyone was. You can learn a lot about people from their secrets, you know.' She paused. '"Knowledge is power", remember, Franks?'

'Well, that's for sure.' Frankie was still stunned. 'I can't believe you didn't tell me.'

'It wouldn't be a very good confession site if everyone knew it was me, would it? Anyway, Beth approves posts too. It was sort of her idea to start with.'

Frankie looked at her thoughtfully. 'So, between you and your sister, you must know who has posted what?'

'Exactly. Some people are sensible enough to use fake email addresses but most people aren't. And it's weird, but after this long, I'm starting to recognise the tone of some of them – people have distinctive ways of saying things. Sometimes I edit them a bit if I feel it's too obvious that they've posted before. If someone guesses who's posting then it fails the anonymity test, which is kind of the point.'

Frankie was quiet for a minute. Putting the T-shirt down, she put her hands on her hips and pursed her lips. 'I'd be very interested to know who posted that "Josh was no angel" post?'

'Beth approved that one, but I can check. Give me a minute.'

Sorcha's brows knitted as she tapped her phone, scrolling through, scanning the screen. 'Here it is: fifteengreenbottles3@gmail.com.'

Frankie looked at her, taking a slow breath, trying to still her thumping heart.

Puzzled, Sorcha inclined her head, 'What?'

'Patrick plays in the number three shirt. And there are fifteen players on a rugby team.'

Sorcha's mouth formed into an O shape. 'And one of the green bottles has accidentally fallen …'

It took a moment for Frankie to recover. 'Or not so accidentally …'

FIFTY-TWO

Frankie glanced at the clock on her bedside table. It was almost midnight and she and Sorcha were still up. Sorcha was usually fast asleep by ten with her training schedule, but tonight they were both wide awake, running on adrenaline. And now Frankie's mind was reeling from the news that Sorcha was behind the Rave-fess site, *and* that there was a strong chance that Patrick had posted about Josh not being an angel.

Folding the tops she'd scattered across her chair, Frankie tried to work out how she hadn't realised Sorcha was behind Rave-fess ages ago. Sorcha had wanted to know about everyone before she started at Raven's Hill, and she was brilliant at maths and coding and web stuff. And Ollie had told Frankie that lots of colleges had confession sites like Rave-fess and Sorcha's sister Beth was doing her degree at Edinburgh. She'd likely know all about them, and probably how to set one up. *And* she could approve posts when Sorcha was busy in the pool or in class so it didn't look like she could be involved.

Frankie turned to look at her cousin, who was still lying across the bed, tapping at her phone. 'I can't believe it was you all along. What if you'd got a really desperate one? Someone who was about to slit their wrists or something?'

'Obviously if anyone said they were about to do something like that, then I'd tell Ms Cooke. She's the school counsellor – she's qualified to sort out people's problems.'

'But if you contacted Ms Cooke, you'd have to admit to being behind Rave-fess, and then you'd get into *so* much trouble. It doesn't make the school look like they've got their students' mental health sorted, or that they've got much control, when everyone's posting about sex and getting drunk.'

'They aren't really. There was that one post earlier in the summer about getting wasted at that new club, Havana: 'Wish I knew who that gorgeous boy in the Adidas T-shirt was, he was a great shag' or something like that, but it could legit have been one of the Sixth Years.'

'And was it?'

Sorcha shook her head. 'No, it was Ella. She's a bit of a party animal. She was the one who got with that hockey coach too. I still don't understand why Georgia hangs around with her and Amber and Ruth – she's so quiet.'

Frankie shrugged. 'I think Georgia's known Amber forever, and sort of came with the package when Ruth was forming her little posse.'

Sorcha played with her tiny silver hoop earring thoughtfully. 'Georgia seems so nice. I wonder if she can see how awful they are?'

As she spoke, Frankie was running back through the posts she'd read on Rave-fess that had stood out. 'So, who posted that one about a Raven's Park College rugby guy not being straight? That was nasty. Why would you approve it?'

Sorcha screwed up her face. 'Beth approved that one. By the time I saw it, there were loads of comments and it seemed too late to delete it. But – and don't breathe a word of this, obviously – I *think* that was Josh.'

Frankie looked at her, shocked. 'Katie said he didn't like Patrick, but a post like that could cause so much damage.'

'More than was *actually* caused, you mean?' Sorcha's tone was heavy with sarcasm.

'You know what I mean.' Frankie was starting to see a very different side to Josh, the golden boy they'd all thought was so perfect. But as she spoke, an idea occurred to Frankie. 'Can you put up a post asking who might have lost a gold bracelet with an R-shaped charm on it at the party?'

Sorcha looked at her like it was a stupid question. 'Obviously. That's not very controversial, though, is it? I mean, I don't want it to turn into a lost-and-found site.'

Frankie came over to sit next to Sorcha on the bed. 'I have a feeling there might be a bigger story behind it.'

'You're talking about Ruth's bracelet, aren't you? The one with that chunky chain?'

'How do you know it's Ruth's?' Frankie looked at her. Sorcha was full of surprises this evening.

Sorcha turned over, pulling a cushion in behind her head. 'Because she cornered me in the loo last week and was pretty nasty. I think she felt she needed to establish her position or something. But she was wearing it then. I noticed it because it rattled off the basin when she tried to block me from leaving.'

'You never said she'd had a go at you.'

'Didn't need to. I gave as good as I got, and don't forget, I'm the one with the power – I control Rave-fess. Do you remember that post about dating older guys? I checked and that was Ruth. *And* ...' Sorcha paused for effect, 'the one about being dumped by text.' Frankie's mouth fell open as Sorcha continued, 'I could be joining the dots wrong here, but when I saw her at the DART station with Rob Doyle, I reckon they were having a row.'

'Georgia said something about them hanging out. Do you think she was actually dating Rob Doyle, as well as seeing Josh?'

Sorcha's brows knotted like she was figuring it out. 'I think that's a very strong possibility. And it would explain why she was wearing a man's bracelet and not something a bit more tasteful.'

FIFTY-THREE

The minute Frankie got back to the hotel after school on Friday afternoon, she went to find Danny. He wasn't working that night so he'd planned to come in specially to set everything up.

The more she thought about confronting Patrick, the more nervous Frankie became, to the point that she was now feeling positively sick. But she couldn't think of another way to do this and, unless they acted quickly, Rob Doyle was about to have his life ruined for a second time.

Pushing open the door to the audio-visual booth above the conference suite, Frankie found Danny at the mixing desk, adjusting the lighting. He must have been there a while – she could smell his soap as soon as she took a step inside. He was wearing jeans and hi-tops, a faded grey T-shirt straining across his shoulders.

'Hiya. All ready?'

He glanced behind him with a welcome grin, one eye on the window that looked out from the booth over the conference room.

'Almost. I've got all the cameras set up, so we've got the full room covered.' He paused. 'We're going to need to be ready from the minute he arrives, and have someone blocking each of the exits. If Katie covers the fire exit, you can do the main doors, and Jess and Sorcha the stage, then we should be good. You don't want him guessing something is up, getting mad and storming off. If you're all in front of the doors, he'll have to stop.'

'And you've got the tape ready to go?' Frankie could feel her mouth going dry as she spoke.

Danny glanced at her reassuringly. 'I'll be up here the whole time making sure everything's working. I'm going to mic Conor up when he arrives so I can hear everything and record their conversation. The minute Conor gives me a signal, I'll play the audio.'

'And you've edited out the bit about Ruth?' Frankie let out a ragged breath.

'Have you told Katie about that?' Danny's brown eyes were full of concern.

'I don't know how to break it to her, but she did say that she and Josh had had a row before the party. I think that's why Josh wasn't there early to help set up. She said he'd been acting strangely. I think she guessed there might be something going on … but I'm pretty sure she'd never guess it was with Ruth.'

Danny grimaced. 'I've got that section of the audio separated; I hope we don't need it. It's definitely better she finds out from you. You can frame it that Ruth was the instigator, maybe?'

Frankie gave him a side eye. She really didn't think that that would help but she knew he meant well. Not that Josh was exactly an innocent party. 'I'll work it out.' Frankie paused, 'Everyone should be here by six. Will you be ready to run through everything then?'

Danny nodded. 'It's pretty simple, really. You meet Patrick at the main entrance at seven. Tell him you have to pick something up in the conference room. Conor and Katie will be here already, Katie on the fire door, Conor by the stage.'

'He'll guess something's up as soon as he sees Conor.'

'Yep, but he's going to try and bluff it out. He doesn't know that we have that tape. Conor needs to get him talking, ask him what happened.'

'Do you think he'll admit it?'

Danny scowled. 'It's important he doesn't have too much time to think – that Conor keeps the pressure on, asks him why he tried to blackmail Josh.'

'Katie said Josh hated him. Patrick, I mean.' Frankie had been looking out over the conference room, imagining the scene as Danny took her through it. Now she turned to him. 'If we can hit the same nerve that Josh hit that night, Patrick might say enough for the Guards to bring him in for questioning.'

Danny nodded slowly. 'Let's hope he does more than that.'

FIFTY-FOUR

Frankie could feel her palms starting to sweat as she waited for Patrick. She'd texted him earlier and invited him over for a walk down the pier, suggesting they meet at reception. His 'Sounds fun, see you at 7' would have sent her heart into a spin a few days ago, but now it was racing for a different reason.

Would this work? They'd gone over the plan meticulously, looking at every possible scenario. Jess's natural inclination to overthink everything had never been more useful. Sorcha had ended up drawing out a giant flowchart detailing every possibility they could think of, and the next move discussed. What if he tried to run? What if he tried to bluff it out? What if he lashed out?

What if he came up with an alibi that none of them expected?

But as Danny had said, short of him swearing someone else had walked into the kitchen at the exact moment Josh turned his back, picked up the knife and stuck it in Josh's shoulder, there really wasn't a way out of this one. And, if he *did* say that, Jess would be ready to take Patrick through the photos, their time stamps highlighted, to show that they knew where – almost – everyone else was at that moment. Sorcha was sure that would totally freak him out.

Frankie knew it would freak *her* out, and while Patrick might be fast on his feet on the rugby pitch, he'd need to be a genius to come up with a plausible counter-argument supporting whatever claim he'd made to justify his innocence.

If he could prove it wasn't him, then they'd all look pretty stupid. And Frankie was quite sure he'd never speak to her again. But after him asking her all those questions about the Guards the other day in Starbucks, she was absolutely sure that he was more interested in her as a source of information than for her dating potential, and that made her really angry.

'You're like a cat on a hot tin roof tonight.' Sinéad's voice cut through Frankie's thoughts from behind the hotel reception desk as she looked out through the main doors for what felt like the fiftieth time.

Frankie turned to answer her with a grin that she hoped reached her eyes. 'I know, pathetic, isn't it?'

'I hope he's worth it.'

Frankie's tone was grim. 'So do I.'

A moment later, Patrick appeared between the white pillars of the pedestrian entrance, sauntering towards her, his hands in the pockets of his jeans. He was wearing a cream hoodie with the Tommy Hilfiger logo across the chest, and black hi-tops. Frankie knew he couldn't see her yet – from outside, the sun slanted off the glass windows in the porch, turning them into mirrors – so she had a few more seconds. She fired off a text to Danny –

Coming through the gate

– then quickly drafted the one she'd need to send as soon as they started walking down to the conference room.

Her heart was beating so loud now, Frankie was sure Sinéad would be able to hear it on the other side of the reception desk. Part of her wished Jess and Sorcha were here waiting with her, rather than down in the conference room. They'd both coached her at lunchtime with tips to control her nerves. Remembering their advice, she started breathing deeply, in through her nose and out through her mouth. It definitely helped to concentrate on something else. Hopefully Patrick would just think she was nervous because she fancied him – Frankie was quite sure he'd love that.

Her phone in her hand, Frankie sidestepped over to the mahogany desk and leaned her elbows on it so she had her back to the door when it opened. She wanted to look casual and relaxed, not like she was waiting for him.

Sinéad looked up at her from her chair, glancing behind her to the doors. 'He's here. Nice …'

Frankie heard the suck of air as the doors opened, the sounds of the sea and the traffic on the coast road spilling in for a moment.

'Sssh.' Frankie tried to glare at her but Sinéad's expression almost made her break into nervous giggles. 'It's not what you think.'

'Really?' Sinéad's finely plucked eyebrows arched.

'Really.' Frankie drew in a sharp breath.

'Hiya.'

Hearing him behind her, Frankie spun around. 'Hiya, how was school?'

'The usual.' Standing on the huge green and gold monogrammed door mat, Patrick rolled his eyes. He still had his hands in his jeans pockets, and gestured with his head as he said, 'I thought we could get ice cream on the way, and maybe a pizza if you've time?'

Frankie fake-smiled. 'Awesome. I've just got to get

something for my mum in the conference room before we go out. It'll only take two minutes. I'll show you around?'

If he found the request to accompany her strange, Patrick didn't show it. Frankie mentally ticked off the first box on the list in her head.

'It's this way.' Distracting him by pointing at the door, Frankie held her phone in her other hand and put her thumb on Send, firing off the next text to Danny.

'Won't take a minute.' Frankie pulled open the heavy door to the conference wing on the right-hand side of reception. It was the newest part of the hotel, the doors still sticking on the deep green carpet. As she led him down the broad corridor, he glanced into the huge window that fronted the business centre with its bank of screens and glass-panelled meeting pods.

'Wow, that's impressive.'

'It's the most hi-tech on this side of the city, apparently. Means I can't pretend my laptop blew up and I couldn't do my homework, though.'

Patrick laughed. 'Yeah, bummer.'

Swinging around to the left, Frankie could feel her stomach doing somersaults as they got closer to the huge conference room. If she was nervous before, she was terrified now.

'Here we are.' She put her hand on the conference room door.

This was it.

FIFTY-FIVE

Frankie pulled open one of the huge pale wood double doors just enough for Patrick to go inside. She slipped in right behind him as the door sucked closed.

All the furniture in the room had been cleared to the sides, leaving a wide-open expanse of maple wood flooring. Gold banqueting chairs with dark green cushioned seats and backs were stacked against the side wall, and a couple of trestle tables with white cloths on them were pushed back against the long windows on the right-hand side.

It took a few moments for Patrick to realise Conor was leaning back against the stage, his arms folded.

'Yo, bro, what are you doing here?' Patrick sauntered into the middle of the room, smiling.

Conor looked at him coolly, taking a moment to answer. 'I'm here with Katie. She and Frankie are friends. But you know that. Katie has a problem she needs to sort out, so I thought I'd come down to help her.' Conor indicated Katie with his head. She was leaning on the glass fire door that opened onto the car park.

'What sort of problem?' If Frankie's senses hadn't already been on high alert, she might have missed the edge to Patrick's voice, but she could see Conor didn't. Patrick turned back to Frankie, one eyebrow raised. 'Don't you need to get something for your mum?'

Frankie tried to look relaxed. 'It can wait.'

Patrick took a step backwards, opening his arms in an expansive gesture. 'So what is this? Why are Conor and Katie here?' He looked at Frankie like she was somehow stupid, and waited for her to answer.

Frankie's nerves began to turn to anger. Katie had said Josh didn't like Patrick because of his arrogant sense of entitlement, and this was exactly what she was seeing now. She was absolutely sure he had guessed that this had something to do with Josh's death. Was he going to try to bluff it out?

Before she could reply, Conor took a step forwards.

'I thought we were friends, bro, like *good friends*. But it seems you're too much of a shit to acknowledge that.'

He left the words hanging there.

Patrick feigned confusion. 'Everyone knows we're friends – what are you talking about?'

Conor paused. 'More than friends, Patrick. *Boyfriends*.' Conor started to walk towards Patrick until they were just a few feet apart. Conor's hands were at his sides but he was clenching and unclenching his hands. 'I know you've got problems at home, but to deny me like that, with those words?'

Patrick shook his head, glancing from Conor to Frankie. 'What the fuck are you talking about?'

Conor took another step forwards, his voice low. 'I don't know what I'm more disappointed and hurt by. I thought we had something special, that you were one of the good guys, not some murdering bastard who'd stick a knife in his team captain just to keep him off the pitch.' Frankie held her breath as Conor continued. Patrick's face was impassive, like he was taking it all in. This wasn't exactly in the script, but she prayed the mic clipped under Conor's hoodie was picking everything up. Frankie could only just hear what Conor was saying as he continued, 'Did you mean to kill him, Patrick? I mean, what was the game plan there?'

Patrick had gone very still. 'I didn't kill anyone, you're talking total shite, Conor. That weed you've been smoking has finally made you go out of your mind.'

'Oh, I don't think so.' Conor was almost nose to nose with Patrick now, but Patrick was holding his ground, his stance deliberately relaxed. Conor looked like he was about to explode.

Then, looking up over Patrick's shoulder at the audio-visual booth, Conor gave a slight nod with his head. Danny's signal.

The speaker system suddenly came alive with Josh's voice. It sounded a bit muffled but it was clear enough to know it was him.

'Don't you dare. You keep well clear of both of them, or your dad might get to hear about you and Conor.'

Patrick looked around wildly as the next sentence played out.

'What?'

'You think I don't know? You play it straight but you're as gay as he is.'

'What the fuck is this?' Patrick shouted, trying to drown out his own voice on the recording. He knew exactly where this conversation had taken place, and what had been said. And what was coming next.

'That's crap and you know it. I'm not some gay-boy fag.'

'You know exactly what this is.' Conor's voice was shaking. 'This is a recording of your last conversation with Josh. Right before you stabbed him.'

His punch landed square on Patrick's jaw.

'That's for Josh. And this one's for me.'

Frankie cried out and took a step forwards, but it was too late: Patrick was already hitting Conor back, his head down. They both fell over, rolling on the floor, throwing punch after punch until Patrick was on top of Conor, smashing his face with his fist.

Frankie felt like she was paralysed, watching the fight in slow motion. The shock of finding Josh's body, of realising Patrick was a fake, of Ruth blaming her for it all, tumbled around her head, making the room sway.

Then suddenly her brain caught up and she heard Jess and Sorcha screaming. They'd come forwards onto the stage, were standing above the two boys writhing on the ground. But it was as if neither Patrick nor Conor could hear the girls' voices. They were locked together, Conor on his back, twisting and punching as if his life depended on it. Which it did.

Patrick's hands were around Conor's neck.

'Stop, stop, you'll kill him!' Katie's scream cut through the sounds of the fight. Running forwards, she grabbed hold of Patrick's hoodie and tried to haul him off Conor. As if the pressure brought Patrick to his senses, he suddenly released his grip and burst into tears.

'I didn't mean to kill him, I didn't. I didn't mean to.'

FIFTY-SIX

'Honestly, Frankie, I can't leave you for more than five minutes without you getting yourself into trouble.' Ollie shook his head and pulled Frankie into a hug. She could tell from his tone that he was mildly annoyed, but also proud of her. They were still in the conference room, and behind him two uniformed Gardaí were hovering while a paramedic checked Patrick over. Cian and Kai were sitting on the stage, side by side, their arms crossed, glaring at him.

Frankie had never been more relieved to see Ollie and the twins than when they threw open the conference room door and had barrelled in followed by the Guards. She knew her brothers had been waiting in case they were needed, but they got there fast. Danny must have called Ollie the moment things kicked off.

The fight felt like it had lasted a lifetime, but it was probably only a few minutes. *Just long enough for the Gardaí to get here. Thank God.*

Frankie gave Ollie an extra hug, still feeling shaky. She didn't know if she'd ever get over the shock of this week. It just kept on coming, like waves pounding the beach. Ollie looked down at her and gave her a reassuring smile.

Once the Guards had separated the two boys and everything had calmed down, Frankie had explained to them what was happening. Well, she tried to. She wasn't entirely sure she was making sense, but the Guards got the gist of it.

Conor and Katie were sitting well away from Patrick on two banqueting chairs, Sorcha and Jess flanking them protectively. Conor was leaning into Katie's shoulder, her arm around him. Cian and Kai had gone straight to help him up after the fight, checking for broken bones. Now he was holding his arm around his ribs. His eyes were swollen, his nose plugged to stop it bleeding. A paramedic had arrived shortly after the Guards. He'd checked Conor first and given him some painkillers, but he would need an X-ray to see if he'd broken any ribs.

Frankie sighed. Thank goodness Danny had managed to edit the tape so Katie hadn't heard about Ruth yet. Frankie knew she'd have to tell her at some point, but it could wait until after she knew Conor wasn't badly injured.

Across the conference room, the paramedic finished checking Patrick over and stood back, his green uniform toning with the hotel's trademark green wallpaper. He snapped off his latex gloves. 'Nothing broken. All yours, lads.'

The two Guards gestured for Patrick to turn around as one of them put plastic handcuffs on his wrists. Frankie couldn't hear what they were saying, but Patrick's head was bowed as if all the fight had gone out of him.

She was starting to hate him. If he had one milligram of empathy for anyone except himself, he'd never have lunged at Josh with a huge kitchen knife. There was no way Patrick would ever understand Katie's hurt. He didn't even seem to understand Conor's.

Beside Frankie, the conference room door opened and Danny appeared with another Guard, her hat under her arm, her blonde hair pulled back into a ponytail. Danny smiled at Frankie. He looked so ridiculously pleased with himself she could feel a grin creeping onto her own face. 'We got it all. The mic was far enough down inside Conor's hoodie to be protected so we picked up everything.'

A surge of gratitude overwhelmed Frankie. Danny was just the best. If they hadn't caught Patrick's confession after all of this, it would have been a nightmare.

The two Guards with Patrick looked over to Ollie. One of them had his hand on Patrick's shoulder as the other one called over, 'Okay if we take him out the fire exit? No point in creating a spectacle.'

'Will you be all right?' Ollie glanced down at Frankie as he untangled himself from her hug. She nodded and he crossed the conference room towards the Guards, pointing out the fire exit on the far side of the room. It opened onto the back of the hotel, well away from prying eyes. Frankie guessed that their patrol car was already parked out there.

The Guard with Danny turned to her. 'You guys did an incredible job. Danny here gave me a run-down. He played me the video. Very impressive. We'll be able to release Rob Doyle now and charge Patrick Kelly with attacking Josh Fitzpatrick.' She hesitated. 'Kelly may want to press charges against your friend Conor for assault.'

Frankie sighed, grimacing. 'Patrick's dad's a hot-shot lawyer.'

The Guard kept her face expressionless, but Frankie could see from her eyes that she already knew this. 'I've seen him in court. And the pathologist's report says that the way Josh fell pushed the tip of the knife into his heart. If he hadn't fallen, it might not have been a fatal blow.'

'Oh, that's awful.' Frankie's hand shot to her mouth. She could feel sorrow welling up inside her, threatening to spill into tears. She'd been right there when it had happened. Could she have saved Josh if she'd been looking in the right direction? She didn't know how she was going to cope with that question hanging over her. Then she realised what the Guard was saying. 'Does that mean it was accidental? That's what they call it, isn't it – an accidental death?'

The Guard looked back at her. 'That'll be for the courts to decide.'

FIFTY-SEVEN

'I think this is yours, Ruth.' Katie dropped the heavy gold bracelet onto the kitchenette counter in the Fifth Year common room and turned to look Ruth straight in the eye. Even from the sofa, it looked to Frankie like Ruth had frozen. Around them, the whole room fell silent.

Ruth had been looking for her iPad in her backpack when Katie had come in, a hush falling on the room as she had walked through the door. It was Katie's first day back and Frankie could feel the tension immediately. Everyone wanted to hug her, but no one knew what to say.

'I know exactly what happened. I hope you're pleased with yourself. You're almost as despicable as Patrick Kelly. If it hadn't been for you, Josh wouldn't have been in the kitchen and Patrick wouldn't have had that row with him.' Katie gave Ruth a long look. 'I hope you can live with yourself.' Then she turned abruptly, coming back to join them on the sofa. Jess quickly shunted up closer to Sorcha to let her in beside Frankie.

Frankie knew how hard that had been. Katie had held it together, but now she was shaking. For a brief moment, Frankie had thought Katie might have been going to slap Ruth. And Ruth had looked like she was half expecting it.

The silence in the room behind them was like a shock wave; then as Katie sat down, everyone started talking, like a dam had burst. From the sofa, none of them turned around to look at Ruth.

Frankie put her arm through Katie's and squeezed it as Katie flicked a smile back at her. Last week, when they knew for sure that Conor didn't have any broken ribs, Frankie had gone over to see Katie and tell her about Ruth. And the bracelet.

Clinging to her, Katie had just shaken her head as Frankie had explained. Perhaps she was all cried out, or perhaps having Ruth to focus her anger on had helped a bit. But it really felt like the final twist of the knife.

That's when they'd talked about how Katie could

return the bracelet to Ruth – and how doing it privately at home would be letting her off too easy. If it happened in front of the class, everyone would want to know what was going on and they'd learn her part in it. And know exactly what she was like, if they'd been in any doubt before.

Now it was done.

Sitting beside her on the sofa, Katie turned to Jess. 'Tell me about your dad, Jess. I need something to distract me. Where is he now?'

Jess rubbed Katie's arm. 'Well, I thought he was in Afghanistan, but it turns out he was only there for a few days. Now he's at the UN headquarters in New York.'

Katie took a shaky breath. 'Does he tell you what he's working on when he goes?'

Jess shook her head. 'Not often. I think I'd rather not know. Sometimes he tells me before the story breaks so I won't get a shock. Quite a lot of the time I wish he just covered flower shows, instead of wars.'

Frankie could see Katie was beginning to relax as she tried hard to smile at Jess. 'Do you want to be a journalist?'

Frankie could feel the dark chasm opening inside her again. Katie was talking about the future, a future Josh didn't have. All their plans, going to America together, his sports scholarship …

Frankie dug her nails into the palm of her hand. Ollie had said something about Josh being a bright light, about how Buddhists believed that some people burned with such incredible intensity while they were on earth that their time was short. She wasn't sure if she was remembering it quite right, but everything about Josh had been intense: he'd shone on the rugby pitch as well as in school.

He wasn't perfect, but Katie had loved him.

Frankie tuned into what Jess was saying. 'I want to be a human rights lawyer. I think I'll have to go to back to the UK to uni, though.'

Jess had said it carefully, as if she'd realised too that talk of their future was missing one key player. Before Katie could reply, the door flew open and Georgia came running in, waving a piece of paper over her head.

'I got Lady Macbeth!'

Jess laughed, throwing a quick glance at Frankie, obviously relieved that the subject had been changed.

'That's brilliant news, George, you're going to be so good.' Jess struggled forwards on the sofa, standing up so she could see the page in Georgia's hand. 'Wow, and I'm stage manager. How did *that* happen?'

'All that experience.' Georgia grinned at her. 'Come on, let's go and find the others and see if everyone's got what they wanted.' Pulling Jess by the hand, she dragged her out of the door.

Sorcha wriggled into the gap Jess had left next to Katie as Frankie gestured towards the open door with her head.

'I think Georgia's found a new friend, thank goodness. She and Jess get on so well.' Frankie paused. 'You okay?'

Katie hesitated for a moment before she replied. 'As good as I can be.' She closed her eyes and paused again as if she wasn't sure if she should continue. 'Patrick's been released on bail. He's going to plead not guilty.'

Frankie looked at her, shocked. 'Out, now? Not in prison?' Katie nodded as Frankie went on, her voice barely a whisper, 'Not guilty to what, murder or manslaughter?'

Sighing, Katie rubbed her hand over her eyes, her voice shaking. 'Both. The Guards said that he admits that he had a row with Josh, but then he's saying he left the kitchen. He's claiming someone else must have stabbed him.' She glanced at Frankie. 'And it was Josh falling that did the real damage anyway.'

Frankie could feel sadness seeping from Katie like spilled ink. 'But the tape, his confession …'

'I know.' Katie sighed. 'He's admitting he was there – obviously – but the Guards think it could come down to what the jury think.' She took a deep breath. 'They've warned us that he might get off.'

'Oh my God.' Frankie looked at her, speechless.

On her other side, Sorcha winced and shook her head despairingly as Katie continued, 'At least Patrick didn't get to play in front of those scouts. That's something,

I suppose.' Then, obviously not wanting to talk about it anymore, Katie forced a smile. 'How's that gorgeous Danny? I don't know how you kept him so quiet.'

Still stunned by what Katie had said, Frankie blushed. She and Danny had been talking and texting non-stop since the drama in the conference room; it was like they'd known each other forever. 'I'm meeting him later, actually. We're going to film the feral cats on the outhouse roof at the back of the hotel.'

Sorcha did a double take. 'That's real romantic, Frankie O'Sullivan – he knows how to look after a girl. What could *possibly* go wrong?'

EPILOGUE

Out of breath, Frankie looked at the time on her phone again as she paused at the pedestrian crossing outside Starbucks. She'd practically run up the hill, but she reckoned she had just enough time to grab a mocha and get into school on time. She shifted her backpack higher up her shoulder. She hadn't been able to sleep last night, and then her alarm hadn't gone off and Ollie had already left so she hadn't been able to get a lift.

What a great start to the day.

But at least it was Friday. And she and Danny were going to a film tonight. Well, a weird documentary that

Danny wanted to see, but it sounded interesting and it was sort of their first proper date. Frankie felt herself smiling at the thought. She'd been tempted to try to set up a double date with Jess and Matteo, but that could wait.

Looking up to see if there was a gap in the traffic, Frankie drew in a sharp breath. A hearse was crawling around the corner, its gleaming black body reflecting the morning sun, its sides glazed so she could see the coffin inside, surrounded by flowers.

Frankie closed her eyes, her knees suddenly weak, and reached for the pole beside her. Josh's funeral had been one of the most traumatic events of her life, almost as bad as finding him. Hundreds of mourners had filled the church, everyone in their school uniforms. Raven's Hill was so small, that even girls who didn't know Katie beyond seeing her in the school corridors had come to support her, the collective grief like a wave, suffocating and consuming them all. She still didn't know how Katie had got through it – well, she almost hadn't. The rugby team had carried Josh's wicker coffin on their shoulders out of the church and Katie had almost collapsed on the steps.

Suddenly the pipping of the pedestrian light broke into Frankie's thoughts and instinctively she ran across the road. She didn't need a hearse this morning to add to everything else.

They didn't know when it would be, but they still had the trial to face.

And as well as Patrick, Ruth Meaney would be there. She'd left Raven's Hill, but Frankie was dreading Katie hearing the full detail of what had happened that night if Ruth was called to give evidence.

Pushing thoughts of the trial away, Frankie opened the door of Starbucks. She needed to get moving and focus on mocha and maths, in that order, this morning; there was no room for traumatic thoughts right now.

Barely looking at who else was inside, out of habit, she scanned the menu board.

'Hello, Frankie. Running late?' Frankie spun around at the male voice behind her, her mouth falling open in shock. It was the same voice that had kept her awake last night, going around and around in her nightmares.

Patrick Kelly.

'What are …?' The words came out as a whisper, barely formed, her mouth suddenly dry.

He was wearing a jacket with jeans and one of his fancy shirts, the inside of the collar lined with the blue floral fabric that she'd liked so much. He grinned at her, but his smile was cold and hard, his eyes icy. 'What am I doing here? Getting a coffee, obviously.'

She stared at him, speechless.

'Queue's moving, you ready to order?'

Glancing around, she moved up a space. They were

almost at the till. Around them she realised the shop had almost emptied. She whipped her head back to look at him, her shock receding as rage built, reactivating her paralysed brain.

'How can you come in here?' She almost spat it at him.

His smirk made her want to slap him. He leaned towards her conspiratorially and kept his voice low as he replied. 'I'm on bail, Frankie, free to walk the streets, and the DPP is considering the evidence. Or should I say *lack* of evidence. So it might not even get to court.'

Frankie's mind flew back to the conference room, to Patrick with his hands around Conor's neck. 'But the tape ...'

'Isn't forensic evidence. My clothes were clean. And that wasn't a confession, I was confused. Anything elicited under duress is, well ...' He smirked and nodded towards the counter. 'Your turn to order. You better hurry or you won't get in for the bell.'

Dazed, Frankie quickly gave the barista her order. She was so preoccupied she barely registered the sound of a chair scraping back and a movement beside her. She couldn't believe this. How could he come here, to Starbucks, to Josh and Katie's hangout? And what was he saying about evidence? She took a breath, trying to steady her heart pounding in her chest, thoughts tumbling around her head.

'Hi, Patrick, what brings you here?'

Frankie spun around at the new voice. It was Viv, her backpack over her shoulder, her face like thunder. She must have been in the corner when Frankie came in. For the first time Frankie realised Viv was about an inch taller than Patrick, perhaps because right now she had pulled herself up to her full height, her glare like a laser beam. Before Patrick could answer she continued.

'Get out. Right now, and leave Frankie alone.' Viv's voice was low, so threatening Frankie felt like her blood had frozen. 'I know you, Patrick Kelly, and you don't get to make anyone else's life hell like you did mine. You think your dad can get you off a murder charge? Well karma is a bitch, Patrick – trust me, it'll get you. You think you can talk your way out of everything, but all that fancy footwork is going to trip you up.'

'Vivienne …' Patrick's tone was laced with sarcasm, but he didn't get a chance to finish.

Viv took a step towards him so she was leaning down right into his face. 'I'd leave now, really. You're on bail; you get involved in any sort of altercation and you'll go straight to jail. You won't even pass Go.'

Holding her breath, Frankie looked from Viv to Patrick, suddenly aware that the two baristas behind the counter were watching them too.

Patrick took a step backwards. 'Don't worry. I'm not ordering in a place that serves the likes of *you*.' It was loaded with vitriol, but the whole shop seemed to breathe a collective sigh of relief as he pushed past her, slamming the door behind him.

Immediately relaxing, Viv smiled at Frankie, and went up to the counter. 'A double espresso please, I think I need it.'

Behind the counter the barista smiled. 'Won't be a minute.' Frankie looked from the barista to Viv still trying to process what had just happened. A moment later Viv had her espresso in her hand.

'Come on, let's walk down together. Get some air. It won't matter if we're a few minutes late for class. Not the end of the world.'

Picking up her mocha, Frankie smiled gratefully and followed Viv out. She'd liked Viv from the first time they'd had a proper chat at the induction day. Now she liked her a whole lot more.

As they walked across the car park, thoughts swirled in Frankie's head. She knew Katie had said the Guards thought the case could be hard to prosecute, but how could the DPP have any questions over what had happened, about Patrick even getting to trial? Ollie had explained to her that the Director of Public Prosecutions made the ultimate decision about whether a case went to court or not, whether there was enough evidence.

What had he said about his clothes?

Beside her, Viv glanced over, not speaking, as if she

understood that Frankie needed a few moments to herself. There weren't many people in Fifth Year who knew what had happened at the hotel, but Viv had come to ask her. Frankie had sensed then that Viv and Patrick had a history. And she'd been right.

A moment later Viv shook her head. 'He's so awful, isn't he?' Frankie glanced at her in agreement as Viv continued, 'Patrick is the type of bully who covers their tracks and slimes up to the teachers so that they always side with him. To the outside world, he appears to be perfect. He was the biggest reason I missed months of school. I just couldn't face it. I was physically sick with anxiety.'

Frankie slipped her arm through Viv's and pulled her into a mini hug, 'You did the right thing moving to Raven's Hill.'

A smile flicked across Viv's lips, but her face was clouded with worry. 'God, I hope the judge puts him away for a very long time. But what did he say about the evidence?'

'He said his clothes were clean. That was so weird, like he was bragging. Did he mean the clothes he'd worn to the party?' Her arm still looped through Viv's, Frankie stopped walking for a minute, staring down the road as she re-ran their conversation in her head.

Forensics. The word circled in her head like a hawk over carrion. *His clothes were clean.* She was sure Katie had told her that Conor and Patrick had left the party because they'd got caught in the fight. *Hadn't Conor said something to Katie about blood on Patrick's shirt?*

'His shirt.' Frankie turned to Viv as all the pieces suddenly fell into place. 'He said his clothes were clean. But there was blood on his shirt, Conor said so. It had to be Josh's blood. That's what the Guards need. They need his shirt.'

Viv put her head on one side, frowning. 'They must have asked for it. There were loads of photos of him at the party – they'd be able to see what he was wearing. They'd be pretty suspicious if he couldn't produce it.'

Frankie shook her head. She knew exactly what he'd done. 'He's got loads of shirts that look almost exactly the same. I think he gets them from a special place in London. He must have given them a different one.'

Viv raised her beautiful eyebrows. 'Can you prove it?'

Frankie looked at her, her mind processing everything that had happened. 'I think so. His Instagram. You can see them on his Instagram.'

The ketchup. The day she'd taken the photo of them all on the pier he'd got ketchup on his shirt – but later that evening he'd been wearing what had looked like the same shirt, but with no stain. That's what had made her realise that he had more than one, and then she'd noticed that the lining in the collar was slightly different.

Viv looked doubtful. 'He'll have deleted the posts, won't he? He's clever.'

Frankie shook her head, smiling. 'I've got screen-shots.' She blushed; it sounded stalkerish, but she knew everyone did it. And she'd been so busy with Danny that she hadn't got around to deleting the folder yet. 'And if he's taken down the posts, it just proves it, doesn't it? That he has something to hide. If he gave them the wrong shirt, he'd need to explain why. All his shirts have slightly different patterned fabric in the collar, he must have ordered them like that. The Guards may not have realised that he has a load of almost identical ones – I mean, who does?' She looked at Viv, her eyes wide, 'He's got one on today.'

Viv was trying not to grin. 'What did I say about karma? You need to get down to the Guards, Frankie, and tell them. This could be the piece of evidence that swings the case. And Patrick Kelly deserves *everything* he gets.'

ACKNOWLEDGEMENTS

A book is nothing more than a collection of words on paper until it finds a reader, so my first and foremost thanks are to you, my reader, for picking up this book. Thank you for taking a chance on me, and I do hope you loved reading about Frankie, Sorcha and Jess and their world as much as I enjoyed writing it.

If you'd like to explore Katie's house during the party for yourself, we have created it in The Sims 4 – you can find it in the Gallery under the username SBlakeBooks. We will also be creating Raven's Hill School and other key locations, so do follow for more.

If you are faced with any of the challenges that I've covered in this story, you'll find some links that might help at my website www.samblakebooks.com (where you can also join my Readers' Club and get a free e-book). Nothing about being Frankie's age is easy – anyone who makes it look so or who seems to have the perfect life is curating an image, papering over their own cracks. We've all got cracks. But there are lots of people who can help us to fix them.

Every book has an army behind it – I put pen to paper (or fingers to keyboard), but I can only do that after talking to lots of people to make sure that the story works, and then, when it's finished, a whole team helps to polish it to a shine. Finally, book bloggers, reviewers and wonderful booksellers help to get it to you. Every single link in the chain is essential and I'm hugely grateful to everyone in it.

Massive personal thanks go first to Sarah Webb, whose generosity is legendary and whose talent speaks for itself. There is no one more connected in the children's book world. I'm privileged to call her a close friend – it was her advice, 'just keep writing', that landed me my first bestseller. Sometimes 'thank you' doesn't feel like enough.

Mia Roberts and Ciara Murphy, Ava Donoghue, Niamh and Kate Snowden, Vivienne Dodd and Rex Fox O'Loughlin all helped hugely: advising and reading and making sure Frankie's world was authentic. If you've spotted any mistakes, they are all mine.

Thank you to Orla Doherty who connected me to Shona Kerr, head squash coach at Wesleyan College, Stanford, USA, who advised on sports scholarships; and thanks to Casey King, who is always on hand to make sure my Garda procedure is correct.

Dorothy Koomson is an incredible writer who, in a few words, dug me out of a character/plot dilemma. Often it's all there, it just takes someone to point it out for you to see. Dorothy is a very excellent pointer.

The team at Gill have been amazing since the inception of the idea for this story – they've blown me away with their enthusiasm and love of books, their fabulous cover ideas and attention to detail. Huge thanks to Venetia Gosling, Rachel Thompson and Esther Ní Dhonnacha, the wonderful Charlie in design and Claire in PR – and to Seán, for coming to say hello at the Irish Book Awards. I was so touched; I feel like I've been welcomed into the fold.

But I wouldn't be able to do the job I love without the constant support, guidance and wisdom of my amazing agent Simon Trewin – the best agent a writer could have.

All these people have helped bring this book into your hand. Now you've completed the circle. Thank you for reading.